Praise for *Vivian's Decision*

"Heartwarming and heartbreaking in equal measure."

—Goldie Goldbloom, author of *On Division*

"A tender and gripping portrait of a mother and daughter in post-war suburban Chicago. This book becomes a meditation on community, solidarity, and courage."

—Rachel Swearingen, author of *How to Walk on Water*

"Compassionate and immersive. In her riveting debut novel, Della Leavitt shows us the universal and yet deeply personal challenge women face when another child may be more they can bear. As in the best historical novels, *Vivian's Decision* tells a story of the past that is painfully relevant today."

—Mary Kay Zuravleff, author of *American Ending*

"I couldn't put this book down. Its final coda offers a gut punch from which I won't soon recover."

—Lindsay Hunter, author of *Hot Springs Drive*

"It's rare that historical fiction relates so powerfully to current themes. Della Leavitt has written a brave and important story."

—Susan Levi, Off Campus Writers' Workshop director of programs

"It's an immigrant story. It's a woman's story. A love story and a family saga about generations of women faced with an agonizing moral choice made in a time when choices were not only illegal but dangerous to your health."

—Andrea Change, executive director of Guild Literary Complex

"Leavitt has written a fictional family saga reminding us that, especially for women, past is more than prologue. Self-determination requires courage . . . and sisterhood."

—Jill Pollack, founder of StoryStudio Chicago

"Not only a well-crafted historical fiction debut but also a rich and poignant family drama. *Vivian's Decision* will appeal to women everywhere who grapple with how to balance family obligations, religious teachings, personal aspirations, and their own emotional well-being. I couldn't put it down."

—Maggie Smith, author of *Truth and Other Lies* and *Blindspot*

"Vivian's struggles show in stark, but exquisite detail the contradictions inherent in women's lives in the 1950s. Every word on every page rings 100 percent true. Vivian will stay with me for a long, long time."

—Virginia McCullough, author of *Amber Light*

"*Vivian's Decision* is a warm, embracing novel—a text of a time. Set in the Midwest in the fifties, in both city and suburb, the story could be so many women's history."

—Sandra Scofield, author of *Little Ships* and
National Book Award Finalist for *Beyond Deserving*

Vivian's Decision

A Novel

Della Leavitt

SHE WRITES PRESS

Published in 2026 by
She Writes Press, an imprint of The Stable Book Group

32 Court Street, Suite 2109
Brooklyn, NY 11201
https://shewritespress.com
Library of Congress Control Number: 2026900513
ISBN: 979-8-89636-120-6
eISBN: 979-8-89636-121-3

Interior Designer: Kiran Spees

Printed in the United States

For my parents, Sol and Shirley Linson Leavitt,
who loved me, my siblings, and the extended family
beyond measure.

And for my granddaughter, Nora Shirley Bossen.
May you grow up in a country that protects women's
freedoms.

"None of it happened and all of it's true."

—Jeanne Ray, Ann Patchett's mother,

after reading *Commonwealth*

CHAPTER ONE
SUBURBAN LIFE

1956

AFTER VIVIAN Kolson Jacobson uprooted her family to a Chicago suburb, gardening became her refuge from her four young children's incessant demands. She yanked weeds with the same firm thrusts that she used to braid her daughter's hair. When a cawing blue jay swooped low as if to herald the eldest child's arrival and mimic her shrieks, Vivian sprang from her knees and winced to feel an ache in her breast. She pressed her palm against her tender chest, lost her grip on her hard-won bunch of thistles, and stood dumbstruck watching the unwanted greenery flutter among the fledgling pepper and tomato plants. Vivian's haven was shattered.

"Look what you made me do, Irene!"

The six-year-old swatted her temple and screamed, "Little helicopters are buzzing me!"

Helicopters? Funny, how her precocious child viewed these whizzing cicadas. When they lived in the city, Irene loved to spot whirlybirds flying over their apartment building on their way to Meigs Field at Chicago's lakefront. Here, the droning miniatures terrified her. Vivian tried to hide her own squeamishness when she brushed one away from her daughter's crown. Thicker than an adult's pointer finger, the blue-bodied, red-eyed nuisances were hands-down uglier than garden-variety grasshoppers. Vivian had never seen *any* grasshopper before moving out here. She and her husband, Mel, grew up in the cement enclave of Chicago's hardscrabble west side, both children of Russian Jewish immigrants. A report in the local paper had warned that new housing developments like theirs, mushrooming over reclaimed marshlands, would be the hardest hit by the imminent invasion. As predicted, the cicadas arrived in droves, but nothing had prepared Vivian for the messy, noisy onslaught.

Vivian lifted the muslin netting to peek at the baby asleep in his carriage beside her, popped over to prop open the back door to check on the toddler babbling in her playpen, then smoothed Irene's bangs, grabbed her daughter's fist, and with her free hand, commandeered the buggy and steered it into the front yard.

Up and down the block, scores of shouting children jumped rope, launched wiffle balls, played jacks on pristine sidewalks, and loped across virgin lawns in games of hide-and-seek and capture the flag, seemingly unfazed by the swarming bugs. This carefree life among well-to-do children, attending schools in a noted district with a guaranteed path to college and careers, fulfilled Vivian and Mel's dream for their brood. A life far beyond their own reach. They were children of the Depression.

"Mommy, you aren't listening!" Irene stomped her foot and twisted out of her mother's grip. "I want to go inside!"

"The fresh air is good for you. Remember, you've got to watch out for Sandy. You're the big sister."

"I don't want to! She plays with the boys!"

The baby whimpered.

"Now you've done it! You woke up Baby Billy!" Vivian sniffed his bottom.

Irene mimicked her mother's strained look and pinched her nose. "P.U. He stinks!"

Only three clean diapers left. How had she let that happen? She'd never let their supply dwindle so low before. Where was that diaper truck? Vivian's feet felt as rooted as a statue in a child's game of freeze tag. The manic energy she needed to fuel her daily household tasks had evaporated like the water in an unwatched boiling pot. She wasn't herself, but dared not guess the reason. Without thinking, Vivian lifted her free hand to assuage her aching breast, blasting her into clear focus. Can't be! Always a sign of . . . When was her last period? No idea. Her doctor had told her not to expect her cycles to be regular after bearing four children in six years.

Irene tugged her mother's sleeve. "Mommy, I'm scared!"

Vivian stooped down eye-to-eye with her daughter and spoke in an even tone meant to be reassuring. "Remember the locusts from the Passover seder?"

Irene gasped. "Will we have ten plagues?"

Vivian stroked Irene's cheek and held back a giggle. "No, sweetheart, we're not in Egypt. We're in Wilmette."

Irene brushed a flying bug off her knee. Vivian added, "Ignore these locusts. In a few weeks, they'll all be gone and won't come back for seventeen years."

"Seventeen years?" Irene gazed at the sky and then counted on her fingers. "I'll be twenty-three." She paused. "Sandy will be twenty-one. Linda and Baby Billy won't even remember these little helicopters. When they come back, we'll all be too big to be scared."

Vivian smiled at her child's deft calculations, a payoff from Mel's patient drills. His attention to Irene's learning was as diligent as if she'd been his firstborn son. Yet another thing to love about her husband. She shivered to remember the night they'd met, how she'd felt like Cinderella who'd won over the handsome prince. Now, ten years and four children later, Vivian cringed to imagine how she must look to him. She twirled an unruly lock of dark hair around her finger, patted her belly and sucked it in, then squealed when she flung away a cicada that had flown close to her ear.

"Mommy! Are you scared of the little helicopters, too?"

"Mommies don't get scared."

If only that were true. Vivian gingerly touched her chest. Nothing. Thank goodness. Must be all in her head.

A neighbor girl called out Irene's name and waved her over. Vivian kissed her daughter on the top of her head and gave a little push on her bottom toward the playing children. Irene stomped on a dead cicada splattered on the walk and cried "Gotcha!" before dashing off to join a game of hopscotch.

VIVIAN EXHALED in relief at the sound of clanking gears when the blue-and-yellow diaper service van turned onto Maple Street. Thank goodness. Fresh diapers on the way. Before maneuvering the baby carriage up the walk, she paused to admire their brand-new house in the midst of the sprawling block of the development. They'd selected a trilevel model with slick cream siding and black trim with a ribbon of bedroom windows ringing the second floor. During construction, she'd urged Mel to authorize a change to the original plans and divide one bedroom into two rooms to accommodate the arrival of their fourth baby, due to arrive shortly before their move. Generous glass panes on the first level welcomed sunshine into the combination living-dining room, bringing the outdoors in. The grand double front door with brass handles erased Vivian's memory of the peeling paint in the entryway of the tenement where she'd grown up. She felt lucky to live here. Most days, she reveled in her mastery of the chaos of being a mother to so many, but not today. At Billy's wail, she recoiled at his discomfort but had to push herself to hustle into the house to change him.

As soon as she opened the door, she choked at the ubiquitous stench of ammonia released by urine-soaked diapers. How could her little darlings create so much filth? Vivian couldn't keep herself from crying "Phooey!" when wiping reeking messes off their tiny, doll-like bottoms. If only her children were out of diapers. She yearned to regain her freedom. Toilet training was tedious, mandating constant vigilance to be ready to snatch up the child at precisely the right moment when she displayed the telltale signs and lift her over the toilet seat. Vivian groaned. Two trained, two more to go.

Even with the diaper service, the automatic washer and dryer ran nonstop. Vivian offered up a quick thanks for the convenience of in-home appliances, remembering how laundry chores in their city apartment meant maneuvering an oversized canvas bag filled with dirty clothes down two flights and wheeling it to the laundromat three blocks away. She shouldn't complain about her relative life of ease. And what about the onerous laundry days of her youth when they'd hauled water up three flights to heat, soak, scrub, wring, and hang the clothes on lines stretched between buildings? That era felt as far away as the lives of pioneers who traversed the American frontier in covered wagons. Thank goodness she lived in modern-day Wilmette.

Billy almost squirmed out of her arms when Vivian bent over the playpen rail to kiss Linda, who was blissfully cooing at her stuffed rabbit. How Vivian loved each one of her children, more than she believed she ever could have. She climbed the half-flight to place Billy on the bassinet, smiling to remember her witticism when she dubbed him her "change of scenery" after diapering three girls in a row. But she wasn't as clever as she thought, laughing at the memory when she'd dodged his arcing shot of pee that nearly caught her in the eye. She'd had to learn to cover Billy's naked penis with a spare diaper before pinning on a new one. Wasn't that what a good mother did? Adapt?

At a loud yelp from downstairs, Vivian sprang out of the baby's room to peek over the banister and gasped at the sight of Linda diving headfirst over the playpen's guardrail. Vivian sprinted down and roughly scooped up the toddler, who was crawling toward the carpeted stairs leading down to the den. Vivian trembled and bit her lip to keep from shouting. Linda couldn't understand the fright she'd caused her mother, who'd pictured her toddler cracking her head open on the tile floor. Linda screamed when Vivian grabbed her before taking the stairs two at a time, holding her breath until Vivian exhaled in relief to see that Baby Billy hadn't moved.

He lay serenely on his back with his toes in his mouth while Vivian expertly pinned his diaper. Then he dropped his foot and added loud cries in solidarity with his sister's wails. Amid this chorus, Vivian balanced the writhing toddler and the howling baby, one on each hip, marched back downstairs, and set them both in the playpen. Did Linda have to be changed, too? She'd have to wait until the diaper truck arrived.

Vivian sank heavily onto the couch nearby, holding back tears. She lit a Pall Mall and took a deep drag. She exhaled toward the ceiling and said aloud, "I can't take this anymore!"

Smoking calmed her. She blew a lazy ring toward the ceiling and blamed herself for dismissing Irene's fears about the cicadas. She should go easier on her precocious child. Irene must feel like Dorothy in Oz, dropped into a foreign landscape teeming with armies of insects. Irene must miss the city. Vivian did, too.

There had been a wealth of conveniences near their high-ceilinged, vintage apartment in the redbrick courtyard building in Chicago's Lakeview neighborhood. Despite the scarcity of postwar housing, Mel had scored a great place for them through his family's Maxwell Street connections. In the city, the kosher meat market, Woolworth's five-and-dime, and National Tea grocery were all nearby on Broadway. The US post office was within walking distance on Clark Street. Vivian had her hair done in the beauty shop in the Surf Hotel on the corner. When she was too tired to make lunch, she splurged and bundled up the girls to take them out to O'Connell's on Diversey for a quick bite: juicy hamburgers, buttermilk waffles, chocolate phosphates, and blueberry pie. The best.

Out in the suburbs, Vivian was stranded. Six days a week, Mel drove his Oldsmobile, the family's only car, down to grimy, crowded Maxwell Street where he and his brothers worked long hours at Jacobson Brothers, the business Mel's father and uncle established after selling vegetables on pushcarts upon their arrival in Chicago from Chernigov, Russia in 1906. Jacobson Brothers began as a grocery, then a delicatessen, and now, a busy tavern in the hub of the port-of-entry marketplace. Downtown Wilmette was beyond walking distance from their home. Vivian was often lonely. She missed her husband and adult conversation. The all-consuming nature of caring for the children and their new home had begun to overwhelm her.

Mel tried to pitch in on his day off, but he was only home on Wednesdays. Vivian envied him as the even-tempered "good parent": the arithmetic teacher and card game player. Vivian was thrust into the role of traffic cop, always on the brink of blasting a piercing whistle. She hated to hear herself raging at the kids. Soft-spoken Mel rarely raised his voice. The girls adored him.

THE DOORBELL chimed in a shower of sweet trills, unleashing renewed cries from the playpen. The screen door banged open, followed by a boisterous call of "Di-ia-per Man!" ricocheting through the house, propelling Vivian off the sofa, leaving her cigarette burning in the ashtray, and dashing upstairs to retrieve their stinky, lumpy bundle. The lanky, black-haired man with a greasy lock falling onto his forehead followed to help her lug the unwieldy bag downstairs. Then, he raced out to his truck to exchange her family's mess for a towering stack of folded, sweet-smelling bleached cloths and returned to bound back up the stairs to leave them in the baby's room. At last, the little ones had quieted.

Before he ran out again, Vivian asked with a catch in her voice,

"Could you add another stop? Make it three times a week?" She hoped Mel would OK the extra expense.

The diaper man shifted from foot to foot.

"Please?" she begged coquettishly, and combed her fingers through her brunette perm.

He pushed back his unruly shock of hair and looked at his feet. "You'll have to call the office, Mrs. J. You know they do all the routes."

He must have noticed her eyes welling. The diaper man shoved his hands in his pockets and said, "I guess I could give you another dozen. But just today, mind you. You sure do use 'em up fast."

Vivian wanted to hug this middle-aged man with his too-long greaser 'do, the only adult male she'd seen since Mel left home hours earlier. She'd ask Mel tonight, during their private dinner hour, to be sure they could afford her impulsive request. Her husband kept a detailed household budget, accounting to the penny for their expenses: mortgage, real estate taxes, utility bills (electric, gas, water, and sewer), milkman's deliveries to the tin box outside their back door, landscaping, snowplow service for the driveway, and each piece of stylish modern furniture Mel's cousin, the interior decorator, suggested they buy. Mel separated these costs from the allotment he gave Vivian for her needs and the children's: new clothes, shoes, haircuts, and toys. Mel kept the diaper service and doctor's bills in the house account.

Doctor's bills. She'd almost forgotten about her scare in the garden. Impossible, but she'd need a test at the doctor's office to be certain. Didn't everyone say you couldn't get pregnant while nursing? Most of the women she knew bottle-fed their babies, but Dr. Goldblum was insistent. Breastfeeding offered the best odds for a healthy child. Vivian followed his every instruction to the letter. She'd continued nursing ten-month-old Billy longer than the others, not wanting to release her last baby. He'd *better* be her last.

Don't panic. Behave normally. Do laundry. Cook dinner. Pick up the toys and blocks before Mel got home. He liked order and hated stepping around a jumbled mess. Fix her face. She must look a fright. Try on her new shade of Revlon's Super Lustrous lipstick to masquerade as an alluring woman to disguise the frazzled housewife inside.

AN HOUR before Mel was due home, Vivian nursed Billy, fed the others a quick dinner, and loaded their dirty dishes into the Hotpoint dishwasher. Irene and four-year-old Sandy sat on the floor playing Go Fish! while Vivian put Linda and Billy down to sleep and then went upstairs to the master bedroom's en suite bathroom to freshen up. She patted on pancake makeup, brushed on blue eye shadow and black liquid eyeliner, curled her lashes before adding thick layers of black mascara—careful not to smudge—then styled her hair and sprayed it with Aqua Net. After deftly applying Revlon's new Fire & Ice, she took a tissue to blot her lips and looked into the mirror, smiling in approval of her artistry. For a finishing touch, she added a slight spritz of Chanel No. 5 to make herself feel elegant.

When the *chug-chug-chug* of the automatic garage door resounded through the house, Irene and Sandy shrieked, "Daddy's home!" and hugged him around the knees as he entered the den directly from the garage. Laughing, Mel handed each of the girls a pack of Wrigley's Juicy Fruit gum before shaking them off to climb the half-flight to his waiting wife. Vivian was also thrilled to hear the garage door finally rise, but a little jealous because she never received such enthusiastic greetings from her girls. Mel pecked Vivian on the lips, brushing his rough beard against her cheek. He never left or returned home without meeting her mouth with his. Mel's scratchy face, already two hours beyond his five o'clock shadow, aroused her. She leaned into him, breathing the pungent, familiar whiff of the man she loved. A blend of congealed aromas from the grimy Maxwell Street tavern permeated his clothes: stale beer, spicy corned beef, and the lingering stench of cigarettes. Although none of these odors reflected Mel's own habits, except his rare indulgence in a good Havana cigar, they combined to brand him with a lingering reminder of the unsavory environment where he spent his long days away.

VIVIAN WENT back into the kitchen to put their dinner on the table as Mel went through his routine. He glanced through the day's mail before making a beeline to the basement to unlock the liquor cabinet. A half-filled bottle of Glenlivet Scotch stood next to an empty shot glass. He poured himself an ounce and savored it to take the edge off his hectic day. Home was where he found peace. He then padded all the way up to the bedroom level to bend and kiss the sweet faces of his sleeping son and toddler. What a wonderful wife he had! She expertly cared for their children and still looked like a knockout at the end of the day. He rubbed his hand through his thinning hair. Some days he couldn't believe his good fortune. On his long drives home, sometimes he pictured his worst fear. What if he came home to find Viv and the children had vanished? That sounded like something from the movies. He sipped the last drop and let it roll around on his tongue. It was bad luck to even imagine such things. Believe it. Vivian, their children, and this home were really his.

A bit drowsy after his frenzied workday and long commute, Mel settled into his comfortable green upholstered chair in the living room to read the evening paper. Every night he stopped at the same newsstand at the corner of Jackson and Halsted and tooted his horn twice to alert the newsman. Out he ran to the driver's side of Mel's Oldsmobile with the populist *Daily News* evening paper in hand, never the more conservative *American*. After pocketing a nickel tip, the newsman touched the brim of his cap before trotting back to his makeshift shed. Irene and Sandy crept up the stairs and punched at the newspaper that hid Mel's face. Mel tried not to laugh, pretending not to notice the rambunctious girls.

Vivian chased them away, saying, "Daddy's tired!" They raced back to the den, laughing, even when she scolded, "Keep your dirty fingerprints off my white walls!"

Still giggling, the girls tuned to one of their favorite programs. Depending on the day of the week, *Gunsmoke*, *Lassie*, or *The Adventures of Ozzie and Harriet* flickered across the black-and-white screen. Tonight, it was *I Love Lucy.*

Mel looked around his modern living room feeling grateful to have left the hubbub of Maxwell Street's colorful street corners behind. The loud, dirty city was where he spent his days—everyone had to make a living, didn't they?—but Wilmette's quiet, pristine scenery was where he spent his nights. He was thankful that Vivian had given him the push he needed to move out here. Without her foresight about what was best for their family, he wouldn't have been bold enough to leave his clannish extended family in the city to move to this shiny suburban home with his sexy wife, surrounded by their four bright children. The king of his castle, indeed.

In the kitchen, Vivian finished preparing the dinner for the two of them: broiled skirt steak, mashed potatoes from scratch, and canned green beans. She wasn't much of a cook. Even simple meals took her full concentration, unlike Ethel, her older sister by nine years, who had cooked for the whole Kolson family for as long as Vivian could remember. Their ma had made the best chicken soup but left the rest of the meal preparation to Ethel. For a wedding gift, Ethel had bought Vivian *The Settlement Cook Book* and inscribed it, *To Baby Sis, you gotta learn to cook sometime.* The cookbook became Vivian's bible, covering all the basics: matzoh ball soup, potato pancakes, brisket, roast chicken, and how to perfectly time a soft- or hard-boiled egg. Preparing these dishes was her first step toward becoming the paragon of the Jewish homemaker she aspired to be.

As they sat together at the table, Mel looked into his wife's deep brown eyes. "Are you feeling all right? You look pale."

She pinched her cheeks to add a little color. "What a day! Almost ran out of diapers. We really need to up the service to three times a week. Can we do that?"

"Sure, our budget can stand it." Mel stroked the top of her hand. When Vivian twisted her fingers away from him, he looked puzzled. "Is that all?"

"The kids got to me today. I yelled at Irene." She decided not to mention how Linda nearly fell down the stairs.

"Why? What'd she do?"

"She refused to play outside. She's afraid of the cicadas. Called them little helicopters."

Mel chuckled. "Helicopters! Our clever girl. No wonder the Wilmette schools moved her ahead to skip kindergarten and start in first grade."

"Don't laugh. She was terrified."

"Was she? Irene was brave enough when I took her to the zoo. Roared right back at the lions."

"Stop it. I don't blame her. These ugly bugs give me the creeps, too."

"Aw c'mon, they're not too bad. I saw one on Halsted Street today."

"Only one? You're kidding. Here, they're everywhere you look. And big."

"Big? What's big?" said Mel. "Judy the Elephant was Sandy's favorite at the zoo."

Vivian clutched her stomach and burst into tears, remembering how it felt to be as big as an elephant before her babies were born.

Mel put down his fork. "Viv, what's wrong?"

"Nothing," she said, sweeping her bangs off her face. "Too much baby talk all day long. Sometimes I feel like I'm losing my mind. I feel like an awful mother."

"Don't say that. You're a terrific mother."

She held back another round of tears. "More mashed potatoes?"

He nodded, swallowed the last morsel, and handed her his plate. The spare tire around his middle was expanding, but Vivian still found him handsome and would never refuse him. She dutifully went to the stove and lifted the lid off the pot. She glanced at their neighbors' glitzy invitation to their son's bar mitzvah still taped to the fridge. Yes, it had been a night to remember. They'd been giddy to feel they truly belonged on Maple Street. She'd dieted for weeks to squeeze back into the black sheath with the lace top from before having Billy. She'd drunk the extra glass of wine Mel had poured for her—or was it two? The sudden memory of their passionate lovemaking late into that night jolted her. Could that have been when . . . ? She stared at the date on the invitation. March 17. That long ago? She glanced at the wall calendar. Today was April 28. She dropped the lid of the pot with a clank.

"Ouch!"

Mel jumped up. "Vivian?!"

She motioned for him to sit and sucked on her finger. "It's nothing. Just burned my pinky on the electric cooktop. Still used to our old gas burners."

"You've got to be more careful."

"I'm as careful as I can be," she said in a shrill tone.

Mel grimaced and sat.

"Careful? How can I take care of myself when I don't have a moment's peace all day?" She choked back a sob as she walked over and slammed down the refilled plate in front of him.

Mel had no idea what it was like to be here with the children all day, every day: refereeing arguments, patching skinned knees, mopping spills, cooking to please picky eaters, soothing their fears, surrounded by whining and wailing.

He wiped his mouth with his napkin. "Calm down. I don't like to see you upset."

Calm down? He doesn't know the half of it.

"What's for dessert?" he asked in a low tone.

"Jell-O. With fruit cocktail."

"Red Jell-O?" he asked.

She nodded.

"My favorite," he said.

Vivian couldn't help but smile. She couldn't stay mad at him. Everything she made for Mel was his "favorite." He tried to boost her confidence in the kitchen. She knew she didn't compare to his mother, who had been an excellent cook. And there was Ethel, who loved to point out her shortcomings. Bossy ole Ethel had an opinion about everything.

Mel stood to embrace his wife. She relaxed into his arms. He kissed her deeply but stopped abruptly when they heard Irene's and Sandy's voices mingling with the canned laugh track that mimicked a live TV audience. Mel and Vivian locked eyes.

Irene's imitation sent Sandy into wild giggles. "You're funnier than Lucy Ricardo!"

Mel murmured, "Aren't our girls swell?"

Vivian nodded, dabbing at her eyes as Mel walked away to his easy chair to finish reading the paper. She was glad he wouldn't see her tears.

Yes, they're swell. They'll be grown before we know it.

If only her darling girls could remain naive and never grow to face adult women's age-old dilemmas. For only a moment, Vivian let herself imagine that she was, in fact, pregnant again. How she'd loved to bring home her darling newborns, each with a glowing face and nascent awareness. Each one unique. Then, why so gloomy? She twisted her wedding rings around and around. Her throat constricted. She felt deep in her gut that another one would be too much—push her over the edge. How could she admit this to Mel? He might think she was unfit to be a mother to the children they already had. Indeed, today had been a day when she'd wanted to escape from them all.

When she was single and worked as a secretary in the storefront office at the edge of the Loop, if she needed to boost her spirits, she'd hop on the streetcar and buy a new hat at Marshall Field's. Those days were over. There was no way to escape from life here on Maple Street. As a mother of four, she knew it was unlikely, but she still held out a glimmer of hope to someday find a way to follow her dream to go to college and become a schoolteacher. She couldn't be pregnant again. Another baby would dash those dreams for good. It would be like inserting a jackstraw onto a wobbly tower of Pick Up Stix—Irene and Sandy's favorite game—only to watch the structure collapse in a heap. Torn between being a good mother and a good wife, Vivian felt she was losing ground on both. Another baby might upset the perfectly arranged home she and Mel had made for their family in Wilmette. She'd have to forget about the prospect of a fulfilling future all her own.

She needed a cigarette.

Mel called out. "Viv, I'm beat. Can you get the girls ready for bed?"

Of course she could. Wasn't that her job? If she didn't, who would? What choice did she have? But why was everything always up to her?

Vivian took a deep breath and called, "Girls! Bedtime! Get in your pj's and brush your teeth!"

"Five more minutes?" wheedled Irene.

"I said *now*!"

Vivian put the pans into the sink to soak. She'd come back downstairs to finish washing up when the kids were asleep. The house had to be perfect for Ethel's visit the next day. She couldn't take any extra criticism from her sister. Not now.

Vivian touched her palm to her chest. Nothing. No aches. She exhaled loudly.

She must not let her imagination run wild. She must put these fears out of her mind.

Everything would work out.

It had to.

CHAPTER TWO
ETHEL'S VISIT

SUNDAY, 1956

AS THE commuter train sped northward from Chicago, a kaleidoscope of iridescent green trees soon replaced the city's grimy alleys. Ethel Kolson, sporting her unfussy Buster Brown haircut, *tap, tap, tapped* the toe of her firmly tied, sensible shoe against the seatback ahead. A frowning man in a chic fedora turned and glared at her, but Ethel stared him down. What highfalutin notion had gotten ahold of her sister to convince her husband, a real doll making good dough at his Maxwell Street joint, to move way the heck out to Wilmette? Couldn't Viv be satisfied in Rogers Park, closer to Ma? Sure, people were leaving the city right and left, but Ethel couldn't see what the big deal was about these snooty suburbs. Thank God her sister hadn't moved closer to that Kennelsworth, or whatever it was called, where everyone knew Jews weren't welcome. Hadn't they had enough of that growing up next to the Poles, Italians, and Irish on the west side? Ma had fled for her life to escape the pogroms in Old Russia. No doubt about it, the same haters were here in America, but sure as shootin', Ethel wouldn't go looking for them.

Ethel clambered off the train at the Wilmette station before it roared away, horn blaring, belching a trail of sooty smoke as a reminder from where they'd come. Ethel coughed and reached for a Lucky Strike before swatting away a flying bug as big as a Pontiac.

Vivian had warned her about these darn locusts. Worse than the plagues of Egypt. Ethel elbowed herself ahead of a man stinking of cigars to grab the only waiting cab and muttered her sister had better learn to drive if she wanted to live out where God left his shoes.

When the driver stopped in front of 336 Maple Street, Ethel hopped out, kicked the door shut, and said in a huff, "Whadd'ya mean, 'Is that all?' You're lucky to get my extra nickel for the lousy ride."

Vivian cringed and gave Ethel a withering look, hoping the neighbors hadn't heard her sister's rough remarks. Vivian wore tight turquoise pedal pushers with a diaper slung over her shoulder and stood on her front walk, cradling the baby. She stomped on a cicada, then examined her new beige espadrille hoping she'd avoided a stain. Ethel probably blamed her for these swarming insects. But what could she do? Not her fault. This was the life out here.

Ethel was on her day off from her job at the fanciest dress shop on Oak Street. She smiled broadly and took long strides toward her younger sister. Her string-bean build in baggy, plaid, cuffed trousers and no-nonsense haircut was in stark contrast to Vivian's compact buxom shape and smooth pageboy. No one would ever mistake them for sisters. No matter how different they might be, their fierce kinship was solid.

Ethel stopped and stared. She trusted what she saw. Unmistakable. Viv was more zaftig than usual.

Zaftig?

At the dress shop where she worked, men came to outfit not only their wives but their mistresses too. It was Ethel's job as head seamstress to notice a customer's unexplained curves. She heard the women whisper about where to go if they found themselves in a jam. Would Vivian know? Hoo boy! Her baby sister better wise up fast, better not make their ma's mistake. Vivian deserved a better life than Ma. Ethel knew all too well the burdens too many children placed on a family.

Irene skipped up to her. "Aunt Ethel! It's you!"

"Who d'ya think? The man in the moon?" She pushed away Irene's outstretched arms. "You're too big to pick up anymore."

Irene sniffed and ran back to the group of children on the sidewalk to rejoin a game of tag. When one of the bigger boys tagged her "it," Irene started to cry.

"Aw, c'mon, don't be a baby," he teased.

Vivian took a few steps toward her next-door neighbor's son. How dare he pick on Irene?

"Leave 'em alone," said Ethel. "The sooner your girls learn to stick up for themselves, the better off they'll be."

As the mismatched sisters walked into the house together, Ethel complained. "Took me two hours to get here. I always forget what a hike it is from the city. You sure you like living way out here?"

Vivian rolled her eyes. Same ole Ethel. Her sister never changed. She reached up to put her hand on Ethel's shoulder. "I love it here. But it can get lonely. Thanks for making the trip." Vivian led her toward the cozy kitchen.

Ethel plopped onto a chair, then pulled out her pack of cigarettes and lighter before tossing her pocketbook onto the floor. "Any coffee made? You oughta at least be able to make coffee."

Vivian sighed. "Relax. Coffee's perking. I want your honest opinion of our new couch. Take a look and tell me the truth. Does the new green-and-orange upholstery go good with my avocado shag carpeting?"

"What if I say it doesn't? Will you send it back?"

Vivian groaned. "Don't be such a grouch. Really, it's good to see you. Being around these kids all day can make me crazy."

"You said it, not me." Ethel reached for the coffeepot. "Got any real half-and-half?"

"C'mon, Eth. Isn't milk good enough? I can't stock everything."

In her playpen in the formal dining area alongside the kitchen,

Linda let out a high-pitched wail. Vivian jumped up, but Ethel motioned for her to sit. "Let her cry. Can't run to them at every peep." Then Baby Billy let out a yelp and began to squirm in Vivian's arms. Ethel pointed to the kitchen chair beside her. "After you put Mr. Chubby Cheeks in his crib, come back and take a load off."

"OK, OK. In the meantime, help yourself to schnecken."

Ethel shook her head at the packaged pecan rolls arranged neatly on a dish and gave Vivian her familiar "that all ya got?" look. Vivian wasn't surprised by her disapproval, but there was no way she could get to a bakery. And home-baked goods were out of the question. No time.

Ethel reached for her lighter and lit up. When Vivian returned, she asked, "Is this an ashtray?" She pointed to a clean dish painted with foreign words written in curlicued script. When Vivian nodded, she traced the gold-colored rim with her finger.

"Fancy-schmancy. Where'd you find it? The Salvation Army store?"

"My interior decorator brought it."

"Oh, I get it. *She* bought it at Salvation Army, marked it up ten times, and sold it back to you. La-di-da. Ain't you the grand lady? And Mel Jacobson puts up with this? I never took him for a chump."

"Mel wants me to be happy. Don't you want nice things?"

"Not enough to hunt up a husband. After Pa, I wouldn't take my chances on any man. With my luck, I'd wind up with some dumb schmuck I'd be waiting on hand and foot and still have to work to pay the bills. Wait. Don't sit. Let me look at you." Ethel blew out a long stream of smoke. "You're looking more and more like Ma every day."

Vivian sucked in her gut. "I'll take that as a compliment," she said and quickly sat. "Why?"

"I think you know damn well why," said Ethel as Irene ran through the front door.

"Mommy, I gotta go wee-wee!"

Vivian whispered loudly, "Quiet, Irene! Baby Billy's sleeping. Use the downstairs bathroom." Irene squealed and ran, gripping her crotch.

Vivian leaned toward Ethel and spoke in a low tone. "Watch yourself. I don't want Irene to hear your foolish talk."

"Foolish talk? Take your head out of the sand, baby girl." A serious look crossed Ethel's face. "I wasn't much older than your Irene the summer when Ma was such a wreck."

Vivian took a last drag on her cigarette, exhaled, stubbed it out, and took a nibble from her sweet roll. "What are you saying? What happened with Ma?"

Vivian's neck felt tight. Eagle-eyed Ethel. Never missed a thing.

SUMMER, 1923.

HANNAH KOLSON prayed it wasn't so. The all-too-familiar signs were impossible to ignore any longer. Nauseated, she ran to the hallway toilet and rapped an urgent staccato to hasten whoever lingered inside. When a youngster dashed out, head down, tying up his pants, Hannah rushed in and slammed the door, scrambling to let down layers of undergarments to check for the blood she knew wasn't there. After heaving bitter vomit into the pot, she stood upright and shook her fist at the light trickling in through the haphazard ceiling slats. "Aren't four enough? Dayenu!" Panting, she shoved her fist into her burning mouth, lest her boldness anger God.

Knock, knock! Three other families shared this toilet. It was never vacant.

Hannah hurled another round of her mealy breakfast into the commode, groaning to consider all that would lay ahead if she survived what was surely a fifth pregnancy: endless nursing, buying back baby clothes she'd given away twice over, extra mounds of laundry stained with spit-up, and added commotion at all hours. All to care for a new, wailing infant disrupting their already overcrowded flat.

She imagined the wooden diaper pail in the corner unleashing a wicked grin. Hannah gagged with a whiff of its putrid breath. Purging that filth was her most despised chore, the neighbors' collective duty to appease the city's roving sanitary inspectors. Would she have to add cleaning this sludge bucket to eight-year-old Ethel's mounting tasks? She already burdened her only daughter with a heavy household load. But who else did she have to help her? Her sons did nothing. Just like their pa. Life in Chicago was rough. Tougher than Hannah had imagined.

With God's help, Hannah had been kept safe from bearing more children for five years. By feigning sleep, or worse, she'd tried to stay away from her husband Abe at her most vulnerable times. Abe left his bed for hers whenever he pleased, ignoring all risks and the Jewish laws. For an extra precaution, Hannah followed a whispered tip passed around the shul's women's balcony: After relations, squeeze Lysol into your private parts and rinse with water. She hid the apparatus and its stinging solution from Abe. If only she had her Mama with her. Back in their Russian village, Mama had told her the midwife had herbs for these emergencies, such as when their young neighbor was impregnated by her uncle. Hannah had been warned against another childbirth. Who could save her life in this foreign Chicago? Where was God?

Knock! Knock! Knock!

"Sha! Quiet! I'm coming."

Hannah hurried out of the water closet, straightening her skirts. "Oy, a woman's lot."

When she reentered the flat, Hannah called for Ethel to put on her Shabbos best and dress Max in his good shirt, urging her to hurry before the older boys came home from the rabbi's cheder class.

"Where are we going, Ma?" asked Ethel. "It's only Wednesday."

"Don't ask, my little mamele. I need your help. Don't let Max make a noise. You know how the neighbors complain."

Five-year-old Max ran screaming all the way down to the first floor, banging on the glass-paned front door to try to push it open. Ethel caught up to him and grabbed him as he strained against her grip. Hannah was huffing when she reached them and scolded, "Max, today, of all days, you must behave! Ethel, mind your brother!"

By noon, they reached the corner of Twelfth Street. Dense heat turned the air to vapor, causing water to stream from Hannah's armpits. She patted her underarms, grimacing at the stains on in her long-sleeved cotton blouse, worried that someone might see droplets sprinkling onto the sidewalk. As the trio trudged along, they passed the barber shop, kosher butcher, hardware store, delicatessen, dressmaker's, and shoemaker's repair shop. At the greengrocer, Max pressed his nose onto the window until Ethel pulled him away by his hair. Hannah ignored her son's yelps and focused on her plan, vowing never again to beg God for anything if she could find a way out of this emergency.

Hannah's hands shook when she heard Ethel shout, "Stop, Max! Stop!"

Screeching streetcar brakes pierced the heavy air. Passengers screamed. Hannah squeezed her eyelids shut and, as if summoned, saw the anguished blue eyes of the Polish mother on the next block. Hannah shuddered as she remembered how this woman's son lost his leg under a streetcar's wheel last month. All rivalries had ceased as the neighborhood's Jews, Poles, Italians, and Irish mourned the tragic accident as one.

Hannah's eyes flew open when the conductor yelled, "Lady! You're lucky I didn't run him down! Your boy coulda been killed!"

Tears of relief washed away the vision of the Polish mother's sorrow. Her Max was spared. She would not share the Polish mother's pain. Not on this day.

Her stomach turned over as she shook Ethel's shoulders. "What did I tell you? Watch after your brother!"

Ethel grabbed Max by the collar. With her other hand, she gave him a little potch on his behind and waggled her finger, mimicking Pa when he got angry with Ma. "Max! If I told you once, I told you a hundred times! Never, never, never run away from me!"

Max strained to bolt again until Ethel lifted her arm as if to strike him, and he quieted. Then, she changed from little mother to little girl and skipped alongside Hannah, holding her mother's hand and gripping Max's fingers tightly with the other.

Hannah chastised herself for being so hard on her daughter. Wasn't Ethel but a child herself?

Ethel and Max ran ahead. Hannah called out to them to turn onto Crawford Avenue. Ethel yelled, "Now I know where we're going! Daubert's store! Can I get a penny candy today? Can I, can I?"

"Yes. After we finish with the druggist."

"The druggist? Are you sick?"

Hannah's voice wavered. "No, but I need something from him. You must ask for me in your best English."

Again, Hannah yearned for her own mama. She wished she didn't have to ask her American daughter to beg for something she couldn't understand.

The bells attached to the door of Daubert's tinkled a pleasant *ring-ring, ring-a-ling-ling* announcing their entry. No other store in the neighborhood rang out such a tantalizing, high-pitched tune. Ethel lingered inside the door and gazed at the counter with a lineup of all her favorites and more: Wrigley's Juicy Fruit and Doublemint gum, Tootsie Rolls, Baby Ruths, and Hershey bars. Max strained to reach into the row of barrels filled with more of the treats they coveted: long ropes of red licorice, paper dots, waxen bottles filled with sugary liquids, lollipops, and jelly beans. He lurched and stuck in his hand to grab a fistful, but Ethel jerked him back.

Ethel held him tight and begged, "Ma, can we get two candies today?"

"Let's wait and see. Now hand over your brother." Max resisted, holding tight to Ethel's grip.

"But Ma, you know he minds me better."

Hannah clucked her tongue and held out her hand. Ethel obediently transferred the apple-cheeked boy's sweaty palm into her mother's cracked fingers and warned, "Listen to Ma!"

Hannah led the way over oak floors strewn with sawdust, passing shelves crammed with assorted hairpins, spools of ribbons, sewing needles, thimbles, cards of buttons of various shapes, and every imaginable color of thread. Small pouches of specialty cough remedies mixed on the premises caught Hannah's eye. She eased her grip on Max, who stood on tippy-toes, straining to reach up and grab a key chain adorned with a White Sox baseball charm. Ever alert, Ethel pushed his damp fingers away and slapped his wrist. Max wound up to punch his sister, but Hannah stood between them to prevent a fight.

At the back of the store, Hannah pushed Ethel up to the druggist's high counter. The man peered over it through gold wire-rimmed spectacles with lenses so thick they obscured his eyes. He frowned and cleared his throat.

"What can I do for you today, Mrs. Kolinsky? Is everybody well?"

Ethel answered. "We're the *Kolsons* now."

The druggist chortled. "Oho, aren't you the clever girl? You must be citizens. So soon?"

"Yes, Pa said he gave us all a good American name."

The druggist's tone shifted from solicitous to taunting. "What is it with you people? Come to this country and breed like rabbits. We'll be outnumbered in no time." He slapped the counter with his palm and stared over Ethel's head and met Hannah's eyes with a scowl.

Hannah bent and whispered to Ethel. "What is this *outnumbered*?"

Ethel replied in Yiddish, "Ignore him. He's a mean man."

Hannah whispered again and gave Ethel a little push. "Go on, ask. Ask him for something to bring on my courses."

Ethel hesitated and looked back at her mother. She twisted the end of her long brown braid. "Bring on your *what* . . . ?"

"Just ask the man what I tell you to ask," said Hannah with a slap on Max's wrist to stop his fidgeting.

The druggist tapped his pestle. "Out with it, child. What does your mother need?"

Ethel lifted her head and drew in a deep breath. "My ma wants to know if you . . . if you have something"—she looked back at Hannah, who waved at her to continue—"to bring on her—"

Hannah set her lips in a tight line. Her eyes beseeched the stern druggist. As Max squirmed, Hannah took a deep breath and prayed this hostile American would have the same herb the old midwife had in their Russian village. With her free palm, she motioned to surround her still-invisible, rotund belly.

Ethel's mouth fell open. "Ma! No? Are you—"

"My, my. Aren't you the bright little girl," said the druggist, smoothing an errant blond strand to cover his balding pate.

Hannah placed her hand on her daughter's shoulder. Ethel lifted her face and rapidly repeated her mother's request. The druggist clucked his tongue and spat on the sawdust floor.

"You Jews! At least the Italians and the Irish fear their pope!"

At the word *pope*, Hannah spun Ethel toward the door. "We must go."

"Speak English!" The druggist pounded his fist. "If you want to be real Americans!"

Ethel turned around and jutted her chin at him. "I *did* ask you in English!"

"Girl, tell your mother if she doesn't want this baby, I'll take him!"

Hannah unleashed a Yiddish curse. "You should get so sick as to cough up your mother's milk!"

Ethel gasped and covered her mouth. "Ma, that's terrible what you said!"

"Enough with your foreign gibberish," the druggist hollered. "Get out! You can go to your Maxwell Street ghetto to get what you want! You don't need to come to me!"

Max broke free and bolted toward the front of the store. Ethel dashed after him. When Hannah reached the children, Max had already pulled a fistful of lollipops out of the barrel. Ethel pried open his stubby fingers and pulled out several, but he clung to the last few. Ethel looked longingly at the candy counter.

"Only one," said Hannah.

Ethel took a Baby Ruth. Max gripped his last lollipop.

Hannah reached into her pocketbook, but the stout German woman at the cash register surprised her when she waved her palm and said, "No money today, missus."

"T-anks you," said Hannah, trying out her English. She hurried the children out of the door as the bells tinkled a harsh goodbye. Putting a hand on her heart, Hannah said, "See, my brave girl with the good English, God is watching over us. Everything will be all right."

With lips covered in chocolate, Ethel asked, "Ma, are you sick?"

Hannah shook her head. "This morning's breakfast bothered my stomach."

Ethel looked puzzled. "Same oatmeal we eat every day." She stopped and asked, "Why did the druggist get mad? Didn't he have the medicines you needed?"

Hannah stared into her daughter's bright face. "Maybe he had, but not for me."

"Why? Because we don't have the money to pay?"

"Not the reason."

Ethel hugged her mother around the waist. “Ma, are you going to have another baby?”

Hannah pushed her arms away. “Why do you think so, mine daughter?”

“I heard you vomiting this morning. Miriam downstairs told me that’s how it starts.”

“Miriam doesn’t know everything,” said Hannah. “Only God decides whether we will have another one or not.”

“What about Pa? Doesn’t he have a say?”

Hannah froze. “Don’t tell your Pa about this.”

“Why not? Won’t he want a baby?”

“What about you, Etheleh? Do you want I should have one more?”

Ethel remained silent. Their three-room flat was already cramped and noisy. Hannah often took sick to her bed, leaving Ethel to take over.

Ethel stared at her feet and answered, “Maybe another girl. We have too many boys.”

Hannah tweaked her daughter’s cheek. “True, my wise daughter. Too many.”

They hurried back to their building. Max was quiet, sucking on his lollipop.

“My friend Dena’s family has a restaurant on Maxwell Street,” said Ethel. “Will you go there, like the druggist said?”

“Hush,” said Hannah. “I’ve seen their restaurant. Close to the maternity clinic. But Liza Jacobson doesn’t talk to me in shul. She sits with the politicians’ wives.”

“She’s nicer than you think,” said Ethel. “Dena brought me home one day after school. Her ma bakes good cookies.”

Ethel took Max’s hand and they skipped ahead. Suddenly off-balance, Hannah stumbled on the uneven sidewalk but caught herself before falling. She shouldn’t have asked her daughter to beg that uncaring druggist for such a thing. But wasn’t Max supposed to be her last?

She'd almost died that night. God might not spare her again. Without thinking, she called out, "Keinehora!" to keep away the evil eye. Sweating and breathing hard, she stopped and smoothed down her skirts.

Ethel ran back without releasing her grip on Max. "What's wrong, Ma? I heard you call 'Keinehora.'"

"You hear everything, don't you, my little American? Don't you worry about me."

Ethel and Max hugged their mother's waist.

A tear escaped Hannah's eye. "My dear kinderlach. And you, my strong daughter, what would I do without you in this foreign Chicago?"

SUNDAY AFTERNOON, 1956

"WOULD A German druggist really have taken in a Jewish baby?" asked Vivian. The stale pecan roll hardened in her stomach, feeling tougher than a piece of leftover liver.

Ethel finished her sweet roll in one bite and leaned back to balance the chair on two legs before tapping out another cigarette from her pack. Vivian took her napkin to wipe away a nut dangling on her sister's lip.

"It don't sound believable, but I remember what he said. I was young, but I had big ears."

"And Ma cursed him? Are you sure?" asked Vivian. "Ma doesn't raise her voice to anyone."

"I heard what I heard."

"Tell me." Vivian's leg shook with the *shpilkes*. "Could that baby have been me?"

Ethel took a few drags on her cigarette before she spoke. "For once, little sister, figure it out yourself. You think I've got all the answers? C'mon, let's go sit on that new couch of yours. Isn't that what you invited me here to see?"

Vivian stumbled as she tried to balance her coffee cup and saucer, teetering until Ethel took her elbow to steady her and usher her into the living room. Vivian's thighs trembled as she sat close to her sister on the couch and held her breath. Ethel pressed her palms against the seat cushions and caressed the shiny fabric.

"Your decorator has good taste," she said and leaned back with a sublime look on her face.

Vivian exhaled in relief. She lit a cigarette and blew it out forcefully. Her sister's approval meant the world to her.

Sandy burst in through the door. "Mommy, my knee is bleeding. Awful Chuckie pushed me down! I need a Band-Aid."

"Honey, were you teasing him again?" Vivian turned to Ethel and said, "This one is just like you. Hold on, Eth, I've got to take care of her."

Vivian took the stairs two at a time to the upstairs bathroom, returning with a wet washcloth, a small bottle of Mercurochrome, and two Band-Aids. After gently wiping dirt and gravel from her daughter's knee, Vivian applied the stinging orange liquid, causing Sandy to emit only a faint yelp.

"Be tough," Ethel said to her niece as Vivian snapped a Band-Aid into place and smoothed it gently over the scrape.

Sandy wiped away a tear with a muddy hand. "Kiss it, Mommy. Make it all better."

Vivian complied and gave the child a little push toward the door. Sandy dashed out. The screen door slammed behind her.

Vivian called, "Irene! Are you still downstairs?"

A tiny voice wafted up from the den. "I'm reading *Blueberries for Sal* one more time before we take it back to the library."

"Outside! Now!" said Vivian.

Ethel jabbed her elbow into Vivian's rib. "If you think your Sandy is like me, then that Irene is your carbon copy. Always with her nose in a book." Ethel stubbed out her cigarette. "Don't sit down. Let me have a look at you." She put her hands on Vivian's waist.

Vivian pushed her hand away. "Stop it. What are you doing?"

"You know damn well what. I'm a seamstress who studies women's shapes all day, every day. Unless it's from living the good life out here in the suburbs, I'd bet dollars to doughnuts you're in the same pickle Ma was way back when. Doncha use a diaphragm?"

"None of your business what I do."

Ethel snorted. "Don't kid around with me. With all these kids, aren't you worried?"

"Leave me alone. Anyway, I'm nursing. I can't get pregnant now. Besides, it's too early to tell. I'd need a test at the doctor's."

"From what I see, you'd better get over there pronto. Listen to me, baby girl, if you don't want to have another kid, don't have one. My customers talk about it all the time. From the looks of this place, Mel makes a good living. Go find somewheres safe. It's not like it was in Ma's day."

"What do you know?" said Vivian. "It's not as easy as you think—"

"What's stopping you? You wouldn't be the first. Ask your sainted doctor if he'll do it himself."

Ethel had a point. Dr. Goldblum was her god after all he did for her before she had Irene. If Ethel's sharp eyes were accurate, Vivian would have to rely on Dr. Goldblum to come to her rescue. Why couldn't Ethel be wrong just this once? Even when they all lived under one roof on the west side, she spied every unwashed dish and every wrinkled shirt.

Ethel glanced at her watch. "Look at the time! I can't miss my train."

The doorbell rang. Jackie, the next-door neighbor. "I'm headed to the store. Can I pick up anything for you?" She knew Vivian didn't have a car.

"Thanks, but I don't need anything right now. Come on in. Meet my sister Ethel." She waved Jackie across the threshold.

She sashayed into the living room and extended her hand. "I'm Jackie Reisman from next door."

"Ethel Kolson." She reached out to shake. "The bossy older sister."

Jackie laughed. "I've got one of those myself."

"But I'll bet you're not a Goody Two-shoes like Viv here."

"Watch yourself," said Vivian. "Jackie doesn't need your opinions."

Jackie held up a palm like a crossing guard. "Vivian is all right by me."

Ethel guffawed and jabbed at her sister's upper arm. "I guess she's a keeper, but you don't know 'er like I do."

"How about giving Ethel a ride to the train?" asked Vivian.

Jackie smirked. "Sure thing. Give us time to compare notes."

"Good deal!" said Ethel, and snatched up her pocketbook.

Vivian put her hands on her hips. "Don't believe anything my sister says about me."

Baby Billy began to yowl. Vivian glanced at the wall clock as she hustled up the stairs. "Time to go, or you'll miss that train. You're a lifesaver, Jackie. I've got two fresh Jell-O molds in the fridge. Why don't you take one home for Hank and the kids?"

"You sure? Gee, thanks. I don't have anything for dessert tonight."

Ethel hugged her sister with a grip so tight that a small cry escaped from Vivian's mouth, surprising them both. "Take care of yourself, baby girl. Remember, if you need me, you know where to find me."

ON THE ride to the station, Ethel said, "I'm worried about my sister. Stuck way out here all day long with all those darn kids."

"Give her credit," said Jackie. "She's stronger than you think."

"I've always wanted the best for her, like she was my daughter, not my little sister."

"She's lucky to have you in her corner."

"Watch out for her, will ya?" said Ethel as she scrambled out of the car. "And thanks a bunch for the lift."

ETHEL CAUGHT the train with only minutes to spare. The trip back to Chicago whizzed by faster than the ride out to Wilmette. Her head pounded as she gazed numbly at the blur of leafy trees, surprised to feel a fat tear slide down her cheek. She wiped it away roughly with the back of her hand. What was this? She never cried. Hadn't she tried her best to navigate the family hardships to give Vivian a clear path to college to become a teacher? None of the other Kolsons had aimed that high—certainly she hadn't—and she recalled how she'd itched to quit school. Couldn't leave fast enough. But Viv ended up following the crowd. Marrying Mel Jacobson was OK for her, but not the sort of life Ethel wanted for herself. She'd let a man into her life only once, not long after she was done with school: a fling with a card shark from the pool hall where their older brothers hung out. When the jerk dumped her after she refused to stay overnight with him, Ethel swore off men for good. Would this chump take responsibility if he got her in trouble? Not a chance. What did she need a man for? She had the freedom to come and go as she pleased. Cook and clean only for herself. Keep up her own bills and take care of only her well-being unless the day came when Ma needed her. Yessiree. She liked it this way.

No doubt about it, Mel Jacobson was a mensch and a solid provider from a decent family, head and shoulders above their pa, but now her baby sister was knocked up again. Plain as the nose on her face. Too many kids and another one on the way. As far as Ethel could tell, Viv was already in over her head. Repeating Ma's crisis. Ethel felt like barfing.

The train made an abrupt stop at Evanston's Main Street station, and Ethel's forehead clunked onto the seatback in front of hers. Cursing, she rubbed the bruise. When the customers at the shop came back after taking care of their "problem," they were no worse for the wear as far as she could tell. As the saying goes: Viv made her bed, let her lie in it. Ethel took a clean handkerchief from her pocketbook and blew into it with two loud honks. A well-dressed man across the aisle stopped leafing through the Sunday *Tribune*, the rich folks' paper, and glared. Ethel stared back, raised an eyebrow, but restrained herself from flipping him the bird. Viv claimed she had the life she'd always dreamed of in that Wilmette house. But did she really? Her sister would have to solve her own problems. Ethel couldn't take charge of her baby sister the way she did back when they were under the same roof. No more coddling. Ethel blew her nose again, surprised to find her cheek was sopping wet.

Why was she crying?

CHAPTER THREE

THE MOVE TO MAPLE STREET

1956

ETHEL MIGHT be disapproving, but Vivian was happy in Wilmette. Who could have imagined that the Jacobsons would settle in so well?

In 1947, when Vivian and Mel married, Mel's mother, Liza, remained in the deep grief of widowhood. She relied on Mel, her eldest, more than her other four children. Vivian admired her husband's dedication to his mother and did her best to be a dutiful daughter-in-law, but Liza could be critical of her. She found Vivian's fascination with fashion to be frivolous and disapproved of what she considered Vivian's overspending on dresses, shoes, handbags, and hats. She'd mutter, with Vivian in earshot, about how her son works hard for his money. Despite this, Vivian faithfully followed Mel's encouragement to visit her mother-in-law to try to become closer, learn her recipes, and sit with her to pore over the family scrapbooks. Liza always cried at one photo where she stood alongside a sad-eyed, raven-haired woman and told Vivian this was her late sister-in-law Addie, a beautiful woman both inside and out.

IT WAS only when Liza passed away in 1955 that Mel was freed up from tending to his mother's needs: paying her bills, delivering orders from the pharmacy, or renewing the lease on her apartment. He could spend more time with Vivian and the children after his long hours at work. Vivian was secretly relieved, but Mel was morose and missed his mother greatly. Vivian tried her best to console him. Soon she was pregnant with their fourth and took this opportunity to convince Mel to search for a home in the suburbs. They'd long outgrown their Lakeview apartment, but Mel never would have agreed to abandon the city while his mother lived nearby.

Vivian relished the lush greenery of suburbia, a world away from the city. She was convinced that the excellent schools would lead her children toward the college and career opportunities that both she and Mel never had. Mel's siblings owned homes in the city's Rogers Park neighborhood, but after the war, Vivian's brothers had moved from the city they perceived held no future for them, seeking new horizons in Los Angeles. Of the Kolsons, only Ethel, Ma, and "Aunt Ruthie" (Ruth) Lavin remained in Chicago. Abe Kolson had been long absent from the family and down on his luck when they learned he had been killed in a tavern brawl. Vivian grieved for her pa. She was ready to move out of the city limits for good.

As always, Mel wanted to please his wife. He took off from work on the occasional Sunday to crowd the family into his Oldsmobile to go house hunting in the suburbs. On one trip, Vivian urged Mel to stop in front of a stately two-story brick home with an OPEN HOUSE sign in front. The house stood in the middle of a winding, shady street, set back from the sidewalk, with a sweeping lawn and a gracious, wraparound porch, only a few blocks from the beach. With a playground on the corner and a short walk to the elementary school, this would be an ideal place to raise their children.

They climbed the steps and walked in. The realtor was busy with an older couple and motioned the Jacobsons to explore the second floor. Irene and Sandy raced each other up the stairs. Mel carried

Linda. Vivian lumbered behind, lingered on the landing, and gazed out of the window onto a grand backyard, lovelier than she could have imagined: a sturdy fence to ensure the children's safety and prevent them from running into the street, a lush flower garden with potential to cut blooms every day for their table, and a sunny patch to plant vegetables, reminiscent of the victory gardens during wartime. Upstairs, two spacious bedrooms faced the front lawn, two others the backyard. The older girls argued about which bedroom they would claim. No more sharing. The two bathrooms had old-fashioned fixtures, but there were appealing turquoise tiles in the master bath that she and Mel would share. On her way back downstairs, Vivian sat for a moment on the cozy window seat, a feature she remembered from her favorite children's books, never dreaming she could live in a home with this comfortable nook. She pictured Irene nestled in that space, reading . . . and for a moment, felt jealous of her daughters, the advantages they would have compared to what she'd missed. She chided herself. Doesn't every good mother want her children to have a brighter future than she had?

Vivian overheard the prospective buyers explain they were from Kenilworth seeking to buy their daughter and her new husband their first home. Vivian looked at Mel in surprise. Who could afford to buy a house for a gift? When the front door closed with a click, Vivian scolded Irene and Sandy for playing too close to the unlit fireplace. Mel waved Vivian over to talk to the realtor, a classy-looking middle-aged woman with her hair set in a tight, platinum blonde helmet that framed her face. She frowned at the laughing children and glared at Vivian's tentlike maternity top with the blue polka-dotted bow at the neck as if she had never seen such an outlandish blouse.

Mel asked her to confirm the price. When the realtor named a figure five thousand dollars higher than what they'd overheard her quote the couple who had just left, he looked perturbed. Vivian trusted her husband's business sense; nothing like her pa's, who'd always scrambled to make the rent. Mel never overspent. He had savings from before he was drafted and socked away much of his army pay during the war. He was financially solid.

When Mel challenged her, the realtor tossed her head and said, "It doesn't matter. Your family would not be happy here."

"What do you mean?" Vivian asked. A house this size would fit their family with ease.

"Easy, Viv," Mel said. "I'm beginning to understand how things work out here."

Vivian heard a rare, angry timbre in her husband's voice when he confronted the realtor. "What do you know about what will make our family happy?"

The woman pursed her lips and looked back at Mel. "You must be from Chicago. People on the North Shore recognize this street is in a restricted area."

"Restricted to who?" Vivian spoke up. She felt a contraction and placed a hand on her belly.

"Sit down, honey," said the realtor, pointing to a chair next to the archway into the living room. "You're Jewish, aren't you?" She didn't wait for a reply. "I hate to be the one to burst your bubble, but this area is off-limits to your family."

Vivian couldn't believe what she was hearing. Both her parents and Mel's fled Russia to escape the tsar's conscription and his Cossacks' murderous pogroms against the Jews. But that was both an ocean and a generation away. She and Mel were both born in Chicago. Growing up, she was no stranger to hatred against Jews in clashes with the Poles, Irish, Italians, and Greeks of their west side neighborhood. She remembered during Easter week, someone chalked "Christ Killers" on the sidewalk in front of her family's apartment building. Every Halloween, their fence was ripped down. At her secretarial high school, when Vivian was elected vice president, the principal said, "Congratulations. We've never had a Jewish class officer before."

Although he meant this as a compliment, Vivian hated being singled out, as if her Jewishness mattered more than her hard-won accomplishments. Didn't Mel fight overseas to help to win the war against Hitler? America was a free country. That's what Vivian's pa always insisted. Restricted areas? Why couldn't they buy a house wherever they wanted, wherever they could afford it? How could anyone tolerate such blatant discrimination?

The agent put her hand on Vivian's shoulder. "Let me get you a glass of water. You look flushed."

Vivian gulped down the water, feeling hot tears sting her eyes.

"There are new housing developments close to the Edens Superhighway expansion," the realtor said. "Why don't I show you one of those models next week?"

Vivian uttered a word of protest until Mel covered her hand with his soothing palm. "Don't say no before we have a look, dear. Maybe we'll find something we like."

When the agent confirmed that the development near the Edens was still within the prestigious New Trier Township School District, Vivian agreed to review the plans of the model homes, somewhat disappointed at the skimpy room sizes compared to those of the old homes east of the highway, but didn't raise an objection. When they visited the area, she despaired at the naked streets, devoid of all greenery. Sprinklers waved back and forth over precious rolls of sod straining to take root for new lawns. It would be a long time before any home here would grace the cover of *House Beautiful*. However, Vivian did appreciate the sleek lines of this development's modern homes, unlike the cookie-cutter, garishly painted houses they'd driven past in other developments. Perhaps they *could* find something she liked.

Vivian selected a plan for a trilevel home with graceful proportions. The efficient kitchen was small, but the Hotpoint dishwasher was worth the price of the house. "If we buy this house on Maple

Street, our family will fit with no room to spare." She patted her expanded belly and said, "This one must definitely be our last."

"If you insist," said Mel. "But watch out. I can't keep myself away from you." Vivian giggled. He gave her a quick kiss. "No one can say I don't love you."

Mel was pleased with the developer's favorable mortgage terms and made the deal. He was happy that they would be the first owners with everything brand-new.

"I want to take you and our children away from the dirty city."

Vivian tried to see it from Mel's point of view—everything pristine, shiny and clean. She'd never liked to visit him on chaotic Maxwell Street with peddlers raucously hawking their wares and the congealed odors of open-air stands grilling *traif:* barbequed ribs, Polish sausages, and pork chops. Drunks meandered in and out of Jacobson Brothers at all hours. She'd long wanted to pretend that Mel wasn't enmeshed in that world all day long.

He squeezed Vivian's hand. "Maple Street is closer to the highway. Easier for me to drive to work."

At least he would come home at night to Wilmette. Vivian relished the idea that they would be suburbanites, joining many others leaving the city in this postwar world, seeking optimism in the new atomic age.

THE JACOBSONS moved to 336 Maple Street in August 1955, a few weeks after Billy was born. Given his increased commuting time, Mel left extra early on the morning after the move. With stacks of boxes piled everywhere, Vivian didn't know where to begin. Too much to do. She sat for a moment on their worn, cushy brown couch and lit a cigarette. At the cascading ringing of the new doorbell chimes, Linda began to wail. Vivian almost cried, too.

She opened the door to a trim woman with keen eyes and dark

hair coifed in a stylish flip, wearing coral pedal pushers and a bright, floral scarf knotted around her neck. By comparison, Vivian felt frowsy with her hair still in pin curls and a whimpering baby in her arms.

"Good morning! Are you Vivian Jacobson? From the Maxwell Street Jacobsons?"

Did everyone know their business? May as well hang a salami on their doorknob. Vivian was not proud to claim their seedy heritage now that they'd moved to Wilmette.

She frowned. "Yes, that's us."

The woman's voice had a cheery note. "Thought so. My husband's uncles have a shoe store on Maxwell Street. I'm Jackie. Jackie Reisman. Hank and I live next door."

Vivian exhaled, happy to share the connection. She'd feared suburbanites would look down at them for their association with Maxwell Street. When she glanced around her helter-skelter living room with boxes everywhere, she sighed. "Please excuse the mess."

"Doesn't bother me. Moving in takes time. Look, I won't keep you. Promise. Here's a casserole to welcome you to the block."

The woman extended the covered casserole dish, but with the baby in her arms, Vivian couldn't reach for it. The baby let out a yelp. He needed to be fed. "Really, Jackie, you shouldn't have."

"No trouble. How's about I put this right into your fridge?" Vivian took a few steps toward the kitchen, but Jackie pushed ahead of her. "Don't mind me. I know the floor plan of every home on the block. You picked the biggest model. Do you like tuna noodle casserole? It's not strictly kosher. Is that a problem?"

Vivian's cheeks colored. "It's fine. We decided not to keep kosher anymore now that we've moved to Wilmette." There. She admitted it. Vivian still felt a little guilty for the change. Her mother disapproved.

Jackie laughed. "You'll fit right in. I grew up Catholic but learned to keep kosher to please my late mother-in-law." She winked. "At least, we followed the rules when she was alive. Our world is different from our parents', isn't it?"

Yes, a different world. "Tuna noodle casserole sounds terrific. If you must know, anything I don't have to cook myself is terrific." They laughed together. Vivian liked Jackie. She hoped she would become a friend.

"Do you have kids?" Vivian asked.

Jackie smirked. "If you haven't figured it out already, everyone on Maple Street has kids. Yeah, we've got two. A boy and a girl, nine and seven. That's it for us. Sometimes I feel like I'm pulling my hair out with our two. Especially Chuckie. He can be wild."

Vivian smiled. She felt proud to announce, "We have four. Irene, Sandy, Linda, and this is the baby, Billy. But that's it for us. Don't get me wrong, I love each one, but many days I think my life would be a breeze if I only had two."

Vivian wondered if she looked as tired as she felt, standing next to this perky neighbor. She wished her pressed powder compact were close by to peek at her face, certain that her lipstick needed freshening.

Jackie surveyed the scene. "We all have our trials, but I do understand why you needed the biggest model. You've got a lot on your plate. Anything I can do to help, just ask. My door is open. That's how I was raised."

"Gee thanks. I might need a lift into town every so often. My husband takes our only car to work."

"Don't tell me? No car of your own? You'll be stranded. Listen, call me whenever you need a ride. I mean it, don't give it a second thought. Welcome to Maple Street. I'm sure you noticed we don't have any maple trees on the block." Jackie laughed, a deep, throaty laugh. "Or any trees at all."

"Hard not to notice," said Vivian. "In Chicago, we lived near Lincoln Park."

"Lucky you." Jackie headed toward the front door. "Listen, the neighbors are taking up a collection to plant sugar maples on both sides of the street to live up to our street's name. They say sugar maple trees grow fast."

"They'd better," Vivian said with a laugh. She tried to imagine a time when towering maple trees would line the parkways. She'd probably be dead by then.

"We're asking for twenty dollars, but anything you can contribute will be fine."

"Sure, count us in. I'll get a check from Mel when he comes home tonight." Vivian lifted a weary hand. "Great meeting you. Thanks again for the casserole." Sandy raced up from the den looking for her jump rope. Linda crawled close to the stairs. Billy started to cry. "Much as I'd like to talk, I've got to get back to all of this."

Jackie took a long look around the room. "I don't know how you do it. Remember, don't hesitate to call me. I'll write down my number here on your phone pad. Don't bother to get the door. I'll let myself out."

Jackie Reisman was a gem.

From the street, Vivian heard the ping of a wiffle ball hitting a plastic bat. Those lightweight balls couldn't break a window, could they? Their living room picture window would cost a fortune to replace. She sent Irene and Sandy to play outside. The village hadn't poured the sidewalks yet. With no boundaries to contain them, dozens of children spilled into the street, pausing their games to slowly step aside only to let the rare car pass by. Look how free they were to run and play.

Vivian tried to picture the time when tall sugar maples would grace the street. Her throat constricted to remember how they were turned away from the snobby restricted areas with towering trees. She wouldn't want to live where her family would be shunned. Not likely to find a Jackie Reisman in that part of town.

The realtor had been right. Their family would be happy on Maple Street.

And they were. Until the next spring.

CHAPTER FOUR
SHABBOS DINNER

FRIDAY, 1956

IRENE AND Sandy held hands and danced in a circle singing their lyrics to the ring-around-the-rosy tune. "We're going to Bubbe's and Aunt Ruthie's tonight! We're going to Bubbe's and Aunt Ruthie's!"

On Fridays, Mel came home early from work to pick up the family and drive them back into the city for Shabbos dinner at Vivian's mother's apartment. She lived on the second floor of the two-flat in Rogers Park owned by her friend Ruth Lavin. Ruth lived on the first floor.

Vivian got the youngest two ready before she dressed to avoid any unforeseen messes that would force her to change clothes. Irene loved to dress up, but Sandy, a tomboy, no matter how she loved the weekly family dinner, resisted putting on a skirt until Vivian insisted, saying Bubbe liked to see the children wearing their best clothes on Shabbos. Aunt Ruthie didn't mind, but Vivian wanted to avoid Ma's criticism of how she dressed her children. Especially tonight. She was grateful that Sandy did not utter one word of complaint. Vivian chose Sandy's favorite orange top to wear with the skirt. Then, Vivian packed what she hoped would be enough diapers for Linda and Billy in the oversized tote that Mel would carry. He'd be home in less than an hour. She'd have to hurry to get herself ready.

Standing in her brassiere and panties, Vivian stared into the mirror before selecting her outfit. Turning sideways, she saw what Ethel's keen eyes had spied before anyone else had. Vivian could no longer ignore the soft roundness of her belly, no longer hold on to a glimmer of hope that it was only a vestige after having Billy last July, or too many Oreo cookies with the girls. From now on, she'd have to stick strictly to cottage cheese. With her girdle, she could keep anyone else from suspecting. Just in case, Vivian selected a silky blouson top—not too clingy—and tried to force the zipper of her good pencil skirt all the way to the top, but settled for two inches below her waist, grateful the blouse would cover the gap.

She patted on fresh pancake foundation, shaded her brows with a deep brown pencil, added a swath of blue eye shadow, and painted even, thin rows of liquid eyeliner to the corner of her eyes. She curled and compressed her lashes before brushing on wet black Maybelline mascara. Dammit. Smudged her eyeliner. She'd have to start over on her left eye. She teased up the crown of her hair and spritzed it with hairspray. The finale was her signature slash of Revlon's Fire & Ice lipstick—a bold shade that made her feel daring and in control. Two quick squeezes from the Arpège atomizer added an air of elegance. Her nails looked terrible—always chipped—and she painted on a quick, good-enough touch-up. She blew on them, willing the polish to dry, before heading downstairs to try to relax and, at the same time, keep an eye on Linda, who was cruising around the living room furniture.

Five minutes later, the garage door rose with its uneven *chug-chug-chug.* The older girls cried, "Daddy's home!" Mel rushed upstairs for the kiss-kiss with his wife, saying, "Gorgeous as ever," and then ran up to their bathroom, stripped, and showered. He dressed in the clean shirt, tie, and trousers that Vivian had laid out for him on their bed, because she couldn't trust her color-blind husband to select his own ensemble. The older girls waited by the garage door, already arguing about who would sit next to the window in the back seat behind

Mel. Sandy liked to pretend she was driving the car. If Irene lost the argument, she'd claim the seat next to the other window. Linda always sat in the middle in a harness. In the front passenger seat, Vivian squeezed her arms around Billy, keeping him tight to her lap.

Thirty minutes later, Hannah greeted them at the door, as always, with presents for her granddaughters. Tonight she had hand-crocheted dolls. Irene and Sandy argued over who would have the one with yellow braids. They'd give Linda the one they didn't want.

"Girls!" Aunt Ruthie scolded. "Time for dinner."

"Wash hands!" called Vivian.

"Where's Aunt Ethel?" asked Sandy.

"Playing cards," answered Hannah and shook her head. "On Shabbos, no less. That one does what she wants. Always has."

The clatter ceased when they gathered around the table. Hannah blessed the candles to usher in the Sabbath. Mel chanted the kiddush blessing over the wine, then passed the cup around for everyone to take a sip. Sandy scrunched up her face. "I want grape juice." Vivian coaxed her to take a tiny sip. Then, all together, they recited the blessing over the bread.

Irene clapped her hands. "This is my favorite night! Bubbe makes the best chicken soup."

Hannah and Aunt Ruthie went to the kitchen to prepare to serve the meal. Vivian followed. Hannah brought the first bowls of soup into the dining room, leaving Vivian alone with Aunt Ruthie, who gave Vivian a quick once-over and said, "I talked to Ethel last night. She shared her suspicions with me."

"But I won't be sure until I test at the doctor's."

"Don't delay," said Aunt Ruthie. "When you know, we must have a heart-to-heart."

"Is it about what happened with Ma when Ethel was a girl?" Vivian placed the bowl of soup on the counter. Her hands were shaking. "Ethel gave me a hint. Is that what it's about?"

Aunt Ruthie put a finger to her lips. "Let's find time to talk soon. Just the two of us."

Thank goodness Aunt Ruthie wasn't afraid to talk openly about the topics others dodged. Wasn't she the first one to answer Vivian's questions about how babies were made? Vivian was tired of being protected as the youngest child, as if she couldn't understand. Wasn't she an adult and a mother of four children?

"Come out to Wilmette. See our new couch."

Hannah walked back into the kitchen. She sputtered. "New couch? When will you be satisfied with your beautiful home?" She picked up two more bowls filled with still-steaming chicken soup and noodles. "Help me before the soup gets cold." As they walked back to the dining room, she added, "How much can you ask from your husband? You'll make him old before his time with new furniture."

"Mother Kolson, please," said Mel. "Don't worry about us. We can afford it. I want Vivian to be happy. She's good about keeping to our budget."

"As long as you don't take on more than she can handle," said Aunt Ruthie, who sat next to Vivian and covered her hand with hers. "I remember your mother's troubles when we first met. With so many children, keeping up a household can be overwhelming. Of course"—she turned her head to Vivian—"you had a good-for-nothing father."

"Please, Ruth," said Hannah. "Not in front of the kinderlach."

Irene and Sandy ran from the table to the living room to play with their new dolls.

Vivian's body tingled with the warmth of Ma and Aunt Ruthie close by. There was something about sitting around the table with the Shabbos candles aglow that bound the family circle tighter. Vivian worried what Mel would think of her if she told him she feared she was pregnant again but didn't want another. She felt like an ungrateful, unworthy mother to admit this. She pinched a wrinkle of skin near her wrist to feel a prick of pain. *This cannot be true. It must be a false alarm.*

Another child now would delay new options for her and extend the time when all of the children were in school. No chance to be a sales clerk in downtown Wilmette to earn her own money to buy things for the children or herself outside of Mel's budget. No chance to find a way to somehow salvage her dreams and begin college part-time. Vivian hadn't told Mel that she had sent away for a catalog from the northside branch of the teachers' college. She remembered how her teachers at Bryant Elementary School had encouraged Vivian to set her sights on higher education and Ma would rest her palm atop Vivian's head and say, "My mama would be proud. In this free country, you could study at a university." Now that Vivian had her own children, would Ma discourage such grand plans? Women were expected to stay home now that the war years were over. Every magazine ad and TV show depicted smiling homemakers. Vivian felt her gut clench. Not every day at home was a happy one.

FRIDAY NIGHT was the time for the family to share memories, stories, and secrets. Vivian calmed herself, rested her hands lightly in her lap, and stroked the band of the silver watch that Mel had presented to her on their second wedding anniversary. She gazed into the blue and orange flames flitting around Ma's battered, tarnished candlesticks, the heirlooms entrusted for safekeeping by her mama to take to America. Whenever Hannah gently placed these candlesticks on the table, tears filled her eyes. Sometimes at these Shabbos dinners, Ma told stories about her mama: how she'd taught her the women's prayers and purification rituals about what it meant to be a Jewish wife and mother. During Vivian's childhood, Hannah was often sickly and left Ethel in charge of teaching Vivian such lessons.

She suspected that Ethel had decided to skip many details, if she ever knew them at all.

"Tell me about the time you met Aunt Ruthie," Vivian asked. Her ma rarely spoke of those days. Tonight, when Hannah stood to brush crumbs from the tablecloth where Irene and Sandy had been sitting, she said something Vivian had not heard before.

Hannah bowed her head. "She introduced herself to me at shul."

Vivian turned her head from one woman to the other. "She did? Why?"

Ruth put her napkin on the table. "Your mother was a learned woman. And bold too. Willing to stand up against those gossip-mongering yentas."

Hannah winked at Ruth. "Soon after we met, I invited my new friend to our flat for Shabbos lunch. I needed a woman to confide in."

Ruth let loose her unmistakable, throaty laugh. "I was only too happy to come and meet your family. Although it was during Prohibition, your mother brought out a bottle of slivovitz—plum brandy. Remember how Abe got angry wondering where you got the bottle? I thought I would choke holding back my laughter. She told your father that the rebbetzin gave her the bottle at Purim."

"The rebbetzin? The rabbi's wife had brandy?"

Mel said, "Always legal to have liquor for religious purposes."

Ruth nodded. "I remember how your older brothers ran from the table, like your daughters did tonight. They were a handful. Ethel was your mother's only helper."

Hannah looked somber as she swept crumbs from the table into her napkin. "What would I have done without my hardworking daughter?" Absentmindedly, she brushed the tablecloth again, although there were no more crumbs. "But she was only a girl herself."

"Where was I?" asked Vivian.

Hannah glanced at Ruth.

"You weren't born yet," said Aunt Ruthie.

Hannah dabbed her eyes with her napkin. She grew solemn and gazed at the ceiling as if speaking to someone who was not in the room. "There was so much I didn't yet know about your pa. He hid his bad habits, and his union shenanigans made him unpopular with the bosses. He went from job to job, leaving us short of money. He always complained he had too many burdens."

Vivian felt the burn of tears. "Was I a burden?"

Hannah grabbed her daughter's hand. "No. You must never think such a thing. You are my treasure. My miracle child."

Mel stood up. "Viv, get the children ready. I'm tired. I've got to go in early tomorrow. Thank you, Mother Kolson, for the beautiful dinner."

Vivian still had tears in her eyes as she walked to the front closet to gather the children's coats. Hannah followed, gripped her hands on her daughter's shoulders, and looked her in the eye. "Don't cry, my beautiful child. A mother's life is a hard one. Always was."

"I'm OK. Please, Ma, don't worry."

Aunt Ruthie pulled Vivian aside. "Take care of yourself. I'll drive out to see you tomorrow. We'll talk."

After Vivian, Mel, and the children went home and the washing up was complete, the Shabbos candles burned down, transmitting bits of light in an unintelligible Morse code. Hannah and Ruth sat together in the living room and drank another cup of tea, content to sit together in silence. Hannah missed stirring her usual milk into her glass, but she wouldn't mix in any dairy foods after eating a chicken dinner. The old traditions remained strong.

"I don't envy my daughter," said Hannah. "A young mother with so many little ones does not have an easy life. And I can see from her round face that she is expecting another. The face is always where it shows first."

"Ethel called," said Ruth. "She noticed changes in her sister's shape."

"That one has eagle eyes," Hannah said. "Always did."

"I'm worried for Vivian," said Ruth. "Different from how I worried for you when we first met. Your Abe cared only for himself. Not for your health. Vivian has a good husband, but from what I see, she's overwhelmed."

"Abe was not so different from many husbands of our time. Vivian will be OK. Mel Jacobson is a mensch."

"Even so," said Ruth, "when it comes to bearing a man's child, even the kindest man may insist on imposing his will. I've seen it more times than I can count. No man can truly know how a woman feels. Vivian must trust herself not to overextend her limits. She shouldn't be afraid to say, 'No more.' That's my advice. I'll tell her so when I drive out to Wilmette."

"You were never shy about keeping your opinions to yourself. But watch what you say. My daughter listens to you. On something so important, she must make up her own mind."

The two women sat staring at the candles as bubbly globules of uneven, lacy wax dripped and hardened on the silver candlesticks. In the darkening room, Ruth began to hum an old melody under her breath. The tune announced the weekly arrival of the day of rest, entreating the Shabbos queen to enter their home like a groom woos his bride. Hannah sang the words while Ruth harmonized until the candles burned out.

Hannah sighed and said, "So many mysteries in this life. I always felt my mama from the next world brought you to me when I needed you most." She rested her head on Ruth's shoulder. "I'll never forget those days. I trust you to say to our frantic young mother what I cannot."

Ruth smiled and looked into Hannah's brown eyes where the last glint of light from the candles remained. "But look at all the good that came from those troubles."

SUMMER, 1923

EVERY SHABBOS morning, the Kolson family walked together to their shul on Chicago's west side. Abe walked briskly ahead, the three boys jostled and pushed each other. Eight-year-old Ethel danced in and out between them. The air was stickier than cotton candy. Hannah struggled to keep up. With each step, she felt as if she were pushing through bread dough.

"Why so slow, Alice?" asked Abe.

Hannah stopped, panted, and struggled to catch her breath. "Slow? After four children, I'm not the fresh chicken you married. How many times must I say to stop with this 'Alice'? The name inked on my papers means nothing to me."

"I tell you again and again, Alice. We live in Chicago. Use your English name."

"Why should I? I'm the same person I was in Russia."

Why couldn't Abe Kolson see her for who she was? By the time their three sons raced each other into the males-only sanctuary, Abe was already engaged in a heated debate with a union comrade. Ethel shouted after her brothers to settle down and then waited for her ma at the foot of the stairs leading to the women's balcony. A thin smile slipped from Hannah's lips as she made her way to her daughter, Hannah's only comfort. Ethel scurried up the well-worn, steep treads to the U-shaped upper level built near the rafters to keep musky, female scents far from the main sanctuary, lest they distract the men who participated in the rituals below. What folly! Abe Kolson was a nonbeliever; he never focused on the service. He only came to shul to placate his wife and jaw about politics with whoever would listen.

Hannah trudged up the stairs, halting halfway, and then panting when she reached the top. Ethel waited and skipped up to their usual seats, but Hannah shooed her further to sit in the top row.

"Why up here?" Ethel questioned.

"Don't ask. Sit."

"Can't I go by Dena?"

"Maybe later," said Hannah with a solemn look on her face.

The balcony was a noisy hubbub with women greeting one another and chattering as they caught up on the week's activities. A slight woman with reddish hair styled into a sleek Marcel wave took a seat in the row ahead of Hannah, looked back at them, and scowled. Had they taken her usual spot? This woman wore a smart, charcoal, double-breasted blazer and pink blouse in striking contrast to the others who, like Hannah, were clad in drab serge dresses or white blouses with long dark skirts. Hannah couldn't remember having seen this woman before, but several women recognized her, pointed, and tittered. Every aspect of this odd woman's appearance marked her as a bohemian: bright-cheeked makeup and blue eye paint. She wore no hat, as if to flaunt this indication of her unmarried status. But this irreverence paled when she unpacked a black-and-white tallis from a royal blue velvet pouch hidden inside her oversized purse. She draped the ceremonial shawl around herself as if it were a cozy winter scarf, murmured the Hebrew blessing, and kissed the fringes twice in the ritual strictly reserved for men.

Hannah gasped and pushed Ethel's face away. "Don't look!"

At Hannah's caution to her daughter, the shameful woman turned around, put a finger to her lips, and winked. The sparkle in her eye hinted that she welcomed Hannah to join in her rebellion. Hannah shivered, surprised how she felt drawn to this unusual woman, feeling the need for a co-conspirator.

Heavyset, prematurely gray-haired Liza Jacobson stood up from the front row and turned to face the top rows. She jabbed her sister-in-law in the ribs and waved her hand upward, her voice echoing throughout the balcony. "Look at that woman, Addie. She's a disgrace."

Delicate Adeline Jacobson, with dashing dark eyes, tried to get Liza to sit down. She whispered loud enough for Hannah to hear.

"Everything they say about her must be true. Wearing a tallis? Another one of her outrageous behaviors. I hear her boyfriend is married!"

Liza's voice boomed. "What did we do to deserve such punishment? To pray alongside a woman who acts like a man?"

Addie nodded. "That Ruth Lavin is a shanda, a true scandal."

Hannah's eyes widened. Ruth Lavin. So that was her name.

Ruth splayed out her fingers from under her chin with a gesture that screamed, "Back off!" and pulled the tallis tighter around her shoulders.

Hannah wished that she dared to be as bold as this feisty woman.

As the men below rattled through the singsong morning prayers, Ruth added her throaty contralto to the cantor's clarion chanting, lifting her voice as if she hadn't heard any derisive words. Behind her, Hannah swayed with the rhythms of the familiar melodies, mesmerized. She added high notes to harmonize with the tallis-clad woman as if she and Ruth were the only two in the women's balcony, singing a private duet. When Ruth unleashed a barrage of trills in a melody of her own making, Hannah quieted, willing herself invisible. Her purpose was clear.

Hannah clutched at her abdomen, feeling nauseated, ruing the day when she first heard the name Abraham Kolinsky. Why had she agreed to the *shidduch*, the match that her brothers arranged? Had they genuinely believed Abe would make a good husband? If only her parents had been with her in Chicago, Hannah was certain they would have insisted on a more suitable match instead of a poor *schneider* —a tailor who'd won higher wages after the 1910 Hart, Schaffner, & Marx strike that spawned the Amalgamated Clothing Workers of America. Perhaps she should forgive her brothers, because a twenty-five-year-old woman could become a dangerous burden.

Now a mother herself with four children, thirty-seven-year-old Hannah Kolson yearned to collapse into her mama's bosom, pour out her worries, and confide her fears. Hannah trembled to think how today's bold plan might have outraged her traditional papa, but certain that her mama would have convinced him that a desperate woman was justified to defy the law. Ever respectful of his wife's insights, her stern papa might have relented to protect his dear Chana, their only daughter.

Ethel tugged at Hannah's sleeve. "Ma, you aren't paying attention! The rabbi is opening the Ark to take out the Torah."

"I know the order of the service." Hannah's words were sharp.

Ethel stamped her foot. "Can't I go sit by Dena Jacobson?"

"Go. Go now."

Hannah watched Ruth entwine the fringes of the tallis around her fingers and heard her moan, lost in her prayers. A cold rush of air surrounding Ruth rose toward Hannah, who recognized her mama's distinctive whispers. "Dear Chana, when the cantor lifts his voice into the highest register, he brings God closest to us."

Hannah prayed that God must understand and answer her plea.

Downstairs, the rabbi held the Torah scroll in his arms, closed his eyes, and proclaimed aloud the watchwords of faith: "Shema Yisroel, Adonai Elohenu, Adonai Echad."

Hear O Israel, the Lord is our God. The Lord is One.

Hannah trembled. The time was near. After the Torah reading and the scrolls were dressed to return to the Ark, Hannah focused on the *t'khine* she'd selected from the set of women's common prayers. The prayers passed down orally from mothers to daughters and she remembered her mama, who had taught her each one. Hannah strained to keep her morning meal settled, closed her eyes, and filled her lungs with air, listening closely to the cantor. His voice rose higher and higher. He stood in front of the open Ark and unleashed a string of sweet falsetto notes:

"Atz Chayim Hee. The Torah is a Tree of Life. Restore us O God, as we were before."

The cantor stretched out the last notes: *as we were before.*

Now!

The pulse in Hannah's temple throbbed. Shaking, she took a sharp breath and began to utter her biblical namesake's fertility prayer:

"O God of Israel, accept my prayer, just as You accepted the prayer of our mother, Hannah, when she prayed to banish her barrenness."

Hannah dared to add one word to transform the prayer from holy to profane:

"Please God, may I *not* bear the child I carry in my womb to full-term."

Sweating, she whimpered and sobbed at her audacity to let those words leave her lips. Would God ever forgive her? She pulled her breath into the deepest part of her low abdomen, willing her prayer to float out through the roof and up to the heavens. God must understand how she feared for her survival and the hardship to bring another babe into their household where the others already didn't have enough. A compassionate God must understand, different from the narrow judgments of men in their community. In a hushed tone, she boldly repeated the forbidden words, "May I *not* bear this child to full-term!"

Hannah heard a gasp. Ruth's tallis fluttered. Impossible that the striking woman had overheard because Hannah sent her prayer heavenward for God's ears alone. No one would believe the outcast woman if she claimed to have heard pious Hannah Kolson praying to lose a baby and calling upon God to intercede in this way.

To Hannah's horror, Ruth Lavin stepped into the aisle and moved up to Hannah's row, motioning her to scoot down. Reluctantly, Hannah shifted, brushed away her stinging tears, and vacated the seat on the aisle for this interloper. In the book of Samuel, when the matriarch Hannah wept and prayed silently to bear a son, her anguish was mistaken for drunkenness. If indeed Ruth had heard her, would she think Hannah crazy, a *meshugenah*? How could she explain?

At the conclusion of the service, when the women began scurrying toward the stairway, Hannah tried to jostle past Ruth to meet Ethel, but Ruth blocked her way.

"Please," Hannah said. "My family is waiting."

Ruth held up her palm. "Stay. I heard your prayer."

No. Can't be. A strand escaped from Hannah's thick brown bun, and she tucked it back in under her tan cloche hat. Hannah was a full head taller than the diminutive Ruth, who stared up at her with a knowing gaze, but not an accusatory look. Suddenly overcome with dizziness, Hannah sank back onto the bench, and her hand flew to her breast.

"What prayer?"

"You know the one."

If Ruth heard her alter the *t'khine* prayer, she must think her shameful—more shameful than a woman who wears a tallis. Hannah rose, stiff-backed.

"The word you added," said Ruth. "Shocking."

"I didn't mean for anyone to—"

"To hear? Don't worry. Yes, shocking to many. But not to me. You must understand, I'm different from these small-minded women." Ruth gave Hannah a sly look. She let loose a burbling laugh that resounded through the balcony. Hannah studied this curious woman. Reluctantly, she added her own sad laughter.

Hannah looked around to see if anyone was watching.

"I'm Ruth Lavin." She extended her hand to Hannah. "Surely you've heard the gossip about me. And you are . . . ?"

Hannah did not accept the handshake. "I'm Hannah. But not like Hannah from the Bible."

Ruth laughed again. "Tell me, Hannah-not-from-the-Bible, how did you become the rare woman in this balcony who is fluent in the liturgy?"

A rush of feelings brought Hannah back to her childhood when her father taught her the Hebrew alphabet, bragging that she was as smart as any firstborn son. "My papa, of blessed memory, believed I should study Torah alongside my brothers. My mama was a scholar among women. She taught me poetry and literature, not only in Yiddish, but in Russian, too."

"Wise parents," said Ruth.

"Both of my parents have gone on to Olam Haba, the next world. How I miss them. The Cossacks slaughtered everyone in our village soon after my brothers and I left for America."

Hannah's hand shook and swiped her sleeve over her eye. Ruth took out her handkerchief and offered it to Hannah, who accepted and wiped her face.

Ruth said, "I'm an orphan, too, but never knew my parents. My mother died in childbirth. My father ran off. I never learned where. My uncle took me in until he died and I landed in the Marks Nathan Jewish Orphans' Home. The people at the home told me I must have compassion because a man cannot care for a child alone, but I never forgave my father for abandoning me."

This Ruth Lavin had her own *tsuris*, her own sad troubles, but as an American, she could never understand what it was like to live in Russia with everyday terrors of unexpected, violent pogroms.

Ruth continued, "I envy you your scholarly mother and forward-thinking father. He would have had a different outlook from those alta cockers, those old men downstairs." Ruth tipped her head down toward the main floor. "They live in a new world, but their minds are stuck in the old one."

When Ethel dashed up to them, Hannah put her finger to her lips to silence Ruth. Ethel's expression gave her the appearance of a little woman, not a child. She was almost as tall as Ruth, but Ruth's electric presence made her appear taller. Ethel twisted her long braid around her fingers, intently watching Ruth neatly fold her prayer shawl and place it into the velvet pouch.

"Why do you wear a tallis?" she asked.

Hannah shushed her daughter, but Ruth held up her hand. "Let her ask. I like a girl who's not afraid to speak up. You're a good helper for your mother, aren't you? What's your name?"

"Ethel."

"A solid name. Ethel, you have gumption."

"What is this *gumption*?" asked Hannah.

"Don't worry, Ma. Gumption is something good, isn't it?" Ethel's eyes locked onto Ruth's.

"Yes, it is. Keep asking questions. Don't lose your curiosity." Ruth squatted down to eye level with Ethel. "Do you think it is wrong for me to wear this?"

Ethel hesitated, then looked up at her ma, and then directly at Ruth. She shook her head and said, "No. But I've never seen anyone up here wear one."

"Do you want to hear my secret reason? I've never told anyone."

"Yes, tell me!" Ethel clapped her hands.

"I wear a tallis because God listens to men's prayers more than he does to women's. Maybe I could fool him."

Ethel laughed, but Hannah became cross. "Our all-knowing God could never mistake you for a man."

Ruth looked solemn. "Why must men and women carry such different burdens? What do you think?" she asked Ethel.

Ethel pulled at her braid and then flipped it over her shoulder. "My brothers have it easy. No laundry chores, no scrubbing floors, no cooking dinner, no washing dishes."

Hannah was dismayed to hear Ethel's list. Another baby would only place more burdens upon her precious daughter.

Ruth pulled herself to her full height. Her startling blue eyes probed Hannah's brown ones. "How many others do you have?"

Ethel answered. "Three brothers."

Dena waved goodbye to Ethel and Liza Jacobson called out, "Mrs.

Kolson! Beware the company you keep! You should know better than to make the acquaintance of that hussy."

Hannah felt emboldened to stand alongside Ruth Lavin. She called back to Liza, "Long ago my mama taught me: 'If I am not for myself, who will be for me?'"

Liza pulled her daughter Dena toward the stairs.

"Now you see why I sit in the back, to try to avoid those meddling women," said Ruth. "My time in shul is for my own purposes."

Ethel pulled Hannah's sleeve. "Let's go. Pa will be angry."

"You go on ahead," said Hannah. "I'm still talking to Missus Lavin."

"*Miss* Lavin," corrected Ruth.

"Al-ice! What's keeping you? Come down here!"

Hannah began to scurry. "My husband. I must go."

"Wait. Why does he call you 'Alice'?"

Hannah sighed. "I tell you, sometimes I forget my own name. I was born Chana Teichman. When I arrived at Ellis Island, Alice was the name they inked on my papers. In Chicago, when I married, I became Hannah Kolinsky."

"And now, you're Hannah Kolson? Too many names for one woman. Is Abe your second husband?"

"If only I'd had another. Abraham Kolson is my first and only."

Ruth looked puzzled. "But Kolinsky? Or Kolson?"

"Another foolishness. When Abe got his citizen papers, he wanted an American name and changed it on his own without warning." Hannah shook her head. "Shortened it, and added 'son,' in honor of the great President Wilson, as he called him. A good American name. Suddenly, I was Hannah Kolson. We already had four children."

Ruth chuckled and said, "So your Abe wants to be the president? Keeps you guessing, doesn't he?" At Hannah's faded smile, Ruth grasped her hand. "I'm sorry. Not funny. Let's talk again soon."

"ALICE!"

Ethel ran toward the stairs.

When the girl was out of earshot, Ruth stepped in close to Hannah and whispered, "Tell me the truth. Why did you change the words to pray for an end to your pregnancy?"

Hannah gasped at Ruth's brazenness to speak the words aloud, but was grateful that her daughter was too far away to overhear. Dare she bare more secrets to this stranger? She took a deep breath. "Five years ago, an American doctor warned another childbirth might kill me." Then she spat out, "Pu, pu, pu!"

Ruth's eyes flashed. "What's with 'pu, pu, pu'? Are you trying to ward off the evil eye? Don't tell me a learned woman like you is superstitious? If you fear another pregnancy, you must do more than pray for it to end."

Hannah checked again that Ethel had disappeared down the stairs. "Even if I could survive another birth, we already have too many mouths to feed."

"Many families are feeling the pain of caring for too many hungry children," said Ruth, her eyes brimming. "I can take you to someone who can do what you prayed for today." Hannah looked stricken. Ruth added, "Don't worry. He's not a butcher. Remember, it's not a crime to be desperate."

Hannah squeezed Ruth's hand. "Why would you help me when we met only today?"

"Why *wouldn't* I help you?" A sorrowful look passed across Ruth's face. "When I was sixteen, my best friend Irene couldn't get the help she needed. She found herself in the family way after a staff worker at the Home forced himself on her. Irene couldn't face bearing his child. She took her own life. I come to shul every Shabbos to feel her close to me and hear her voice."

Tragic. This American woman may be odd, but she has great *ruchmanes*, compassion. Hannah thanked God to have had the courage to pray aloud for the unthinkable because God must have heard her prayers and sent this American woman to her. If she was a tallis-wearing rebel, so be it. Her mama had always encouraged her to trust her instincts. Hannah shivered. Goosebumps lifted the hair on her forearms. Could she trust Ruth Lavin? What Hannah sought was against all laws, but from the whispers she'd heard in the market and elsewhere, it was not uncommon among women from every immigrant group here in Chicago to find ways to end an unwanted pregnancy. She'd overheard two Italian women talking about a sister who found someone to end her tenth one, and the Polish woman married to the building's handyman cried to a neighbor how she'd had to hide from her husband what she'd done. When the Greek assistant to the hatmaker confessed such a deed to her priest, he told her she would be forgiven if she became a godmother to another woman's child. Hannah wasn't the only woman to face this crisis. She must go forward and act alone. Abe must not know; never too many for him. She had to stay strong. Didn't she survive crossing the ocean in the lowest deck where people retched for days from morning until night? And the night she delivered her Max? She'd survived that too.

Ruth asked, "Shall we meet next week?"

Hannah felt sick. "Will I be safe?" God forbid she should leave her children without a mother. "Will God punish me for going against His will?"

Ruth clasped her hand and said, "We are only human. We live our lives on earth in the best way we can. A merciful God expects us to act, not live out our days in fear."

How different Hannah's life would be if she were not always afraid.

Hannah said, "I live on Polk Street, two blocks east of Independence. I'll look for you on a bench in the park across the street."

Ethel was already downstairs. Abe was pacing in the lobby. "Where's your ma? Never in my life did I think I'd put one foot onto that balcony, but if she won't come down, I swear I'll go up there and—"

"Don't be angry. She was talking to the woman who wears a tallis."

"Wears a . . . *what*?"

Ethel pointed at Ruth, who stepped off the bottom stair, smiled at Ethel, and opened the door to the summer heat.

"*That* woman? I've heard about her." He waggled his finger. "I swear I'm going to give your ma a good talking-to!"

"Wait, Pa. Here she comes."

Voices swelled below as Hannah began her descent. She rushed to place her foot on the first tread, careened, and grabbed for the railing, suddenly woozy. Would she bring curses upon her family if she followed Ruth Lavin and took this risk? Put both her life and her family in danger? She swayed and gripped the railing tighter, overcome by the memory of her hazy delirium of the harrowing, near-death childbirth five years earlier.

A thundering "Alice!" penetrated her trance, and she shook herself into alertness. She teetered and wobbled, almost falling, until she righted herself halfway down the flight of stairs and stopped to plant both feet firmly onto one tread. From beyond the grave, she heard a chorus of her parents' voices mixed with the sages', encouraging her to fight for her own well-being ahead of others'. She had to save herself. "Your husband will never understand!" she heard Mama whisper. Hannah must gather the strength to prevent Abe from overpowering her. Hannah smoothed down her blouse, straightened her hat, took another step down, then another and another, firmer, faster, with increasing purpose until she reached the ground floor and stood face-to-face with Abe.

"Wife, why so late? I'm hungry!"

"For once, you listen to me, Abe Kolson. I will do what I must do."

How unlike her to say such words to Abe. Outside into the humid air, Hannah took a deep breath. Wispy clouds streaked across the blue dome of the sparkling sky. The landscape felt like an unfamiliar terrain although she'd walked this same stretch of pavement hundreds of times before. Hannah took long firm strides and looked ahead toward the cacophony that was Independence Boulevard, even on Shabbos, the day of rest. When she reached the intersection, she spied Ruth Lavin, who gave her a snappy, triumphant salute. Hannah grinned and returned the gesture. She'd found an American woman to trust. From the next world, it must have been Mama who sent Ruth Lavin to be her ally.

LATER FRIDAY NIGHT, 1956

MEL CAREFULLY maneuvered the car onto the Touhy Avenue ramp to head north on the Edens. The hum of the Oldsmobile motor rising and falling created the rhythmic *whooshing* that always lulled the children to sleep. They rode together in silence. Mel kept his eyes on the road while Vivian imagined Ma's troubles as a young wife and mother. Aunt Ruthie must remember that time. How much would she share?

Back home, Mel read bedtime stories to the older girls until after repeated urgings, they chanted the Shema prayer together and Mel turned out their bedroom light. Vivian settled Billy and Linda in their cribs and met Mel in the bedroom. She began to undress, but her neck stiffened when Mel touched her lower back and urged her to "press the lock." Their locked bedroom door signaled to a wakeful child that she was barred from entry unless it was urgent. Mel and Vivian would be horrified if any of the children caught them making love. Most nights Vivian enthusiastically accepted Mel's overtures. Some nights she was bold enough to initiate their intimacy. But not this night.

"Mel, please," she said and pushed his hand away as he cupped her breast. She slipped into their bed, under the sheet, her eyes moistening. "There's something I've got to tell you." She gulped. "It's hard to say."

He lay down next to her, his arms encircling her. He stroked her thigh. "You can tell me anything. You know that, darling."

Again, she gently moved his hand away. It wasn't fair to keep this from him any longer. "I don't want to be pregnant again." She gripped his shoulder.

His body tensed. "Don't you have your diaphragm?"

"No . . . I mean . . . I'm afraid it could already be too late."

"What are you saying?" He stared at the ceiling and cracked his knuckles, one at a time. "When was your last . . . ?"

Vivian's voice broke. "I . . . I'm not sure. I'm not regular."

"Can't you count?" Mel's words held an unusually harsh tone that she rarely heard from him, certainly not with her. A sob escaped from her throat. He turned on his side to face her and brushed a tear from her eye. "I'm sorry," he said. "I don't mean to blame you. I should have known. You're curvier, more sensitive. Crying at the drop of a hat."

Vivian reached for his hand. How well he knew her. The darkened room hid her strained expression as she whispered, "Didn't we agree?" and then louder, "No more children?"

Mel made a noise as if something were stuck in his throat. "We have no choice. We'll have to make do. As my pa would say, 'Man plans, and God laughs.'"

She turned her head away from him. "Not funny."

"Didn't say it was. But sometimes, we must take what comes." Mel's voice sounded strained.

The moon shone in through the window, half-lighting his face—the face Vivian had grown to find more beautiful than any other. He stroked her imperfect nose. Her kind husband, the man who loved her for who she was. But since they'd moved to Wilmette, she no longer felt like the confident beauty who he fell for ten years earlier. That radiant woman had disappeared amid the daily drudgery of an overloaded housewife's life.

Vivian was afraid to tell Mel how she'd left the bathtub tap running that morning and water had spilled all over the floor. Or how she'd left Linda for only a minute to run down to the basement to transfer another load into the dryer, and upon her return, the toddler had rolled down the stairs. Linda was unhurt, but Vivian's chest squeezed to imagine what might have happened. What if Linda had broken her arm? Or worse? Vivian would never forgive herself for being too frazzled to watch over her children. She couldn't focus only on one, fearing that the others might suffer. Vivian was afraid to tell Mel how many days she rarely had a moment to catch her breath. She felt suffocated by the seemingly endless number of tasks that piled up, one after the other, all day long, day after day. Vivian might walk into the older girls' room and stand transfixed, her head whirling, and forget why she'd entered, then rush out to calm a crying baby. Upon reaching his crib, she was surprised to find herself holding the pillowcases that belonged on the girls' twin beds. Her patience was worn as thin as an old sock. One enraged look sent Linda wailing before Vivian uttered one word. No wonder. The child couldn't understand why leaving a stuffed animal on the living room couch made her mother so mad. Vivian hated to feel that she had become a monstrous witch.

She sniffed away a few tears. "I'm a bad mother."

Mel put his index finger on her lips. "Don't say that. You're a swell mother. You take care of everyone, including me." He held her cheeks in his palms. "Let me look at you. Remember how happy we were when Irene was born? We drank champagne for a month."

She smiled, not meaning to. "Of course, I remember. We bought our first television set."

He stroked her arm. "We were prepared to stay home every night with our new baby girl and never go out again." They laughed as Mel went on. "After Sandy came along, I bought cigars all around. Before we knew it, we had another little rascal, our Linda. And then, finally a son to honor the memory of my pa." Mel squeezed Vivian so tightly she lost her breath.

She gripped his arm. "But this time, it wouldn't be good news. I don't think I can handle another."

"Do we need to hire help?"

Vivian let out a deep sigh. "You know we can't afford anyone. Not with our mortgage and everything else: sod for the lawn, clothes, shoes, and toys for the kids. And Billy's growing so fast . . ." They lay silent for a few minutes.

Mel said, "Do you think I can't support another child?"

"No, it's not that. Do you remember when you told me you had to give your employee five hundred dollars for his girlfriend's abortion, but not to expect our money back?"

"Of course, I remember," Mel's words were clipped. "Why are you asking about this now?"

Her shaky fingers alighted on Mel's hairy forearm. "His girlfriend was OK afterward, wasn't she?"

"Fine. Don't tell me. *You're* not thinking about doing *that*, are you?"

Her breathing became uneven. "If I have a positive test, well, I . . . I want to ask Dr. Goldblum if he would . . ." There, she said it.

Mel snorted. "How could you? After all he's done for us?" His voice rose.

Vivian put a finger to her lips. "Not so loud." She jerked her thumb toward the girls' room.

Mel's voice stayed strong. "I can't let you put yourself in danger." He released Vivian from his embrace with a sigh.

"Do you love our children?" she asked.

"Of course." He paused. "But I love you more." His voice cracked. "I've never told you about what happened with my Aunt Addie."

"Who is Aunt Addie?"

He brushed the hair away from her face. "Now's not the time to tell you about her. A tragedy. Broke our family apart. Please don't do anything rash. I need you. We all need you."

She began to weep. How had a girl like her, who had grown up with nothing, found a man like Mel Jacobson? Better than any schoolgirl's imagination of an elusive Prince Charming. He didn't have movie-star looks and wasn't a rich Jewish doctor, but he was the kindest, smartest, most levelheaded man Vivian could have dreamed of to be her husband. And he loved her—Vivian Kolson Jacobson. His love reinforced her strength. She wanted to please him, to be a good wife, but even more essential, to be a good mother.

She didn't want to alarm Mel. Nothing was definite. Not yet. "I'll have to get a test at the doctor's office before I know for sure."

"But you do know, don't you? Even without the test?"

Yes, the familiar physical symptoms were intermittent, and she couldn't deny Ethel's keen observations. But Vivian still held out hope that this was all in her head; that the queasiness, tender breasts, and emotionality would disappear. She took a deep breath. There would be no pretending after a positive test.

WHILE MEL slept, Vivian shifted from side to side. She couldn't get comfortable. In the early years of their marriage, when her body had threatened to deny her the fulfillment of motherhood, she'd yearned for the day when she'd be a loving, patient mother surrounded by doting babes. She was grateful for their four beautiful children, with the house in Wilmette an unforeseen bonus. When they first moved to Maple Street, many mornings she awoke in amazement, thrilled to be lying next to Mel Jacobson, a steady provider from a good Jewish family whom she loved and who loved her. Mel's love for her had made her strong and confident.

Lately, too many mornings she awoke with a sinking feeling that began by snaking down her neck, through to her gut, and on to her quivering loins. Trembling, she had to force herself to rise to meet another demanding day.

CHAPTER FIVE
HANNAH'S CRISIS

SATURDAY, 1956

EVERYTHING FELT different in the daytime. The usual morning hubbub took over their home. Vivian yelled at Sandy because she refused to put on the clothes she'd selected for her. Irene whined because she couldn't find her library book. Where did Mommy put it?

Mel had planned to leave early; instead, he poured himself another cup of coffee as he pondered what Vivian had shared the night before. He scanned the headline of the *Sun-Times*: "33 Injured as CTA Bus Rams House." Viv had been right: Their family was better off in Wilmette, away from the perils of the city.

He drummed his fingers on the table, shuddering to recall what Viv planned to ask the doctor to do. Would it shatter their Maple Street home and mirror today's disastrous headline? He wasn't ready to agree to her plan, but on the other hand, if he insisted on a fifth child, would Viv blame him if it were too much for her? He'd never forgive himself if she lost control and did something drastic.

Before going out to his car, Mel loped upstairs where Vivian was making the girls' beds, pulling the sheets taut. He kissed her longer than his usual quick goodbye.

Vivian's eyes welled up as she gripped his upper arms tightly. "What do you think we should do?"

"Don't jump the gun. Wait until the test. Please, honey, I've got to go to work now. We'll talk more tonight."

The rest of the morning, blurry-eyed Vivian felt as if she were sleepwalking through her daily routine, each step as if she were trudging through waist-high snow. The older girls' laughter bubbled up from the den, enthralled by the Saturday morning cartoons, Bugs Bunny and Donald Duck. Their voices became muffled as if Vivian's head were underwater.

Until the ringing phone startled her alert.

Aunt Ruthie. Thank goodness.

"I can be at your house by one thirty."

Vivian had long counted on her ma's dear friend's guidance. This was also Vivian's chance to find out more about what Ethel had hinted at. Aunt Ruthie must surely know the whole story. Vivian hurried to settle Linda and Billy for naps, plumped up the pillows on the new couch, straightened the magazines on the coffee table, and hustled to the basement to start another load of laundry.

RUTH LAVIN took off in her two-toned, red-and-white 1955 Chevy, driving along winding Sheridan Road, and contemplated how much of Hannah's story to share. Yes, it was time Vivian knew more, but she did not want to betray her friend's confidence. But certainly, Vivian must realize she was not the first woman to face this crisis.

When Aunt Ruthie arrived, Irene and Sandy were outside on the sidewalk. Irene gave a quick wave, not wanting to interrupt bouncing the ball in their singsong game, "*A* . . . My name is Alice."

Vivian ushered her into the house. Aunt Ruthie refused the offer of coffee. She motioned her to sit on the new couch. "Where shall I begin?" said Aunt Ruthie and grasped Vivian's hand. "When we met, your mother was as frightened as a sparrow whose baby had fallen from the nest."

"Why was she afraid to be pregnant?" asked Vivian. "Too dangerous?"

Aunt Ruthie hesitated.

"In those days, every childbirth was dangerous."

1918

DURING THE last weeks of her fourth pregnancy, Hannah Kolson's ankles swelled as big as melons, unrecognizable as her own. She had to lift one foot to meet the other on each tread of the staircase up to their third-floor flat. In the final weeks, Hannah couldn't leave her bed. The downstairs neighbor and her teenaged daughter Miriam did the Kolinsky family's marketing and household chores.

Finally, labor began. Hannah was jolted awake at midnight, feverish, pulse racing, her hair soaked as if she'd emerged from the Division Street bathhouse. She begged Abe to fetch the midwife.

"Too soon," he said, smoking his pipe. "The crone will ask me for money we owe from the last time—money we don't have."

Contractions racked through Hannah's body, worse than any she'd experienced before. Day turned into night and back again to daylight. When Hannah began talking gibberish, Abe became frightened and gave the neighbor a quarter to bring the midwife.

When the midwife examined Hannah, she chucked Abe's ear. "You should have called me sooner, Abe Kolinsky! I can't help your wife now. Go at once and bring the American doctor. He lives above his office at the corner of Roosevelt and Crawford. I'll stay with Hannah until he arrives."

"How much must I pay this American doctor?"

"Go!" cried the midwife. "Do what I say! *Go now!*"

When the tall, red-faced doctor arrived, he touched Hannah's scorching brow and pinched her swollen ankles. Hannah screamed when he opened her legs. The American doctor praised the old midwife, saying, "You did the right thing to call me here. You may have saved this woman's life, and her baby's too. Go home. I'll take over."

The midwife dashed for the door, muttering "Pu, pu, pu" to chase away the evil eye.

The doctor shook his head. "These superstitious Jews!"

Hours passed. Severe pains plunged Hannah in and out of consciousness. She cried out, and her parents appeared as angels hovering around her bed. They assured her she would not join them in Heaven on this day. It was not yet her time. Hannah's aunts, uncles, and even the village healer joined her parents in a chorus that sounded like birds trilling among trees' rustling leaves. "Chana, dearest Chana, stay strong."

Hannah awoke to see a strange, sandy-haired American man with a fleshy, flaming face as astonishing as the prairie fires in the wheat fields back home. A blue-eyed dybbuk, a monster? She steeled herself to expect the worst, until with relief, she heard the yowl of an infant. She stiffened when the tall man came near until he placed a smiling babe in her arms. A baby boy with a sweet round face, blood on his scalp, and wet black curls. Where was the midwife? She clutched at her son, lest this American devil take him away.

"This must be your *last* baby," the doctor pronounced. His tone of finality frightened Hannah. "Do you understand me?"

Last baby? Yes, she understood his words, but why? What had she done wrong? Hannah led her child to latch onto her breast, where he greedily sucked as if Hannah herself had rescued him from the bulrushes. In truth, she did not rescue him; he had rescued her. This child was her savior, her Moses, her people's great redeemer. She would name him Moshe. She strained to sit, but let out a yelp when the sharp pains through her private parts pushed her down. Moshe gave a soft cry as he fell off her breast, and Hannah laid her head on her soaking pillow with her baby beside her. She squeezed her eyes to hold back tears when the doctor gently lifted her bottom to place a clean towel beneath her. Was God speaking His truth to her through this American? Perhaps he was not a dybbuk, not a devil, but an angel with a gentle touch who brought her from Heaven's door and back again to this life. Hannah smiled up and saw, as if for the first time, shreds of peeling paint crisscrossing the ceiling. Life in America was not the glittering golden medina Chana had dreamed of in their Russian village. Dreams as foolish to her now as if they'd belonged to another woman. In Chicago, she was no longer Chana, but Hannah, lying in the bed of her west side flat, holding a beautiful newborn baby boy. Her children gave her life meaning in this foreign land. They were her golden treasures.

When the doctor called for the father, Abe slunk into the room and cast a sideways glance at his wife, whose eyes were locked onto those of the sucking infant.

"Thanks God," said Abe. "God smiles on me with another son."

The doctor placed both palms on Abe's shoulders, shook him fiercely, and stared into his stubborn dark eyes. "No more children! Do you hear me, mister? Your wife's life is at risk!"

Abe wriggled out of the doctor's grip, squared his shoulders, and said stiffly, "Ach, what do you want me to do? I just look at her, and she is with child again."

Hannah squeaked in protest. Abe Kolinsky knew that he did more than just look. He came to her whenever he pleased. He had no respect for the fertile time in her cycle. She sputtered a Yiddish invective and fell back onto the bed.

"Sha! Quiet, Alice!" Abe demanded.

Angry to be called by the English name, Hannah cursed Abe, but the effort burned her private parts with jolting pains. As Hannah sobbed, the baby wailed, too. She tried to calm him. "Shush, my little Moshe. I'm here."

Abe loomed over the bed. "Listen to me, Alice. Learn English. He is not Moshe. No more Yiddishkeit names. We will name him Max because we live in America. I'll soon be a citizen of this great country. You'll see. Everything will be okey dokey."

Little Ethel pushed the door open and dashed across the room. Had she heard her mother's childbirth screams? Hannah was overcome with sadness to think that one day her daughter must feel a woman's pain.

The doctor's voice filled the room. "Do you understand me, Mister Kolinksy? No more babies! Childbearing is too dangerous for a diabetic!"

Diabetic? Hannah looked up at Abe with brimming eyes, begging for the translation.

"Ya," he said, wiping his mouth with the back of his hand and spitting into the chamber pot. "The sugar problem. Same as your brothers."

The doctor buckled his black bag and muttered, "Immigrant wretches! Bringing more dirty children into our city where every day, people are dying with flu!" At the door, he turned back to them and cried, "Don't call me back here again!"

1956

"BUT MAX was born before she met you," said Vivian. "What was different when you met?"

Aunt Ruthie looked drained. "Can I have one of your cigarettes? I'm trying to give it up, but . . ."

As Vivian handed her the pack, Billy let out a faint cry from upstairs. Vivian stood to go to him, but he quickly fell silent. She sat down and picked up the pack to shake out another cigarette for herself. Aunt Ruthie took two quick puffs and edged closer to Vivian, whose hand was shaky as she set her burning cigarette in the ashtray. Ruth took a deep inhale and blew the smoke toward the ceiling. What right did she have to divulge her friend's anguish, even to her dear daughter? Vivian deserved her mother's guidance to navigate her own all-too-familiar, female predicament, but Ruth knew Hannah balked to discuss intimate matters with anyone except Ruth. Yet Ruth felt about Vivian the way her Italian friends felt about their goddaughters: as if she were another mother for her.

Ruth Lavin was never one for pretenses. "Yes, dear, it *is* time you knew more. Come, sit closer to me."

Vivian's gut tensed as she scooted toward Aunt Ruthie. She took a deep inhale and waited before a long exhale.

"After Max, your mother did everything she could to keep herself from another pregnancy. Tried ridiculous things that she'd heard about from the women at the shul. Of course, nothing works perfectly. Your father was demanding. That's why, when she was certain she was pregnant, she was frantic, wanting to make it go away. In shul, I overheard her praying for a miscarriage."

Vivian gasped. "No! Was she carrying me? Or another one?"

Aunt Ruthie stubbed out her cigarette and stared at Vivian. "Why does it matter? I knew she needed help."

Upstairs, the children were uncharacteristically silent as Vivian pondered the question. *Did* it matter? Wasn't she alive and Ma's favorite? But she remained unsettled. "Tell me. I'm an adult. And a mother. I have a right to know."

Ruth took a long drag and let out a column of smoke toward the ceiling. "I wanted to help. My friends at the Dil Pickle Club knew about a man."

"The Dil Pickle Club?"

Aunt Ruthie's eyes took on a faraway look, as if she weren't sitting beside Vivian on Maple Street. "A haven for the avant-garde. A bohemian club like none other. A salon where writers, actors, and intellectuals gathered to hear political speeches, read poetry, and perform plays. The club was far from your mother's neighborhood. Far, not only in miles, but in ideas. Many women I knew had gone to the man who I took your mother to see."

"*You* took her to this man? Had you gone to him, too?"

Ruth Lavin stubbed out her cigarette. "This is your mother's story. Not mine."

SUMMER, 1923

AFTER THE older boys went to school, Hannah hurried out to meet Ruth Lavin, who was waiting on a bench in the park across from the Kolsons' building. Hannah kept Ethel home that day to mind Max in the downstairs neighbor's flat. Her daughter never complained about missing school. Hannah disapproved of her attitude, but what could she do? She needed her.

Ruth stood and waved as Hannah approached, and the two women linked arms. Hannah's face was blotchy and bloated in the heat. A gurgle rose from her gut, loud enough for Ruth to hear.

Ruth grasped her hand. "I told you not to eat breakfast."

"Just a few small bites of leftover noodle kugel." Hannah touched her belly.

Hannah pulled her hand away. No one fretted about her like this Ruth Lavin did, as if she was the sister Hannah never had. They rode the streetcar downtown before transferring to the Milwaukee Avenue line. Hannah sat by the window and fanned her face with her gloved hand to keep from getting sick. She wasn't familiar with these streets. She'd never taken this line before and asked Ruth where they were headed.

"Better I don't say. Remember, when we arrive, use my last name. Today you are Hannah Lavin."

Yet another name? Too many changes. When they passed a towering sculpture in the middle of a square, Hannah pointed and asked, "Is that the new Logan Square monument?"

Ruth nodded. Hannah's brother had told her about this bold celebration of Illinois's one hundred years of statehood. It was a wonder, but Hannah was not impressed. Only one hundred years? Tsarist Russia was many centuries old. America was still a new country, filled with the bravado of the young.

After they traveled for over an hour, Hannah's face grew ashen. Finally, they alit from the streetcar with Ruth leading the way. They turned down a residential street and stopped in front of an ordinary greystone.

A young boy stopped throwing a ball against the stoop next door. "I betcha I know where you're going," he said. "Ring the bell for Boone."

Ruth gave him a dime. "Stop being a smart aleck."

"Gee, thanks, lady!"

They rang the bell. A buzzer released the door, and they proceeded to the second floor. A woman with a bootblack thick braid wound around her head like a crown answered the door, but she was no queen.

She greeted them in a harsh tone. "Which one of you is Hannah Lavin?"

Hannah looked at Ruth and took a shaky step forward. The woman ushered them into an elegant parlor and pointed them toward a rose satin settee, where the two women sat, knees touching. An unidentifiable, sickly sour scent came from the room behind this one, engulfing them. Hannah felt faint, coughed, and tried to calm her thigh from quivering. Strains of a Bach sonata playing on the Victrola in the corner sent Hannah's heart beating in time to the music until she lurched at pealing church bells that pierced the quiet street. What a contrast to the steady hubbub of their west side neighborhood with its jumble of languages, accents, and the pungent stench of excrement from the horses who pulled carts through the alleys. Was this really a doctor's office? Hannah's stomach cramped with the sense that something was wrong, terribly wrong. She squeezed Ruth's hand more tightly.

The woman beckoned her with a crooked finger toward a carved mahogany desk. Hannah froze, then exhaled in relief when Ruth said, "I will accompany Mrs. Lavin to be certain everything is clear. She is still learning English."

When the woman nodded her assent, Hannah whispered to herself, "Thanks God."

Hannah stood on wobbly legs until Ruth steadied her and gently pushed her into one of the chairs in front of the desk. The woman pulled out a ledger book and filled her fountain pen with ink. She asked Hannah if she had other children and how many. She answered quickly.

When was her last monthly bleed? Hannah shook her head. Ruth repeated the question to her in Yiddish.

Hannah understood before the translation but wasn't certain of her answer.

"At Purim," she told Ruth.

"What's she saying?" barked the woman. "Poor him? Does she mean the father? Tell me, now, what was the date?"

"March 15," said Ruth.

"She's rather far along." The woman tapped her pen on the desk. "Any complications with previous births?"

Ruth hesitated. "Five years ago, an American doctor diagnosed her as a diabetic."

"Diabetic? Dangerous. Any symptoms?" The woman looked at Hannah more closely. "Lightheadedness? Thirst?"

Ruth translated. Hannah shook her head no.

"We'll see what Dr. Boone says."

Hannah remembered the American doctor's warning. Max must be her last. Wistfully, she remembered her joy at the birth of Ethel before him, finally a daughter to help out, how the tiny girl's heart beat in sync with her own. Each child gave purpose to her harsh life in Chicago, the purpose she needed to live each day. Could she risk leaving her dear children motherless?

The woman held out her palm. "One hundred dollars."

Hannah watched Ruth count out ten ten-dollar bills. "Too much," Hannah muttered.

Ruth put a finger to her lips while the woman placed the cash in a desk drawer, entered the payment in the ledger, and motioned them to follow her through oak pocket doors into the next room.

Hannah dragged her feet as Ruth pulled her along. Here, the putrid, gassy odor was more intense. Hannah gagged. The large room was nearly bare. A high examining bed with metal stirrups dominated the space with a shiny metal table holding a pan of instruments resembling knives and scissors aligned in a perfect row. The woman told Hannah to undress—everything off, except her underblouse.

She patted the table. "Hop up and wait for Doctor."

Hannah's hands felt as icy as they did on winter days after wiping off frost that covered their flat's windows. Her fingers trembled as she removed each layer of clothing and then sat sideways on the table to wait with only her toes touching the floor. Ruth squeezed her hand. The doctor entered through a back door with an unexpected grin, surprising Hannah by his youthful look—his wavy blond hair and thick brows. He resembled the son of the Polish man at the newsstand where Abe bought his tobacco.

"I'm Dr. Boone." He spun Hannah around and told her to lie back. "Easy now," he said as he began to guide her bare feet into the metal stirrups, one by one. At the first touch of her toes to the freezing metal, Hannah's foot cramped. She screeched, pulled away, and kneaded her foot.

"Try to relax," he said as he poked at her puffy ankles. "Are they always this thick?"

Hannah flinched again.

"She's a diabetic," said Ruth.

The doctor's face changed to a somber look. "Diabetic? Serious."

Hannah gripped Ruth's fingers and squirmed.

Dr. Boone splayed her legs until she felt like a chicken ready for the oven. She stiffened but tried to imagine him as the neighborhood midwife or the doctor at the Maxwell Street clinic in a futile effort to calm herself.

"Steady," he said. Hannah squeezed her eyes shut. She felt a sharp pain and then a dull ache. "Ask your friend to lie still," the doctor said to Ruth as he pushed his gloved hand deep inside Hannah, who twisted and moaned.

He addressed his assistant. "When was the date of her last monthly?"

"March 15. Or so she says." She clucked her tongue.

"Is she sure? Not earlier?" The doctor shouted at Ruth, who lifted her shoulders noncommittally. Abruptly, he grunted and pulled out his hands. "Too large. Much too large." Then in a softer tone, "Why doesn't she want this child?"

Ruth said, "She almost died during her last home birth. An American doctor warned another delivery could kill her."

"Maybe it would or maybe it wouldn't, but if I go ahead today with this termination, there will be a lot of blood. Does she have somewhere to go afterward?"

"We'll take a cab to my place," said Ruth.

The doctor took a cone and placed it over Hannah's mouth. She squeaked out a protest. "Settle down," he said. "Take three deep breaths. This will be all over before you know it."

Hannah wriggled and tried to pull the mask off her face. As the gas took effect, she kicked violently and reached for Ruth, beseeching her with her eyes. The assistant held her down. Hannah gave a weak cry for her mama before falling unconscious.

Moments later, Dr. Boone replaced the tool onto the tray and lifted the cone from Hannah's face. "Can't do it," he said to Ruth. "Too risky. How dare you bring this ignorant immigrant to me!" His voice rose. "The fetus she carries is too large. She could bleed to death right here on this table." He pulled off his gloves.

"Doctor!" cried Ruth, but he was already washing up at the sink in the back. "How can you put her life in danger to risk another delivery?"

"Stop wasting my time! I know her type. She wants this baby and she doesn't want him. Next time, come to me sooner. Tell her to put her faith in Jesus and pray to survive."

Ruth began to argue as he disappeared through the side door. She held fast to Hannah's hand until Hannah awoke, groggy. Her head felt three times its usual size. She clutched at her belly and wept. How could she have done such a thing? God will surely punish her. Ruth reassured her. Nothing had changed.

Hannah put a hand on her belly and cried aloud. "Thanks God!"

"Get dressed," the assistant said. "Hannah Lavin, or whoever you say you are, pay up, and go buy a new christening gown."

As she waddled toward her pile of clothes to attach her skirts, Hannah shouted a Yiddish curse. "God should visit upon you the ten plagues."

"Are you angry? Dr. Boone might have saved your life," huffed the assistant.

She ushered them out to the front room, hurried them over to her desk, and held out her hand. "Fifty dollars."

"For nothing?" protested Ruth.

The assistant replied, "You took another woman's place. You'd pay another one hundred fifty dollars if he'd done what you came for."

Hannah sputtered as the assistant repeated the fee and tapped her pen on the ledger book.

"What if we don't pay?" asked Ruth.

The assistant opened a desk drawer. Hannah peeked in and gasped to see a pearl-handled revolver with a thick barrel. Ruth opened her pocketbook, removed five ten-dollar bills, handed them over, and clicked the clasp shut.

Hannah's tears filled her throat. So much money. These *mamzers,* these bastards.

Ruth grabbed Hannah's hand and steered her toward the door. Over her shoulder, she called, "Tell Dr. Boone goodbye, if that's really his name."

Outside on the sidewalk, Ruth said, "I'll try to find someone in our neighborhood."

"No," said Hannah. "You did what you could. I'll go back to the clinic. The rest will be in God's hands."

Ruth said, "I'm afraid for you."

Hannah put up her hand. "Not another word. What choice do I have? God will watch over me."

If only her mama were alongside her instead of this Ruth, who had never known her own mother or what it meant to be a mother. Hannah must rely on her mama's wisdom that she carried deep within her. True, her new American friend had good intentions, but Hannah must trust herself to do what's best for her children, her family, and herself.

She recalled her first visit to the Maxwell Street Dispensary of the Chicago Maternity Center when she was pregnant with their eldest, only a few months after their wedding night. Abe sent her to the clinic alone. She'd been fearful because she spoke little English. She was grateful for the kindness of the founder, Dr. Joseph DeLee, a distinguished-looking man with gold-rimmed spectacles and a trim goatee who guided the student doctor and spoke to Hannah in Yiddish. "Childbirth is a natural part of life. If you follow our rules for a healthy diet and regular clinic visits, all will be well. Since 1895, we've safely delivered hundreds of babies in homes all over Chicago."

HANNAH RETURNED to the clinic's familiar waiting room. The yellowing, cracked linoleum floor was unchanged. The same blonde harried receptionist sat at her desk, where the telephone rang non-stop. Hannah gave her name and took a seat alongside a red-faced woman on the cusp of giving birth in Chicago's August heat. The noisy room was jammed with women and children crammed as close together as apples on a pushcart, a cross section of Chicago's newest arrivals: women from every Eastern European country, and also from Italy, Greece, Mexico, and Negroes originally from the South. All in various sizes as they awaited motherhood, shifting their bulk on narrow folding chairs. Toddlers bounced at the edges of mothers' laps. If they slid off, the women scurried to corral them, shouting in a cacophony of languages and accents. A true Tower of Babel, but sharing the common language of discipline: wagging fingers, loud threats, or a quick smack to a surprised bottom with a rolled-up newspaper. Afterward, women resourcefully folded the papers into fans in a desperate effort to keep cool because the two whirring floor units did little to circulate the heavy air. Hannah was musing how she was glad that she did not bring wild Max along today when she was surprised to hear the nurse call her name. So soon?

"Have you been here before, Mrs. Kolson? I can't find your file."

Oy, that Abe. "Look for Hannah Kolinsky. Kolson is our new name. My husband changed it when he got his papers."

"Aha, now you are one of us. Congratulations."

This woman was happy for her, not like the hostile German druggist who'd cursed their newly granted status. These Americans. Each one was different.

When Hannah was called into the examination room, the student doctor read the notes from her last delivery: "Preeclampsia. Diabetes. No more children." The young man insisted she must deliver this baby at the new Mount Sinai Hospital. The clinic would not take the risk of another home birth. Hannah clutched at her throat, chilled by the stories she'd heard from women in shul about the new hospital where they gassed you before cutting open your private parts and pulling out the babies with pliers. The student doctor must have seen her panicked look.

"Cheer up, missus. He'll be a Christmas baby."

Hannah sneered. Christmas meant nothing to her. The only comfort she'd heard was that the new hospital served kosher food. Hannah asked if the midwife would be with her at the new hospital. The answer was no. Hannah shuddered. Would she survive?

DECEMBER, 1923

HANNAH STRUGGLED to get out of bed. She lumbered to the metal heating grate in the floor and stood over it, hoping to claim a *whoosh* of air to tickle her calves and mock her with an illusion of warmth. She shuffled to the hallway toilet and sighed in relief. At this hour, thanks God, no one was inside.

After she returned to the flat, eight-year-old Ethel was awake and asked, "Does it hurt to have a baby?"

Hannah doubled over with a contraction, let out a cry, and sank into a chair. "It's God's way. I don't wish you pain, but I pray that one day you will feel the joy of being a mother."

Ethel scrunched up her face.

Outside the frosted window, a car horn bleated. As arranged, Hannah's brother had arrived to drive them to the hospital in his new Peerless machine. Hannah held tight to the banister and crept down the stairs. Abe trailed behind with the satchel she'd packed the night before.

Outside, Hannah's brother took the bag from Abe and clapped him on the back. "Hurry up, brother-in-law! You're going to be a father again. Hop in! My machine is running!"

"Don't rush me. It's my day off!"

Hannah's brother jabbed Abe's shoulder. "My sister doesn't get a day off!" He embraced Hannah. "Let's get you to Mount Sinai."

Oh, how she'd prefer to stay at home in the comfort of her bed with her own pillow and await the midwife. At the door of the hospital, a no-nonsense–looking nurse with a steep, starched white cap met them in the vestibule and shooed them into the too-warm lobby. Hannah steadied herself on Abe's arm and followed the nurse's thick-heeled white shoes. She choked and coughed at the antiseptic smell that hung thick in the air. When the nurse steered Hannah toward the elevator and waved Abe away, a look of panic rose in Abe's eyes.

"She's ours now!" said the nurse. "We'll give her back to you after this baby arrives."

"Chanaleh, will you be OK in here?"

Chanaleh? Abe hadn't called her by that pet name since the early days of their brief courtship. He must be frightened for her. Hannah pulled back her shoulders and stood as tall as she could manage with her bulging belly. She must survive, not only for her children, but for her poor husband too. What would he do without her? He'd have to marry in haste to find a wife to care for the children or send them to the Jewish Orphans' Home. God forbid, but Abe wouldn't be the first to do such a thing. She thought of her friend and urged, "Get word to Ruth that I'm in the hospital."

Abe pulled his pipe from his pocket and shook his head. "Ach, that woman."

The nurse led Hannah upstairs and showed her to a cot in a room with thirty others. Hannah's contractions were still far apart. She tried to relax and think of this as a holiday. No need to cook, clean, or see to a child's hurts. No husband to bother her to get to bed when she wanted to stay up late and write a letter to her aunt in New York. Hannah took a breath. She was on her own here at Mount Sinai

Hospital. She wondered what it would feel like to be on her own every day like Ruth Lavin.

"A woman shouldn't ask such questions." She could hear her papa scold and see her mama wink.

Hours passed. She dozed on and off until she startled awake, convulsing with contractions with no time to rest in between. Two nurses appeared. Was it afternoon? Night? They poked at her with needles and squeezed her arm on and off in a tight cuff. Hannah's body took over in the waves of excruciating pain that all women forget from one childbirth bed to the next, remembering their purpose only when they reoccur, always surprised by their power.

When Hannah heard "It's time!" two men lifted her onto a rolling bed and wheeled her into a room with bright overhead lights, blinding her. She prayed to survive this delivery without the midwife beside her and called upon God to have mercy and bring her safely through this trial.

A doctor came in holding the tool that must be the one the women in shul whispered about: the horse pliers that pulls the babies out. Hannah lost count of the minutes and succumbed to the increasing pace and intensity of the pains. Two nurses gathered around her bed. One called out, "Blood pressure rising!"

Hannah heard Mama whispering, "Stay strong, my daughter! You will not join me yet." Hannah relaxed. A sign that she would survive.

After many hours, as if in a dream, a baby wailed, and an unsmiling nurse spoke. "It's a girl," she said and handed Hannah a swaddled infant. The newborn peered up at her, as if she'd emerged with full wisdom.

Hannah's mama whispered, "Enjoy your beautiful daughter," and disappeared.

A sister for Ethel! Hannah hadn't dared pray that God would smile upon her in this way. After her bold pleading to lose this baby, Hannah had been certain this would be yet another boy. She chanted aloud the prayer of gratitude to have reached this blessed occasion.

She stared at her daughter with a full head of black hair and asked her forgiveness. Hannah had only wanted to vanquish her from her womb because she feared for her own life. When the infant's eyes locked on hers, Hannah was overcome by the infant's compassionate heart and began to weep.

"Into what harsh American world have I brought you, my miracle child? I will try to make life easier for you. We will have Ethel to help us."

"Are you crying, Mrs. Kolson?" said a nurse with a thermometer in her hand. "Calm yourself. You have a healthy child. Don't despair. What will you name her?"

"She's a Nes, a miracle, in my language. The name of my mother's mother buried in Russia was Nessieh. Tell me, nurse, what is an American name for my precious daughter?"

"Let me think. My niece is called Vivian. The name means 'life.'"

The nurse bustled around her and changed the soaking thick pad between her legs. "I'll go and tell your husband. I'm sure he'll be happy and relieved."

In the fathers' waiting room, the nurse looked at her clipboard and called out, "Abraham Kolson?" She circled the crowded room where a bevy of disheveled men assumed various poses: sitting, pacing, smoking, and reading the newspaper. She called again, "Is Mr. Abraham Kolson here?"

Abe coughed, hit his pipe against the ashtray, and raised his arm. His chestnut hair stuck out in every direction. His white tailor's shirt was untucked and bunched up above his waist.

After the nurse gave him the news, he frowned. "Another girl?" He spat on the floor. "Why does God punish me?"

The nurse's face contorted as she tapped her pen against the clipboard. "Mr. Kolson, your wife almost died delivering your child. Be grateful that she and your daughter are both alive and healthy."

Abe shook his head. "Ach, she brings me another mouth to feed."

The nurse stomped off to attend to the last person on her list. When she spoke quietly to him, he jumped up, burst into tears, and tore his shirt. "No! Can't be! Without my Tillie, how will I live? Who will care for our children?"

The nurse patted his arm. "There, there, mister. You'll find a way. You have a beautiful new son to live for."

The man shoved the nurse. "How could this happen? In this modern hospital?" Sobbing, he sunk back into the chair and covered his face with his hands.

The nurse made her way back to Abe, dumbstruck and staring at the anguished man. "Mr. Kolson, your wife wanted me to tell you that she will name the baby Vivian."

Abe's face softened. He stood and smoothed down his shirt. "At last, my Alice has come to her senses. In this snowy Chicago winter, our new daughter blooms with a good American name. Take me to see my wife and my new baby! My Vivian!"

1956

VIVIAN'S EYES welled as she stared at Aunt Ruthie. "Vivian? So it was me she was carrying on the day you met."

Aunt Ruthie put her arm around her. "Have compassion for your mother. Remember, she is a woman like any other. There are many reasons why a woman can feel desperate to end a pregnancy."

Vivian shook off Aunt Ruthie's arm and began to pace around the room. "What if I had never been born?" Vivian twisted her wedding rings around and around her finger.

Aunt Ruthie motioned for her to sit back down on the couch. She covered Vivian's hand with hers. "But you *were* born. Here you are with us."

Aunt Ruthie was right. She was here in Wilmette with a beautiful family. Vivian felt heartsick to imagine how her gentle, immigrant mother must have been frightened to be in a situation where she feared for her life and understood little English, the language spoken by those in charge. Her ma had been as vulnerable as a locust and just as easily crushed. How bold she'd been to trust Ruth Lavin, initially a stranger, now her lifelong confidante and anchor. Vivian was grateful how Aunt Ruthie protected Ma.

But these were new times. Vivian was a modern woman, born in Chicago. She must be brave and do what she must do.

From upstairs a small voice called, "Mom-mee! I want Mommy!"

Vivian jumped up. "Did you hear that?"

"Hear what?" asked Aunt Ruthie.

"That was Linda calling Mommy. Her first sentence!" Vivian ran up the stairs. "Say it again, Linda. Say it!"

Vivian lifted the toddler from her crib and hugged her. "Yes, Linda. I'm here." She planted kisses all over her face. "Say it again."

Vivian gazed at her daughter as if she were her firstborn. Linda giggled, pleased to have delighted her mother. Vivian prompted her to say the sentence again. Instead, Linda spewed a stream of nonsense syllables. Had Vivian only imagined what she'd heard?

Aunt Ruthie retrieved her coat from the closet and quietly let herself out. Vivian carried Linda downstairs to place her in the playpen, relieved to see Aunt Ruthie had gone. She didn't know what to think about these revelations. So many conflicting emotions. Tears streamed down Vivian's cheeks. Would Ma have died in the attempt to end her pregnancy? Neither of them would be here today. Vivian's breathing came in spurts. She rubbed her palms together, crossed her arms, and hugged her shoulders. Now she knew for certain that she was the pregnancy that Ma had wanted to end. Vivian pinched herself as if proof of her existence.

Vivian didn't have the same physical vulnerabilities as her

mother, yet she was stymied by the same crisis. She was born in this country. How could she have let this happen? Nothing was foolproof, but she should have tried harder to prevent another pregnancy. She loved Mel. Each one of their children was precious. He said he could support another. But she did not want another. Not now. Probably not ever. Vivian stared out of the window at the scraggly plants struggling to thrive in her backyard garden. Had she been too ambitious to believe vegetables could flourish in this clay soil?

"Mom-mee! I want Mommy."

Vivian heard Linda's first sentence clearly. Her heart lifted at those syllables.

I want Mommy. She was forever committed to meet Linda's needs in every way she could. With another baby she feared she wouldn't be able to give Linda and the others what they deserved from a good mother. Vivian felt embarrassed to beg Dr. Goldblum for an abortion, but she had to.

Although Vivian didn't often bother Mel at work, she decided to call him.

"Anything wrong, dear? How're the children?"

"We're all fine. Linda said her first sentence."

"Darn. Missed it again. Don't tell me, let me guess. She said 'I love Daddy,' just like Sandy did."

Vivian put her hand over the receiver to muffle a snort. "Right. Just like Sandy."

"See you tonight," said Mel. "Give Linda a hug from Daddy."

Another milestone. Just like the memories of each of her children's births. Ma never mentioned milestones or her worries. Had she confided in Ethel? Or had Ethel been nosy, listening in? Vivian recalled Aunt Ruthie had said to be compassionate. Yes, her mother was a woman like any other. Ma must have feared for her life, but life with Pa had never been easy.

"Mommy!" Linda cried and raised her arms, straining to get out of the playpen. "I want Mommy."

Upstairs, Billy began to howl. Irene and Sandy ran in from outside.

"Mommy!" Irene called. "Chuckie hit Sandy!"

"Did you tease him again?" asked Vivian. "How many times do I have to tell you not to?"

"I didn't do anything!" insisted Sandy.

"OK, I'll talk to his mother about this the next time we talk. Now, go back outside!"

Vivian sat on the couch and lit a cigarette. When Mel came home, no matter how he tried to coax her, Linda didn't utter "I love Daddy." She didn't say "I want Mommy" either. Not that night.

VIVIAN SLEPT fitfully. When finally she fell into a deep slumber, she dreamt she was at the 1933 Chicago's World Fair, the Century of Progress. She hadn't thought about that wondrous visit in many years. She'd been ten years old, eager to attend the fair after her favorite teacher urged their fourth-grade class to find a way to attend. She was delighted when Aunt Ruthie treated her and Ma to a spectacular day visiting all the sights: the Hall of Transportation with steam-powered and coal-fueled locomotives, and Pullman sleeping cars more luxurious than the rooms in their flat, where passengers slept as they traveled to New York City. Vivian hoped that she would visit New York City someday.

"Sleeping all the way to New York in such comfort?" Hannah was amazed. "I remember my trip. After days at sea where everyone was sick, we landed at Ellis Island, relieved to crowd into a train to Chicago. Not enough seats. Many stood. Nobody slept."

At the open-air stage on the Enchanted Island, Vivian had been mesmerized by the production of *Alice in Wonderland*. How was it that this Alice was a real girl, not a flickering, moving picture? When Vivian panicked after Alice grew so large that she became trapped behind the dollhouse door, the woman nearby poked her and laughed. Vivian cried until Aunt Ruthie reassured her that the theater was make-believe, only an illusion, where the impossible could be designed to appear possible.

Hannah had also felt her stomach clench and whispered to Ruth, "The girl has the same name they gave me at Ellis Island. Am I trapped too? Will I ever get out?"

"Believe in your strength," Ruth said. "I have confidence that you will."

After the show, they walked through the Homes of Tomorrow, marveling at the electric conveniences. Vivian wondered what it would be like if they lived in a flat where everything was automatic. An ice box with no ice? An all-weather clothes dryer? She could not imagine such a life of ease.

Vivian pulled her ma over where a crowd of all ages surrounded another exhibit. To Vivian, it looked like tiny dolls floating in jars filled with water.

Hannah froze. "What is this? Are these real? I think I will be sick," and tried to steer Vivian away. She placed her hand on her stomach and gazed at her daughter. Something about the way Ma looked at her made Vivian feel dizzy too. The room began to spin.

Hannah said, "Come. Sit over there on the bench with me, my miracle child."

Vivian didn't understand why Ma was upset.

Aunt Ruthie pointed to the sign posted next to the display and read aloud: "These are fifty specimens of human babies, all products of miscarriage. The development of the human being from germination to nine months. The product of conception is called an 'embryo' during the first two months of development. At the end of the second month the embryo assumes human form, and from there until birth, it is known as a 'fetus.'"

"Are these real babies?" asked Vivian. "Were they ever alive?"

"Never alive," said Aunt Ruthie and continued to read. "Living fetuses can be kept alive if born after the sixth month of pregnancy."

Hannah clutched at her stomach. "My Vivian, I am grateful you are here."

"Why wouldn't I be?" she asked, puzzled by the look on Ma's face.

Aunt Ruthie answered. "Childbearing is dangerous, my darling Vivian. Many things can happen to the baby and to the mother."

Hannah calmed. "Yes, dear one. It is an awesome responsibility to bring a new life into this world. It takes courage. You must trust in God even when you can no longer hear His voice. You must have strength. And good friends." She looked at Ruth.

Vivian asked Aunt Ruthie why she didn't have children.

"I didn't want any."

"How did you decide?"

"Don't ask her to explain," said Hannah.

"If I could have had a daughter like you, well, maybe I . . ."

"Ma, did you want to have five children?"

Aunt Ruthie broke in. "That's not a story for today, my dear. Let's cherish this day together at the Century of Progress. Once in a lifetime."

Not a story for today. Not today.

NOT TODAY. Not today. Vivian thrashed and threw off the covers, waking Mel. He mumbled to ask if she were all right, but fell back into a sound sleep without an answer. All right, yet all wrong. Vivian ached to shake off the feeling that she'd been captured, colonized, and invaded by an anonymous group of cells that she was powerless to stop. Powerless to stop them from developing like those displayed in the jars at the 1933 World's Fair. They would keep doubling and redoubling unless she mounted an insurrection to vanquish them.

Did she dare?

CHAPTER SIX

THE TEST AND THE REFERRAL

WEDNESDAY, 1956

VIVIAN ALWAYS breathed easier on Wednesdays because it was Mel's day off. He became the extra help she needed most days: lifting laundry, shopping her grocery list and carrying home the bags, picking up dry cleaning, and scouring last night's dinner pans. As the eldest from a big family and working in the family's deli-turned-tavern, he was not afraid to pitch in and took on chores with cheerful efficiency. He did not consider anything to be strictly women's work. Vivian knew she had a gem of a husband. What would she do without him? But given his long work days away on Maxwell Street, she was often without him.

With still no sign of her period, she'd decided it was irresponsible to wait any longer and had called to go to the doctor's office for a pregnancy test on Mel's day off. Mel loaded the children in the car and drove her to the Chicago and North Western's Wilmette station. During the thirty-minute ride from Wilmette into the downtown Randolph Street station, Vivian fidgeted with her watchband and tried to imagine how relieved she'd feel when the office called next week with the results. "Sorry, Mrs. Jacobson, not this time." She heard the words clearly in her mind and let out a sigh so loud, the smartly coifed woman across the aisle looked at her with concern. But what if she was pregnant again? Would Mel be angry? Or delighted to add to their brood? She shivered to remember Ethel's pointed suggestion. Dare she ask Dr. Goldblum to end this? Would he think her ungrateful for all he'd done for her and Mel? She kicked at the seat in front of her, apologizing when the elderly man turned around and frowned. Vivian took deep, calming breaths. No use getting ahead of herself, but why should she punish herself for how she's feeling?

At the station, her high heels clattered over the marble floor as she headed out to the cab stand and hopped into the first waiting taxi, basking in the rare sunny, mild spring day. Before she knew it, another sticky Chicago summer would be upon them. She cranked down the window, yearning to feel the breeze. A few minutes later, she alit in front of an ornate terra-cotta–trimmed building on South Michigan Avenue. Before she opened the heavy brass-trimmed front door, Vivian gazed up and down the avenue, admiring the lineup of elegant, vintage skyscrapers across from the Art Institute, confirming her belief that her obstetrician was among the finest in Chicago.

The elevator operator tipped his cap and smiled as he took her up to the sixth floor. Vivian announced herself to the receptionist, took a comfortable seat in the waiting room, and leafed through *Look* magazine. The nurse called her name and ushered her into the lavatory to collect a urine sample. When Vivian handed in her jar, she trembled and asked to talk to Dr. Goldblum. The nurse brusquely ushered her out, saying the office would call next week with the results. Vivian stopped at the desk, clicking and unclicking the clasp of her pocketbook, saying she didn't mind waiting for the doctor.

"You know how it is, Mrs. Jacobson. He was called away to the hospital. Wait until next week when you'll know for sure." She winked.

One long week. She was familiar with this wait. Before she'd had Irene, Vivian had ached to get a call with the verdict "the rabbit died." As the years went by, Vivian had killed more than her share. She offered up a prayer. Those poor rabbits. Maybe this time, the rabbit would live.

THE WEEK dragged as she knew it would. Vivian dug in her garden with a fury, as if trying to dislodge anything that could be growing inside her. She was short-tempered and scolded the children without a reason. Did they sense their mother's anxiousness? They fell quiet when she came near and made fewer demands than usual. When she burned his toast, Mel scraped it off and ate a few bites anyway. Vivian collapsed into a chair and dabbed at her eyes with a corner of her apron. She was a wreck. Couldn't even make her husband's breakfast.

"It's just a piece of bread," Mel said. He jumped up and bent to give her a quick peck. "Don't worry about me. I'll grab something when I get to work."

Don't worry about *him*? Who was going to worry about *her*?

NEXT WEDNESDAY, 1956

THE DAY arrived. When the phone rang, Vivian was afraid to pick up and let it ring four times until she lifted the receiver and murmured a faint, "Hello." The doctor's cheery receptionist confirmed the pregnancy, adding, "I know Mr. Jacobson will be delighted!"

Vivian panicked. "Don't hang up. I need an appointment with Dr. Goldblum. Right away."

"Right away? The doctor usually waits another month for the first appointment. Don't you remember?"

"I need an appointment. Now."

There was a long pause. Vivian's neck ached, and she clenched her teeth.

The receptionist said, "Let me see here. How about a week from tomorrow? One thirty?"

"Nothing sooner?" Vivian's voice must have betrayed her panic.

"Just a minute, my dear. Hold on."

Vivian doodled circles and triangles on the kitchen counter notepad below the telephone mounted on the wall. The whole page was covered in scrawls when the receptionist returned to the line. "You're in luck. Dr. Goldblum can squeeze you in tomorrow morning at eleven. Got that? Tomorrow, Thursday, May 10. Eleven o'clock sharp."

Already May 10? Vivian counted and recounted. Too many weeks had passed since the night of the neighbors' party. She'd enjoyed Mel's aggressiveness in bed when they came home, but now she was frightened. Why *hadn't* she reached for her diaphragm? The hubris of it all, thinking nothing could touch them and their perfect family here in Wilmette. What would she say to Dr. Goldblum?

When she thought about how to break the news to Mel, Vivian became dizzy. Upon his return with the girls from the library, Vivian motioned him into the kitchen.

"The doctor's office called." She choked back a sob.

"I can hear it in your voice." Mel's lips formed a taut line. "You're pregnant, aren't you? But you'd guessed as much."

"Yes, but now it's definite. I have an appointment tomorrow with Dr. Goldblum to ask if he can . . . well, you know."

Mel grabbed her forearm. "Are you sure about this?" His voice sounded fuzzy.

"Yes, I have to." She let out a sob to see the crumpled look on Mel's face.

His voice took on an unfamiliar harsh tone. "No, you don't have to. Not by a long shot. I won't stop you, but it's not what I want."

Her stomach twisted. Mel didn't say no, but she hated to go against him. She'd have to convince Dr. Goldblum that she needed a way out. He was her only chance.

THURSDAY, MAY 10, 1956

AS SHE waited for the babysitter to arrive, Vivian called Jackie to ask for a ride to the train station, hoping to save the cab fare.

"Last-minute trip? Anything wrong?"

Vivian tried to sound nonchalant. "Nothing special. Just a routine doctor's appointment."

Jackie said, "As chance would have it, I switched my beauty shop day to tomorrow this week. Vivian Jacobson, you are one lucky lady. If you need a ride home when you're back at the station, I'll be here all day painting the basement."

"Gee, thanks, Jackie. I owe you."

"Think nothing of it. You can always call on me. You know I'm happy to drive you when I can."

On the ride to the train, Vivian was grateful that Jackie didn't press her for details. Her best friend on the block was no gossip.

Vivian arrived ten minutes early for her appointment. She picked up the latest issue of *Life* from a stack of magazines on a side table and stared at the cover. Grace Kelly in her wedding dress, the true-life fairytale of the movie star who became a princess. When they moved to 336 Maple Street, Vivian had romanticized that she and Mel lived in a castle in their own private Monaco. Now the clock was about to strike midnight on her Cinderella tale. Would everything disappear and send her back to a grim life on the city's dusty west side? She reached for another magazine on the stack beside her and watched sympathetically as a big-bellied woman rose with a groan and lumbered through the door to the examining rooms. Vivian put a hand on her abdomen that still hid her secret to everyone except sharp-eyed

Ethel. Soon enough, it would be impossible to hide. Vivian leafed through the magazine absentmindedly until she stopped and gasped at a full-page ad of a pink-cheeked, blond infant with wide blue eyes. Nothing like a real baby who woke in the night wailing for a feeding or a diaper change. The woman across from her stared as Vivian tried to restrain her spasmodic coughing as she read the advertising copy: *8 out of 10 mothers who feed their babies a Carnation formula say: 'My doctor recommended it.'*

Not Dr. Goldblum. He never recommended formula.

Vivian trembled when she considered how Dr. Goldblum might respond to her plea. She rehearsed it again silently. *Please . . . I can't . . . Could you . . . ?* She could picture her hero-doctor's disapproving glare. How could he refuse her after all they'd been through together? Vivian sighed in despair.

A woman wearing a brown business suit with padded shoulders looked up in alarm. Should she call the nurse?

Embarrassed, Vivian said, "Oh, no," and returned to idly flipping pages.

The woman furrowed her brow, scowled, and went back to reading *Time.*

When the nurse called her name, Vivian followed her into the exam room, where she received rapid-fire instructions to undress, put on the gown, open to the front, hop on the table, place her feet in the stirrups, and wait for the doctor. He'd be "right in." Vivian complied and twisted her wedding rings around her finger. Right in? The doctor's rooms were always full. There was no predicting if "right in" would be two minutes or twenty. Vivian refrained from putting her feet on the icy metal until he arrived. She pulled her knees up to her chest and covered herself as best she could as she awaited Dr. Goldblum's light tap at the door. Vivian's heart beat with a rapid staccato that pummeled her knees. Nervous and naked, she exhaled in relief when she heard his knock followed by a calm, "Hello again," but didn't look at her face as he reviewed her chart.

"Tell me, Vivian, is this a surprise?"

She hesitated, caught off guard by his candid question. "Actually, yes. I didn't think I could . . . well, you know . . . I mean, I'm still nursing. I didn't think I could get . . ."

"That old wives' tale? Something your mother might say. Vivian, I thought you'd be more modern."

She felt ashamed to think Dr. Goldblum saw her as another ignorant woman who didn't understand how this happened.

"When was your last monthly period?"

Now she really felt stupid. "Not sure."

He stared. Despite him being about twenty years older than Mel, Vivian thought Dr. Goldblum had dreamy brown eyes. He patted her hand. "Not unusual, given your last delivery was so recent."

She exhaled, not realizing that she'd been holding her breath. His reassurance made her feel he didn't think she was completely foolish. A moment later, he returned to his abrupt manner. "Lie back. Let me see how far along you are."

He began a gentle exam. Dr. Goldblum was the first and only one to examine her internally. She couldn't imagine being comfortable with any other doctor. She turned her neck to the side to stare at the familiar framed watercolor in this examination room where two majestic bronze lions stood guard over the Art Institute's masterpieces.

Vivian snapped to attention when he pronounced, "I'd say ten weeks," and took a step back from the table. He pushed his glasses down his nose and scrutinized her over his lenses.

She sat up straight and spoke first, her voice quavering. "I can't do this again."

"Why not?"

"Please. We already have four."

"I'm well aware."

She felt ungrateful to utter the next sentence. This man's surgical skill had made it possible for her to become pregnant at all. "I . . . I don't know how to ask but . . . could you do something about this?" She held her breath as she awaited the answer to her bold question, gripping the sides of the table until her fingers were drained of blood.

He pursed his lips and tapped a pen across her folder. Finally, he spoke. "What are you asking?" The pupils of his dark eyes melted into his irises, hiding his thoughts.

"A way to end . . . to end this." Her syllables were choppy. Her voice trailed off. Her palms felt clammy.

"Are you asking for an abortion?" She looked toward her feet. "Are you certain that's what you want? Have you talked to Mel about this?"

She said, "I have, but we wanted to wait until I knew for sure."

Dr. Goldblum tapped his index finger on her folder as she pulled the sheet more tightly around her naked body. Why cling to modesty? This man had attended to her body when she was in the throes of childbirth pains.

"Tell me honestly, Vivian. Does Mel agree with this?"

"If you want the truth, not really. But he said he won't stop me. Please, Doctor, it's too much for me. I'm exhausted every day. We just moved to Wilmette. There's no more room in our house. I can't take care of everything properly as it is. Some days I feel I can't wash one more load of laundry, make one more meal, change one more diaper. The children are all over the place. I scream at them for the littlest thing. Some days I feel like I'm going crazy." Her voice had a catch. "Do you think I'm crazy?"

Dr. Goldblum tossed the folder onto the counter. A small smile played around his lips. "No, not at all. You're not crazy. You're perfectly sane. Get dressed. I'll be back in a moment."

She pulled on her clothes as quickly as she could, stepped into her pumps, and sat erect in the patient's chair in the tiny room until she heard the tap at the door and rose to her feet.

"Sit." Dr. Goldblum motioned. His even tone was calm, but firm. "Vivian, you must understand. I can't do what you're asking."

She let out a small cry. "Why not?"

"I can't risk my license."

Vivian jumped up, straightened her skirt, picked up her pocketbook, and began to rush past him toward the door.

"Settle down," he said, putting his hand on her forearm. "I can't do this, but I do know someone who can." He took out his prescription pad with his pen poised. "But you must promise that you won't go to this man until you and Mel agree. Your husband is a prince of a guy. I knew him before the war. His family's place is around the corner from the Maternity Center. Jacobson Brothers was my refuge after a long night delivering babies all over the city."

"I promise I'll talk it over with him tonight."

"You must. At ten weeks, you don't have much time left."

He scribbled a few lines, tore off the page from his prescription pad, and handed it to her. Vivian's fingers trembled as she reached for the paper, but Dr. Goldblum's familiar scrawl eased her mind and slowed her racing heart.

"Good luck," he said and held the door for her.

Vivian cringed to think how many times Dr. Goldblum must have heard this plea. How many women had begged him to make a pregnancy go away, either here in his elite private downtown office or at the Maxwell Street clinic? Rich or poor, there were many reasons that a woman could be desperate to end a pregnancy. Hadn't Aunt Ruthie said the same?

Before she boarded the train back to Wilmette, Vivian hadn't glanced at the paper the doctor handed to her. When she read the name and northwest side address, a chill ran through her. A real person in a real place. She pinched her eyes shut with her fingers. Her chest tightened as she tried to imagine what such a procedure would be like. How similar would it be to the excruciating childbirth pains only endured with the hopeful promise of the reward of a healthy babe? Would the aftermath of an abortion leave her bereft with a stark emptiness? Would she punish herself forever if she went ahead with this choice? Or would she feel a grateful relief? How many times a day did she chastise herself for her frenzied mothering, always falling short of the ever-smiling, perfect homemaker Harriet Nelson portrayed on *The Adventures of Ozzie and Harriet*? Mel must agree. It was the only way.

At their private dinner that evening, with the TV blaring downstairs, Mel asked, gripping her forearm, "What did Goldblum say?"

He loosened his grip when she twisted away. "He said he can't risk his license."

Mel exhaled loudly. "The man has sense."

"But he gave me a name of someone who can do this. I want to go. Tomorrow." She let out a deep sigh. "But Dr. Goldblum said you must agree."

"Tomorrow?" Mel tossed his napkin on the plate and stood up.

Vivian motioned him to sit. "Please. Don't say no. Dr. Goldblum said I don't have much time. He said we both must agree."

Mel let out a groan. "How can I say yes? Put my wife in danger?"

"Dr. Goldblum said this man would be safe."

"Who is he? Where is he?"

Vivian retrieved the paper from her pocketbook. Mel shook his head. "I don't know about this."

"Please, Mel. We're crowded in here as it is. Another one in diapers? It's too much. Some days I feel like I'm losing my mind. I call for Irene and when she answers, I realize I meant to call Sandy. Or I call for Sandy when I mean to call Irene. I'm a bad mother."

"Don't say that. Don't ever say that. You're a good mother. But do you think about what *I* want? This would be another one of *our* babies. Are you afraid I can't support another? Business at Jacobson Brothers is slow right now, but we do all right. We could manage."

"But I don't know if I could. I know you give us everything. It's just . . . well, it's lonely here out in Wilmette without any adults around. Except maybe Jackie. And I thought . . . well, I sent for the Chicago Teachers College catalog. I'd hoped to sign up for the first classes in the fall. Jackie is a college graduate. Her sister is a teacher. Why not me?"

"Don't tell me you're saying you want to end this one so you can go back to school? I'm surprised at you." He threw down his napkin. "After all, you're a mother." He gripped her shoulders and stared into her deep brown eyes. His lip trembled. He brushed his face with the back of his hand. Was he crying? "I don't like this, but I said I won't stop you, and I won't. I trust Goldblum. He's a good doctor, but I'm afraid for you, for us. Please, if you must go ahead, wait a few more days. At least, wait until Monday."

"I will. But Dr. Goldblum said if I go, I must go soon."

They didn't say much more to each other that evening. By the time Vivian got the children in bed, Mel was already asleep. Vivian undressed quietly, not wanting to wake him.

They were both sound asleep when Irene knocked at their bedroom door.

"Mommy! Daddy! I had a bad dream. I need a drink of water."

Vivian jumped up but Mel pressed his hand onto her shoulder. "Stay. I'll go."

"Not bathroom water, Daddy," Irene whined. "I want kitchen water."

Mel padded out and Vivian wrapped the blanket around herself, shivering. Mel must think she's a witch. Was he angry? Could he be angry enough to leave them? What would they do without him? She had no way to support herself and the children. She drew in a sharp breath, remembering when Pa left them. But that was different. Or was it? Vivian knew that Jackie and Hank were having problems. They were going to counseling. When Jackie said she and the kids would have to move out of Wilmette if they got a divorce, Vivian had been frightened for her. Life on Maple Street was expensive. Now she was scared for herself. She couldn't lose Mel. Being on her own with the kids would be impossible.

When Mel came back to bed, he reported that Irene was fine. "She said a giant dog was chasing her. A barking dog as big as Lassie. Probably something she saw on TV. Twice I went downstairs for water because the first time it wasn't cold enough. I sat with her until she fell back to sleep. She hardly touched a drop. At least Sandy didn't wake up."

Vivian held back a laugh. "Sandy can sleep through anything."

Mel took her hand. "How true." He yawned and then took her into his arms.

Vivian breathed in her husband's familiar nighttime scent: a singular dusky combination of the children's fresh bedtime smells and the last vestiges of the grime permanently stuck to his skin from his day on Maxwell Street, only half-scrubbed away by Dial soap and masked by sprinkles of the Aqua Velva aftershave he'd slapped on to get ready for dinner.

They kissed deeply for many minutes, and then Mel caressed her shoulders and breasts. She gripped his thick forearms, pressing against the warmth of his hairy chest, and soon their bodies meshed in their familiar grooves. Although he was taller by several inches and considerably fleshier, as the years went on, they'd become like two sides of the same coin. When he entered her, murmuring, "I trust you," his words unleashed her tears. When they finished, they lay silent for a few minutes as he stroked her cheek.

"You're beautiful," he said. "Never doubt yourself. You are a wonderful mother."

Vivian began to sob. Where would she be without him? She hadn't meant to cry. She asked, "What if we'd never met?"

He kissed her again. "Never met, you and me? Impossible. It was b'shert, meant to be. Even if you are dead set on going ahead with this, you'll never lose me."

CHAPTER SEVEN
MOTHER'S DAY

FRIDAY, MAY 11, 1956

VIVIAN PROMISED Mel she'd wait until Monday. At least he didn't say no. She retrieved Dr. Goldblum's note, dialed the number, and set the appointment. Monday at noon. She lit a cigarette and let it burn halfway down in the ashtray before crushing it out with a flourish. *Stop agonizing. This is what you must do.*

Six hundred dollars. In cash. Don't eat anything in the morning.

Six hundred dollars? Vivian felt faint. She didn't think it would be this much. They'd have to wait until next year to sod the lawn. Grass seed would have to do. She'd set the sprinklers out all day long if she had to, to keep away bare patches. They couldn't be an embarrassment to the neighbors. She tried calling Mel but couldn't reach him. "He's outside unloading a truck," said the man who answered the phone. Distracted, she roamed the house picking up toys and gathered a load of towels from the hamper to take to the basement washer.

When the phone rang, she dashed to grab it.

"Mel?"

No. Aunt Ruthie.

"Just checking on you, sweetheart. Remember, your mother and I are expecting you for Shabbos dinner tonight, as usual."

Vivian groaned. "It's been one of those days. I almost forgot."

"Stay put. We'll come to you for a change."

"Really? I'll make the chicken if you bring Ma's soup."

Aunt Ruthie laughed. "Don't bother. We'll bring everything."

When Mel called, he sounded frazzled. "I know, I know. I'll leave soon to be home in time to drive us to your mother's. It's been one thing after another all day long. I'm dead on my feet."

"Don't push yourself. Aunt Ruthie just called. They'll make it easy for us and bring dinner here. Oh, and Mel, I made the appointment."

She heard his sharp intake of breath.

"For Monday. Like you said," she continued. "Six hundred dollars. Cash. Oh, Mel. I'm sorry, it's so much money."

He sighed. "It's not the money I'm worried about. I'll go with you on Monday. What time?"

"Noon. But it's hard for you to take off work. I'll go myself. Besides, I don't want your brothers to find out."

"Viv, please. I want to go."

"Let's wait. I could ask Ma or Aunt Ruthie. After all, it's a womanly matter."

HANNAH, RUTH, and Ethel arrived late in the afternoon. Aunt Ruthie brought a bouquet of mixed spring blooms—yellow jonquils, purple tulips, and white daisies, delighting Vivian, who put them into a vase in the middle of the dining room table. Ethel carried in two pans wrapped in tin foil, one with cut-up roast chicken and another with a savory kugel. "Wanted to be sure we had something decent to eat."

Always the grouch. "Don't think I don't appreciate it," said Vivian, stomping her foot, "but I could have served a fine meal."

Ethel cackled. "Ha! I know your chicken. And I'm glad I brought my noodle pudding. Where's your pot to heat up Ma's soup? How do you turn on this newfangled electric oven?"

Vivian put her hands on her hips. "Why can't you ever say

anything nice? Go make yourself at home with the others. I'll get everything ready." She pointed Ethel toward the living room.

"Did you bring cookies, Bubbe?" asked Sandy.

Hannah assured her there was a big plate of oatmeal cookies.

AFTER DINNER. Mel excused himself to go upstairs and lie down. When Vivian brought out her pack of Pall Malls, Hannah clucked her tongue. "It doesn't look right for a woman to smoke, especially when her husband isn't a smoker."

"Oh, Ma," said Vivian. "These are modern times. Besides, look at my sister."

Ethel lit up a Lucky Strike. Hannah shook her head. "I gave up nagging your sister long ago. She's impossible. She'll never find a man."

"Who says I want one?" said Ethel, coughing.

"Let them be," said Ruth. "Smoking isn't the worst vice a woman can have."

The girls ran downstairs to play the board game, Candy Land. As soon as they were out of earshot, Vivian spoke quietly to her mother. "Aunt Ruthie told me about what you almost did."

"Did what?" asked Ethel. "How come you never told me?"

"You already know too much, my wise child. Let the past stay in the past. I was fermischt, all mixed up. You know I love you all."

"I want to tell you. I made up my mind. Dr. Goldblum suggested someone. I'll go on Monday."

"What does your husband say?" asked Hannah. "Will he go with you?"

"He wants to, but it's hard for him to take off work."

"Darling, please don't go alone," said Aunt Ruthie.

"Don't worry," said Ethel. "I got days coming to me. Only one fitting booked for next week. I'll meet you at the joint."

Coarse as Ethel could be, Vivian wanted her there. She was afraid to go alone. In their childhood, it was Ethel who protected her from the neighborhood bullies. Her sister had always been tough.

"Will you? Thanks. It means a lot." Vivian reached over to give her sister's shoulder a squeeze, but Ethel backed away. Same old Eth. Vivian stood and headed upstairs. "I'll get you the address."

ON THEIR ride home, Hannah scolded Ruth. "If what you told Vivian convinced her to do this, you shouldn't have said a thing."

"She needed to know," said Ruth.

"It's for the best," said Ethel. "Stop treating Viv like a child. This pack of kids is already dragging her down. She'll be safe with her big-shot doctor's man, this Dr. Boone."

Ruth and Hannah both cried, "Dr. Boone! Are you sure?"

"Sure, I'm sure. I copied down the name. What's the problem?"

Ruth took one hand off the steering wheel to reach for Hannah alongside her in the passenger seat. "Can't be the same man."

Hannah tensed. "Impossible. Too long ago. Ethel, you'd better be right about her fancy downtown doctor."

"What's all the fuss?" said Ethel. "My baby sister will be fine. She always is."

Hannah squeezed Ruth's shoulder. "What a thing for a young mother to go through."

"She wouldn't be the first," said Ruth. "You, of all people, must know."

VIVIAN AND Mel cleaned up the kitchen together after settling the children for the night. As they were getting ready for bed, Mel said, "As long as you're going ahead with this, it's time I told you what happened with my Aunt Addie. I don't want you to hear about her from anyone else." He pulled her into a tight hug. Did Vivian detect a sob? She'd never heard Mel cry. "It was the best night for the Jacobson Brothers' business and the worst night for our family. It chased my sister Dena away from the family."

Mel cleared his throat twice and began the story.

DECEMBER 5, 1933

MEL GRADUATED from all-male Crane Tech High School one year after the stock market crashed and began to work every day of the week at the family's delicatessen. Despite the prime location at the corner of Maxwell and Halsted Streets, as the Depression deepened, their business was failing. They tried putting in a soda fountain with no change to their fortunes, but the Jacobson family had hope. Franklin Delano Roosevelt was elected, a president for all the people—including immigrants and children of immigrants, like they were. After he was sworn in, FDR kept his campaign promise by introducing an amendment to repeal Prohibition. One by one, the state legislatures voted to pass this amendment. Thirty-six of the forty-eight states were needed to ratify for it to become the law.

Mel and his sister Dena saw an opportunity. They convinced their pa and uncle to apply for liquor licenses with the expectation that drinking would soon be legal. Months later, the day had finally arrived when one of the remaining states was likely to pass the repeal amendment to make public drinking legal again.

On that day, the temperature hit fifty degrees. A Chicago heat wave. Nineteen-year-old Mel and his sister Dena gasped to see throngs of people lined up in both directions away from Jacobson Brothers. A boisterous mix of everyday folks: Jews, Italians, Mexicans, Negroes, Irish, Greeks, and Poles. Some dressed to the nines, others in work overalls. Men in suspenders and women swishing flouncy skirts, all awaiting the news. They talked, laughed, and clapped one another on the back. Scents of cheap cologne mixed with the sour stench of sweaty bodies pressed close together. Women flirted with strange men; others clutched babies to their breasts, shushing toddlers who grasped at their mothers' ankles. Women urged husbands to run inside to buy sandwiches and soda pop to calm the older children and keep them satisfied.

Mel's father, Harry Jacobson, was awestruck. "God must be smiling on us."

Harry's brother Louie rubbed his hands together. "This will be a good business."

Mel spied Ethel Kolson, whom he remembered from their shul. He'd seen Ethel many times, hanging around their joint's back room with the rough characters who played Hooligan, a twenty-six-dice betting game. Even saw her light up the occasional cigar. Who was that spunky young girl Ethel had in tow? A real charmer. Cuter than Shirley Temple. She was talking to Miss O'Grady, a teacher Mel recognized from Bryant Elementary School. He chuckled. That little one was nothing like her big sister.

Mel stood gawking for another minute before hustling inside to take a shift at the busy sandwich counter. Jacobson Brothers was famous for the best corned beef sandwiches in town. His uncle sliced the juicy briskets paper-thin and slathered the mustard directly onto the meat, not on the rye bread. Everyone in the deli business knew that was how it was done. Mel and Dena worked as fast as possible to keep up with orders from those waiting outside.

When Mel took a break to tune in the radio in the office, the local announcer interrupted the afternoon program of *The Goldbergs*.

"Hey, Chicago! This just in over the wires: Utah votes yes to repeal! We're over the top!"

"Happy Days Are Here Again" rang out across the airwaves.

Humming the snappy tune, Mel hustled outside with the good news. People cheered, hugged, and threw their hats in the air. The crowd rushed the door, but nobody roughhoused or pushed anyone aside. Feelings were sky-high. Everyone had new best friends.

Harry and Louie's American-born brother, Jake Jacobson, showed up and tapped the first barrel. He poured himself a glass and then one for Mel.

"How about me?" asked Dena.

The thick yeasty flavor tasted nothing like the watery beer Mel's pa didn't know Mel and Dena sampled during Prohibition. The strong smell reminded Mel of their ma's kitchen every Thursday afternoon when she baked the family's bread for the week. The cash register rang and rang. They brought up barrel after barrel from the basement. People stood three deep at the bar, clinking glasses to toast one another, the Jacobsons, President Roosevelt, and the great state of Utah.

Harry Jacobson was elated. "We'll stay open all night!"

Suddenly, Louie Jacobson rushed out of the kitchen. "Harry! Take over! I must go! It's my Addie!"

Harry put his hands on his brother's shoulders. His voice broke. "What's happened?"

Louie's knees buckled. Harry caught him before he fell.

Louie's words were choked with sobs. "A neighbor found my Addie on the kitchen floor." His sobbing grew louder. "She's dead!"

Harry lifted him up from under his armpits. "How can this be?"

Louie wailed. "The neighbor said there was blood everywhere. Oh, Harry! I can't live without her? What about our children? Who will care for them?"

Harry grabbed his hat. "Mel, Dena, stay with the business. I'll go with Louie, then home to tell Ma."

FRIDAY NIGHT, MAY 11, 1956

MEL'S FACE was pale as their bedsheet. "Aunt Addie never told Uncle Louie that she was carrying their fifth child. Money was tight in those days. She tried . . . to . . . well, you know . . . She tried to end it herself." He wiped a tear from his eye. "My ma said Aunt Addie wasn't the only woman in the neighborhood who tried this. Some jumped off a high stool, others may have used a tool or a knife. Either it worked or it didn't. Ma said most times they lived but didn't end the pregnancy." Mel's voice was heavy with tears. "My uncle was never the same. My young cousins hardly remember their mother. Aunt Addie was especially close with my sister Dena, who left the family after this tragedy. After she graduated from high school, she moved to San Francisco and became a nurse."

Vivian hugged Mel. "How horrible. For all of you."

"You see why I'm afraid for you, Viv? For all of us?" He squeezed Vivian so tight she couldn't breathe. She pushed him away to ease off his grip and began to cry. Did Mel really want another child? Or was he afraid because of the tragedy with his aunt?

Mel lifted his eyes toward the ceiling and spoke as if Vivian weren't lying next to him. "I've always wondered why Aunt Addie didn't trust her husband? He might have found someone who would have been safe. Uncle Louie and my pa knew everyone around Maxwell Street."

Vivian grimaced. "Don't think about what might have been. You can't go back."

"You would have loved her," said Mel. "She was smart. Strong-willed. Maybe too strong. Independent. Maybe too independent. She had a mind of her own."

Too independent? A mind of her own? Why couldn't a woman be trusted to know her own mind? They were silent for a few minutes until Vivian spoke softly. "Maybe your aunt was afraid her husband would talk her out of it."

Mel sniffed. "Wasn't it his right to share in the decision?"

Vivian murmured in a neutral tone, neither agreeing nor disagreeing.

SOON MEL dozed, and Vivian gathered the covers around herself as she contemplated Mel's indignant questions. Of course, a husband had rights. But it was the woman who bore the consequences. Can any man understand the weight women feel when they embark on the nine-month journey to bear a child? Pregnancy, delivery, and what it means to be a mother? The role of mother endures lifelong. Women's voices were too easily overpowered, unheard by even the most caring husbands. Unheard in a world that demands her to be a perfect mother, to put her children's needs ahead of her own. Of course, Vivian would do anything to keep her children safe and give them the best of life's opportunities. But she had her own needs, her own dreams. Why was she always expected to conform to the unattainable ideal of a good Jewish girl, model wife, and mother? She resented anyone telling her what she could and could not do. If Mel would not be her ally, who could she rely on? Her breasts ached, and she groaned. If she had to, she must trust herself to act alone to do what she felt best for herself and for their family.

SATURDAY, MAY 12, 1956

MONDAY FELT far away. How was she going to get through the days? For lunch, Vivian made toasted cheese sandwiches for the children and added Jays potato chips and apple slices onto each plate. The children's chatter blended into one low roar until Irene's voice grew shrill.

"Mommy, this is the third time I asked you." She sang out the words, mimicking the familiar jingle, "I want a Salerno butter cookie." This sent Sandy into a fit of giggles.

When Vivian brought her another without an argument, Sandy spoke up. "No fair, Irene gets one more. I want another cookie too!"

"I'm not running a restaurant!" Vivian yelled and plunked down the coveted blue box adorned with cascading yellow cookies.

Linda had smeared melted Velveeta cheese across both cheeks. She waved her hands. Irene grabbed a fistful, handed several to Sandy, and lobbed three soft daisy-shaped cookies onto Linda's highchair tray. Irene and Sandy dashed outside. Exhausted, Vivian sank into the chair Irene had abandoned and watched her toddler place the cookies delicately onto her pointer finger, one by one. Linda nibbled around the edges of her stack. Usually, Vivian set a strict limit on their sweets, but today she had no energy to fight her children. Lunchtime at 336 Maple Street was never a picnic. She tried to imagine herself several months from now, struggling to cope with this daily chaos and adding a new baby into the mix. Even if she could manage to toilet train Linda over the next few months, she'd still have two in diapers with the new arrival. She wasn't sure how to train Billy. She'd heard that boys were tougher to coax out of diapers than girls.

SUNDAY, MAY 13, 1956

VIVIAN AWOKE trembling. Tomorrow was the day. She had to stay strong. She met Mel in the kitchen, where he was finishing his coffee. The girls burst in.

"Don't go yet, Daddy! We have something for Mommy." Irene clutched a piece of folded orange construction paper.

"For Mommy?" asked Mel.

"Don't you remember? It's Mother's Day!"

Mel pushed back his chair and looked over at Vivian, who was at the stove retrieving an egg from a boiling pot.

"Every day should be Mother's Day," Vivian grumbled.

"Mother's Day, you say?" said Mel with a chuckle. "Well, girls, let's see what you have here." Irene handed him the paper. "Come on over, Viv."

Vivian placed her own soft-boiled egg in the china holder. She poured herself a cup of coffee and stirred in two sugars. The girls clambered around them.

Irene tugged at Vivian. "I wrote this for you at school, Mommy."

Vivian read aloud, her voice husky.

Happy Mother's Day! I hope this day will be easier for you.
Love, Irene, Sandy, Linda, and Baby Billy

She read the card another time and then kissed her daughters and gave them each a hug.

"The teacher helped us spell words we didn't know," said Irene. "The only word I didn't know was *easier.*"

Easier. Vivian gasped. Sensitive Irene must have picked up cues about how irritable she'd been, as ready to explode as a firecracker with a flame too close to the fuse.

"Beautiful idea," said Mel. "Let's all try to make things easier for Mommy. Especially today." He put his arms around Vivian and kissed her hard.

Irene and Sandy closed their eyes, puckered their lips, and made kissing sounds. "Yuck!"

"Sandy drew the pictures," said Irene. "She's a good artist, isn't she? At least, she's good for her age."

Vivian chuckled at the backhanded compliment Irene extended to her younger sister without an open acknowledgment that she herself could do better drawings. Vivian looked at Sandy's depictions of their family and smiled. She'd drawn a big heart around black-haired Mel with his distinctive, uneven hairline from the permanent hair loss he'd suffered during basic training. Sandy drew herself holding hands with Irene, the two figures looking just alike with Irene one head taller. And there was Linda, confined to her playpen surrounded by stuffed animals, dotted lines streaming from her eyes like tears. Poor girl. When Vivian looked more closely at Sandy's crayoned, crude picture of her, she gasped. There she was with Baby Billy in her arms. Did Sandy draw her purposefully with a pronounced, protruding belly? Was it merely accidental, a wayward line from Sandy's stubby fingers guiding a thick crayon? Or had her sharp-eyed daughter spied her condition the same as Ethel had?

Sandy said, "I drew our whole family. Mommy, I picked a special color for your pretty brown hair."

Vivian's gut cramped as she bent to kiss her dear daughters again. "Yes, that's us. Our whole family."

Perfect as we are. Not one more, or one less.

Mel pushed back from the table. "I've got to get going, girls. How about I bring home a cake and we celebrate Mother's Day tonight?"

The girls clapped their hands. "I want vanilla icing," said Irene.

"Chocolate cake!" said Sandy.

Vivian didn't want to celebrate. Not this year.

After Mel left, Sandy asked, "Is Bubbe your mommy?"

Irene answered. "Of course she is, dumbbell."

"Don't call your sister by that name," said Vivian.

"Does Aunt Ruthie have a mommy?" asked Sandy.

"Everyone has a mommy," Irene said. "Don't be a dope."

"Irene, what did I tell you? No name-calling."

"She should know better. Everyone has a mommy." She kicked Sandy's foot under the table.

"Ouch! She kicked me."

"Girls, stop it!" Vivian sat down and smoothed down her hair. "Irene, it's OK for Sandy to ask. Aunt Ruthie never knew her mommy or daddy. She grew up in the orphans' home."

"That's sad. How did her mommy and daddy die?" asked Irene.

"I don't know," said Vivian.

Sandy said, "Next time, I'll give Aunt Ruthie an extra hug for Mother's Day."

MEL CAME home that evening with a big chocolate cake with vanilla icing from the bakery on Roosevelt Road, a few blocks from Jacobson Brothers.

"Let's celebrate your beautiful mother," he said.

"But the cake doesn't say Happy Mother's Day," said Irene, tapping her fork on the table.

If Ethel were here, Vivian could hear her harsh retort. "Quit your bellyaching. Be glad ya got any cake at all." Vivian could use an occasional dose of her sister's hardheadedness.

Linda tried to wriggle out of her high chair. Sandy reached over to try to stop her, but she crashed down anyway. When they heard her wailing under the table, Vivian bent and shrieked at the blood on Linda's forehead. At Vivian's cry, Linda wailed louder.

"She must have gashed her forehead on the leg of the dining room table. She might need stitches." Vivian was frantic. "Should we call the doctor?"

The celebration ended abruptly.

"We can't call the doctor for every little thing." Mel scooped up Linda and carried her to the upstairs bathroom, returning with a bandage on the toddler's temple. "It's not too deep. Children heal fast. Relax. She'll be fine."

Vivian went to the phone to call Jackie to see if her niece was home from college. Was she available to babysit tomorrow? Jackie's voice took on an unusually high pitch when she asked, "Another emergency?" Vivian stammered about a last-minute chance to have a day with her sister, and could she also have a ride to the station the next morning? When Jackie called back, saying yes, her niece could sit and yes, Jackie could drive, Vivian breathed easier.

In bed that night, Vivian said to Mel, "What a terrible mother I am. Look at what happened to Linda."

"Nobody's perfect. You can't see everything all the time. No matter what you say, you are a good mother. Stop doubting yourself!"

Vivian's feet felt like ice. Mel rubbed them, but they stayed cold. "Are you sure you don't want me to go with you tomorrow?" he asked.

"I'll be fine with Ethel." She kept her voice even to reassure her husband and also to convince herself.

Mel held her close. "My brave wife. I'll be home as soon as I can, but the barman just quit. We're shorthanded again."

Always something to keep him busy at that place. A good thing she was brave, because if she depended on her husband for every little thing like some wives did, she'd really be stuck. By day, she'd been certain this action would be best for her and for their family, but now, in the shadowy night, her confidence waned. The knot deep in her belly tightened. She should have had a smaller piece of that rich Mother's Day cake. The gooey frosting lodged in her gut like it had moved in permanently. Vivian twisted from side to side. She couldn't get comfortable.

Not sure if he were still awake, she asked Mel, as if asking herself, "Are you sure we're doing the right thing?"

Mel had been lying quietly beside her. It was unlike him not to have dozed off first. He stroked her arm as he said, "You remember me telling you about my zayde, the neighborhood Hebrew teacher who came to live with us after my bubbe died? He was so sad without his wife. My zayde taught me there will be many times when you do not know what to do. He taught me that many rabbis take opposite positions but cite the same laws to prove their points. He taught me that the path ahead is not often clear."

"What do you think your zayde would advise us?" she asked.

"My zayde would say we cannot expect God to make the choice for us. We are human beings. We can only do what we think is best. But remember, this is irreversible. We can't change our minds afterward."

Vivian whimpered. "Of course, I know. That only makes it harder."

"Trust yourself. My ma lived through many hardships, both in Russia and after she came to Chicago. No matter what happened, she always went forward. Her last ten years without Pa were especially painful. She had a favorite saying: 'Az me muz, ken men.' 'If you must, you can.'"

"Wise words," said Vivian.

"Ma repeated that phrase many times. She said some days it was the only thing that kept her going. She taught it to me when I returned from the war after Pa died. In those days, there were many times I couldn't face the day."

She squeezed his hand. "The war was a tragedy for us all."

Mel took her into his arms. He could never resist the curves of her body, the softness of her skin. After a few caresses, her brown nipples stood erect. She opened herself to him, and he entered her, thrusting deeper, deeper. Vivian moaned as Mel moved more vigorously, and she encouraged him to continue, on and on, until they both cried out. Panting, they lay spent.

VIVIAN SLEPT, but Mel couldn't close his eyes. He got up to relieve himself, then wended down the hallway, checking on each one of the sleeping children. He decided it was too late to return to bed and went downstairs to finish reading the Sunday paper. An article caught his eye: a warning about thalidomide, an experimental drug given to pregnant women to combat morning sickness, suspected to be the cause of gross deformities such as babies born without arms. The pictures of these children horrified him. He snapped the newspaper shut, grateful that Vivian was rarely sick during her pregnancies.

Thank goodness Dr. Goldblum didn't believe in any extra drugs. Mel believed in science, but he understood medicine could be a guessing game with unpredictable results. After fighting overseas, he knew nothing was certain in this life. Nothing was guaranteed.

Mel thought of the desperate women he'd seen in Europe after the war ended; women willing to do anything to feed their starving children, some burned by the shelling of his own artillery. He was grateful he hadn't seen the survivors of the atrocities in the concentration camps with his own eyes, but had listened when fellow GIs recounted those horrors. Mel was proud of his unit's contributions to save the world from that madman Hitler, but he himself was no hero, nobody special—just an ordinary soldier drafted in a time of great need. He stood and paced, wondering whether he should forbid Vivian from purposefully ending this pregnancy. But what about Vivian's well-being? He wasn't her commanding officer. They were husband and wife. She must be free to act without restraint. Of course, this would be his child, too, but the woman bears the children and cares for them, day in and day out. Thinking about his own mother, he wondered what she would think of this house, of their life in Wilmette. Would she think it too grand? She certainly would have wanted him to live closer to his siblings and their families. But Mel wanted Vivian to be happy, to choose the life she wanted.

Mel padded down to the basement and sat at his small desk where he paid the household bills. He stared at the picture of Ma standing between him and Vivian on their wedding day. Ma was still grieving Pa that night, but she looked lovely in her gown, happy that her eldest had finally found his bride. How he missed his ma. He straightened the objects on his desk: the decorative glass paperweight, letter opener, and fountain pen erect in its stand. He opened the side drawer and picked up the Nazi soldier's Luger he brought home from Germany as a souvenir—no bullets, of course. Mel was always surprised by its solidness, its heft. He'd imagined he might use it to scare off a stickup man on Maxwell Street, but in the end, he did not dare bring it to the tavern's cash register. He was content to have it here, to rest easy knowing that Viv and the children were safe in Wilmette.

In the early morning, he heard Vivian calling for him. "Mel? Where are you?"

He hurried up the stairs. "Here I am. I'm here."

He would always stand by her.

CHAPTER EIGHT

THE GREYSTONE

MONDAY, MAY 14, 1956

VIVIAN BLINKED as she stood at the sink in front of the kitchen window, blinded by the morning sun. Sunny days lifted her spirits and made the compact space feel larger, giving her a brief respite from her churning gut. She appreciated many aspects of their home's design, but the kitchen was too small. As she returned to rinsing the breakfast plates and placing them into the dishwasher, Mel hustled up from the basement with the tallest stack of twenty-dollar bills she had ever seen.

Vivian's voice broke. "It's too much, isn't it?"

Mel placed the cash on the countertop, said, "It's not the money I'm worried about," and put his arm around her. "It's you."

"I'll be fine," she said in a strained voice, not fully believing her words. "Are you sure it's not also the money?"

Mel's voice was indignant. "How can you ask me that? Money is money, but you are my wife. Remember, you don't have to do this. You can call and say you aren't coming. Are you sure you're sure?"

She took a deep breath and said in a soft voice, "I'm sure." She had to be. As she fitted the smooth bills into her pocketbook, she chipped a corner of her fingernail and cried out.

Mel was alarmed. "Vivian! Are you OK?"

She nodded, sucked on her index finger, and with shaking hands, hurried to finish loading the dishwasher. When a cereal bowl slipped out of her grasp, she stared dumbly as it bounced onto the floor and broke into large shards.

She wailed, "Oh, Mel!"

He put up his hand as if he were a traffic cop who could halt her tears. "Please don't cry. It's only a bowl." He bent to carefully pick up the pieces, put them into the garbage can under the sink, and called to the children, "No one goes barefoot in here until we vacuum!" Sandy was upstairs getting dressed. Irene stood by the front door, waiting to walk to school. Linda banged on her highchair tray with her spoon.

Vivian brought Irene her jacket. Her daughter whispered. "Is Daddy angry at you?"

"I'm not angry!" Mel bellowed from the kitchen as he gathered the porcelain pieces into a paper bag to take out to the trash bin in the garage. "I'm late. I've got to go to work."

Mel apologized for raising his voice and lifted her chin to kiss her goodbye, but she turned her face away. "Viv, please don't be upset with me. Not today." He gripped her shoulders to turn her toward him and searched her eyes. "Promise you'll call me as soon as it's over."

She nodded and squeezed his arm, wishing she'd agreed to let Mel, not Ethel, accompany her to the unfamiliar address. Too late to ask him to leave his brothers shorthanded. Besides, she didn't want him to draw undue attention from his family. Her gossipy sisters-in-law already thought they were better than she was. Whatever her sister's faults, Vivian knew where she stood with Ethel. Everybody did. Her strong-willed sister would remain steadfast, even if Vivian began to second-guess herself. Ethel understood all too well what it was like to live in a household overburdened by too many children.

A few minutes after Mel left, the doorbell rang. Vivian's heart flipped. From the playpen, Linda began to wail. Must be Jackie's college-aged niece, today's babysitter. Vivian briefed her and then escaped out the back door, standing in the yard to listen until the crying subsided, relieved it was over quickly. Linda liked this young woman.

On the ride to the station, Vivian was grateful that Jackie didn't press her for details, although she was dying to confide in her, to tell her everything. But she couldn't. She felt filthy and ashamed of her desperation to seek this underground act. She'd never done anything illegal before. Her older brothers were gamblers, but this roll of the dice was different; she was placing her body at risk. What if something went wrong? She would never forgive herself if she ruined Mel's life and their children's, too. She struggled to banish these fears. Everything would be fine.

THE MORNING rush hour had passed, giving her a wide selection of open seats. She chose one far from other riders. Her neck tensed as she held a tight grip on her pocketbook bursting with cash. Her heart pulsated at every stop, debating if she should get off, cross the tracks, and take the next train back to Wilmette. She pinched her thigh, willing herself to stay seated. She could do this. She must. With each of the conductor's calls—Rogers Park, Ravenswood, Clybourn, and finally the downtown station—her breath grew sharper and shorter.

She alit from the train and passed through the echoing cavern of the downtown lobby to exit outside to the cabstand. She got into the first car in line and gave the driver the northwest side address. Even with the sun blazing, the taxi ride along Milwaukee Avenue was grim. The electric streetcars passed the cab, slowed by red lights at every corner. Vivian gazed at the storefronts jammed together, cheek by jowl, some with forbidding iron grates across the windows. The sequence of hardware store, coffee shop, resale clothing establishment, plumbing supply house, discount furniture warehouse, and cut-rate liquor store repeated mile after mile. The scene melded into one long, dreary cityscape as if she were traversing the same dismal street again and again, going nowhere.

When the cab took the traffic circle at the Logan Square monument, Vivian looked up and lit a cigarette. She was far from downtown and hoped Ethel would be waiting when she arrived. She needed her tough-minded sister to embolden her. Vivian's throat tightened, and she began to feel nauseated. She was about to ask the driver to turn around and go back to the downtown station when the cabbie made an abrupt left turn and stopped in the middle of an ordinary residential block. The stately greystones may have been elegant long ago, but now, streaks of green stains left a patina that needed a thorough power washing. Number 5634 stood next to the block's only empty lot, scattered with broken bricks and weeds growing willy-nilly as if no one cared enough to clear them away.

"Are you sure this is the right place?" Vivian repeated the address aloud.

"Sure, I'm sure, lady. Tell ya the truth, you ain't the first fare I brought here."

Vivian read the meter and gasped. Twelve dollars! They *had* traveled far. She peeled off one of the twenty-dollar bills.

"Six dollars and fifty cents back, please," she said, regaining her composure. A ten percent tip. She was always good with figures.

The cabbie took his time counting out the bills. "Thanks, lady. I'm gonna go grab lunch. If you need a ride back downtown after you're done, call me." He handed her a card with a phone number but no name.

Vivian's legs felt weak as she climbed the steps to the building's carved front door, polished with a rich walnut stain, a rare hint of elegance compared to other doors on this block. She glanced first to see if anyone was watching, then lifted a shaky finger to the label BOONE & SON, took a deep breath, and firmly pressed the bell. Aunt Ruthie's familiar watchwords reverberated in her ears: "Throw your shoulders back and lift up your head. No one is any better than you are." How she wished Aunt Ruthie and her loving ma were here with her. Gruff ole Ethel would have to do. Vivian was buzzed in and climbed the carpeted stairs to the second floor. She was met by a stout middle-aged woman with dark brown hair pulled back into a severe bun, wearing a Glen plaid gray suit.

"Mrs. Kolson?"

Vivian nodded, hoping she didn't look as frightened as she felt. She'd decided to use her maiden name to be incognito.

"I'm Miss Satwick. Your sister is waiting for you. At least, she says she's your sister."

Ethel's voice boomed. "None of your darn business who I am."

Vivian exhaled when she saw her sister's imposing figure rise out of a club chair, surprised to note she'd been holding her breath since she'd stepped inside. Ethel wasn't afraid of anyone. An unidentifiable, sickly sweet odor permeated the space. The place reeked. She had a coughing fit, and Miss Satwick asked if she needed water. Vivian declined and looked around, recognizing the layout of a standard two-flat apartment. They stood in the front room that faced the street, wallpapered in an old-fashioned, red-flocked, paisley pattern. The familiar wood-trimmed bay window let in the sunshine to sparkle through dust mites visibly floating through the air. There was a false fireplace complete with a clock atop the mantel. This room also had an imposing oak desk adjacent to a four-drawer tan steel file cabinet. On the walls were framed etchings—inky lines suggesting nude female shapes. Oak pocket doors closed off what was typically a formal dining room. Vivian's stomach tensed when she imagined what went on behind those doors. She put a hand on her gut, feeling nauseated, and strained to will away her growing need to pee, afraid to ask to use the powder room.

Miss Satwick had a pronounced lopsided gait as she ushered them toward the desk. She pointed to a paper.

Ethel grabbed it. “Looks legit,” she said and placed it back on the desk.

Miss Satwick handed Vivian a fountain pen and asked her to sign. Vivian bent over the paper with shaking fingers. Her usually precise signature was wavy, looking nothing like her own, complete with an ugly black splotch after her last name.

“Six hundred dollars,” said Miss Satwick, holding out her palm.

Ethel whistled through her teeth. “Steep. How much can she put down?”

Vivian put a hand on Ethel’s wrist to keep her from interfering. Mel had given her the cash.

“I’ll take two hundred up front.” Miss Satwick tapped her pen on the desk.

“Installments?” asked Ethel.

Vivian jabbed Ethel with her elbow, hoping she’d understand to back off. When the woman opened a desk drawer to expose a pistol, Vivian gasped.

Ethel said, “Give ’er the dough. The lady means business. These folks must be connected.”

Vivian opened the clasp of her purse and counted out ten twenty-dollar bills.

“Sit there.” Miss Satwick waved them over to the two leather chairs. Ethel reached for Vivian’s hand and gripped it tight. Vivian’s knuckles turned as white as if she were clinging to a life preserver while treading water over her head at the North Avenue Beach.

“You’re doin’ the right thing,” Ethel said softly in a rare, reassuring tone. “Ma had too many of us. Everyone suffered. Ma most of all.”

“Did you suffer?” Vivian stared at her sister’s lined face, her worn hands.

Ethel clenched her teeth and said, “I’m no worse for the wear. In those days, we all did what we had to. I’d do anything for Ma. You know that. Don’t you worry about me. Worry about yourself today.”

Vivian yearned for a distraction. No *Life*, *Time*, or *Redbook* magazines here, like those scattered around Dr. Goldblum's waiting room. She wished Dr. Goldblum could have done this for her. She trusted him to keep her safe. She squirmed. She had to pee. Her leg jiggled up and down as she gazed out the bay window covered by an old tree with bright green leaves masking the buildings across the street.

"Why so jumpy?" asked Ethel. "Got the shpilkes?"

"Please, Eth, let me be." Vivian felt trapped. She sucked in her stomach. Her need to pee became urgent. No choice but to ask, "Excuse me, where's the ladies' room?"

Miss Satwick gave her the now-familiar harsh glare and pointed to a door on the wall adjacent to her desk. "Make it snappy."

After she used the toilet, Vivian took a paper towel from the stack on the sink and rubbed and rubbed her hands vigorously as if they would never dry. She examined her raggedy nails, chipped and in need of a manicure. Maybe she could add one to her beauty shop appointment next week. Next week. How would she feel next week? At a fierce rap at the door, Vivian gripped the sink trying not to puke. She did not want to go back into that waiting room with its gassy smell from whatever was going on behind those pocket doors.

Another knock. "Mrs. Kolson! It's time."

Vivian's gut clenched. She opened the door, surprised to see that Miss Satwick had donned a white coat over her charcoal gray suit jacket. Was she the nurse, too? Miss Satwick slammed the door. "Follow me."

Ethel stood and squeezed Vivian's shoulder, adding a little push on her behind. "I'll be right here. Hand me your purse."

Miss Satwick slid open the doors to the next room. Vivian followed, wondering if Mel was thinking about her amid his business's daily hubbub. She stayed away from Jacobson Brothers, not only because Mel didn't want her there—no place for a lady, he always said—but because Vivian didn't like to imagine her sweet, mild-mannered husband spending his days in that filthy marketplace while she was ensconced on Maple Street in a pristine suburb. Her Mel deserved better. But today she yearned to be next to him, even at his smoky workplace, because she ached for his reassurance that despite what she was about to do, she was still a "lady" and a good mother in his eyes. In this place with Miss Satwick, she certainly didn't feel like a lady and not at all like a good Jewish mother.

The room behind the doors was larger than where she'd left Ethel, but even more sparsely furnished. An examining table with stirrups claimed the center of the space with a side table holding an array of steel instruments. Alongside the wall was one flimsy folding chair. Vivian clutched at her white gloves, twisting them furiously, as if she could wring out all of her fears. On this side of the door, the sickening, paint-thinner-like aroma was stronger, an odor so thick that Vivian wanted to grab it with both hands and wrestle it away from her face. But the invisible vapors were impossible to push away. Vivian felt woozy, unsteady, and nearly fainted from the stench until she jumped to attention at Miss Satwick's bark.

"Undress. All the way. Put your clothes there." Miss Satwick pointed to the folding chair before patting the examining table. "Up here. On your back. Cover yourself with the sheet. Feet in the stirrups. Dr. Boone will be right in." Her back was rigid as if standing at attention to guard the space.

Vivian rushed to slip off her everyday tan pumps. She slid out of her camel-colored pencil skirt and crisp blue blouse, quickly folded and stacked them neatly on the chair, and placed her white gloves on top. She unsnapped her garters, carefully rolling down her stockings to avoid runs, and wriggled out of her girdle. Finally, she unhooked her white cotton bra, then crossed her arms in front of her chest in a futile effort to preserve her modesty.

Miss Satwick pounded the table and motioned Vivian to climb

up. She draped the sheet around herself, covering as much of her body as she could, took a deep breath, and silently thanked Mel for not insisting that she carry this one to term. Many men would. At the same time, a geyser of resentment spouted close to the surface of her consciousness. How dare he make her pregnant again! In the moment, a man did what he wanted. Of course, she was Mel's willing partner; wasn't that what a good wife should be? But she had to suffer the unwanted outcome in a way Mel never would. For the first time ever, she felt that Dr. Goldblum had also let her down by referring her to this god-awful place, where she had to put herself at the mercy of this horrid woman and the mysterious Dr. Boone.

Vivian recalled how Irene had asked if Daddy was angry. Her sensitive daughter had detected something was amiss. Was Irene right? Was Mel mad at her? Vivian tried not to be anxious, but she couldn't shake the nagging feeling that Mel had given her the go-ahead—and the cash—but in his heart, he wanted this fifth child.

When a squat blond man appeared from a door at the back, Vivian pulled the sheet around herself tighter. He looked younger than she was. His thick dark eyebrows contrasted with his fair coloring, forming an uninterrupted straight line over pale eyes, giving him a stern look, no matter his mood. He smoothed down his white coat as if wearing a royal robe before striding toward the table on distinctly bowed legs. His smug, self-satisfied grin made Vivian recoil and sit up straighter, still tugging the sheet around her breasts.

"Lie back," he said, "let me have a look-see. How far along are we?"

We?

"Dr. Goldblum said ten weeks." The sheet slipped away, and her palms flew to cover her abdomen.

"Ahh, one of Goldblum's girls. Good doctor, but won't get *his* hands dirty."

The nerve! She was not too meek to defend her noble doctor. She willed her voice to be strong. "How dare you say anything against him! He not only delivers babies at Wesley Hospital but travels all over the city to poor women's homes!"

Dr. Boone clucked his tongue. "So I've heard. Doesn't make him a saint. My father told me about Goldblum and his sacred Maternity Center. Now let's get on with this." With one hand, Vivian gripped the side of the table, and with the other, she desperately clung to the sheet as if it could keep her from taking the next step.

Dr. Boone let out an exasperated sigh. "Relax, dolly. I've done this hundreds of times. Maybe more."

Dolly? Vivian bristled. She looked to Miss Satwick for an ally, but the woman's expression remained neutral. This man was arrogant. What a difference from the ever-polite Dr. Goldblum.

Miss Satwick reached over to roughly lay Vivian onto her back. Vivian pushed her away, remained upright, and grimaced to feel a twinge deep in her low abdomen. "Stop. I can't."

Dr. Boone's voice was harsh. "Cold feet?"

"I don't know anything about you."

"Nothing to know," he said. "No more stalling. I've got someone after you."

He nodded at Miss Satwick, who lifted a cone to cover Vivian's face. Vivian blocked it with her forearm like a quarterback fending off a defensive lineman.

Vivian's breasts began to ache. "What if I die?"

"You won't die," he said and tapped his finger on the instrument tray.

"But . . . I have four children."

"Most of the women I see have children."

With a sidelong glance at Miss Satwick, Vivian began to plan her getaway. Leap from the table, dress as fast as she can—bra, blouse, girdle, stockings, skirt, pumps—and run out of the room to Ethel.

Vivian craned her neck to look over her shoulder and twisted to aim her body toward the chair.

"Come on now," Boone said with a scowl. "Have your husband buy you a diamond necklace when it's all over."

Diamond necklace? Rude. Was he calling her a rich Jew?

He winked again. His sleaziness made her feel dirtier. She averted her eyes from his Maginot Line of bushy eyebrows. She wanted Dr. Goldblum and no one else. Vivian gagged, overcome by the stink of gas.

"Buck up," said Miss Satwick. "There are worse places you could go for this, believe you me."

Dr. Boone gave a disgusted grunt. "Look here, lady," he said. "Are you in or out?"

Vivian did not answer. She slid off the table onto the slick, waxy wood floor and raced for her clothes.

Dr. Boone tossed the speculum with a clank onto the tray, where it bounced and clattered to the floor. He called after her, "Listen. If you leave now, you'll only have one week to return. Afterward, it will be too late. Do you understand? One week."

One week. No matter. She would never come back here.

Vivian dressed as fast as she could, not bothering to put on her hose. Instead, she rolled them into a ball, stuffed them into her pocketbook, and dashed to slide open the pocket doors to the front room.

She heard Dr. Boone mutter as he washed his hands at the sink on the back wall. "Another skittish housewife. Damn prima donnas, each and every one."

Ethel jumped up when Vivian appeared. "That was quick."

"I couldn't . . . I just couldn't," Vivian said in a reedy voice, panting as she reached for her wrist. Where was her watch? Did she leave it in there? Miss Satwick closed the sliding door behind her with a click.

"I've got to go back to get my silver watch!" Vivian's eyes were wild as she tried to push past Miss Satwick and lunge for the door.

"Get your hands off me!" Miss Satwick said, barring the way.

"But I left my watch in there. I can't go home without it."

"Look at you. You're a nervous wreck. It's probably at home sitting on your dresser."

"What about the bathroom?" Ethel pointed.

The door was closed. Miss Satwick shook her head. "Someone else is in there."

"Please, please, I'll wait. Let me check. It was my husband's present for our second anniversary."

"That's rich. Are you pulling my leg?" said Miss Satwick. "Second anniversary! That's a new one. Most women coming here wear a fake wedding ring."

Ethel crossed her arms. "Have a heart. Let her have a look in the john."

"Leave it alone, lady," said Miss Satwick. "You talk a big game, but you're not so tough. If I've seen one, I've seen a million flighty women who don't know what they want."

Vivian flinched, made a run for the bathroom, and jiggled the knob. Locked.

"I told you. You can't go in there. If your watch is here, I'll find it when I clean up. You'll get it when you return."

"I won't be back."

"I predict you will. I know your type." Miss Satwick sauntered over to her desk. "Suit yourself." She tapped the open ledger book with her fountain pen. A lacquered black strand had loosened from her otherwise tight bun. She retrieved a pin from her desk drawer and tucked the errant hair back into place. Ethel took Vivian's hand and led her toward the door. "Hold on," said Miss Satwick. "You owe another hundred."

"What the heck?" asked Ethel.

"Shut up," said Miss Satwick. "I told you before." She pointed at Ethel. "*You* stay outta this."

Vivian whimpered, "But he didn't do anything," as she opened the clasp of her pocketbook and pushed her balled-up hose deeper inside.

"No matter," said Miss Satwick. "Lucky I don't charge you the whole amount. Pay the rest when you come back and the doctor does what you came for today."

Vivian stood up straight and pulled her shoulders back as she rooted around in her purse for the cash. "I'll only be back to pick up my silver watch." She counted five twenty-dollar bills into Miss Satwick's hand.

Ethel harrumphed. "How dare you take advantage of my sister."

Vivian said, "It's OK, Eth. Mel gave me enough."

Ethel pulled Vivian away. "C'mon, let's go. This place stinks to high heaven."

"I called you a cab," said Miss Satwick.

Ethel stuck her tongue out. Vivian became teary-eyed when she recalled Dr. Boone's crack about the diamond necklace. No piece of jewelry could ever substitute for what she stood to lose here in this office. Not even her silver watch. She shuddered to think how close she had come to letting that sarcastic man invade her private parts. Nothing like Dr. Goldblum, who was always a perfect gentleman.

Vivian's legs shook, and she stumbled. Ethel grabbed her hand to keep her from falling. Outdoors, the sun had disappeared behind fluffy clouds, but the air felt fresh. This block looked different now. Children's high-pitched voices rose in shrieks of glee as they played wallball against the buildings. Vivian's heart felt as dull as a knife that had cut through too many loaves of bread.

"Why so sad, lady?" one boy called over his shoulder before he ran through the gangway toward the alley. "Ya look like you lost your last friend."

As they waited on the sidewalk for the taxi, another kid asked Ethel for a dime. She spat on the parkway grass. "No dice, punk."

He waggled his fingers around his ears, stuck out his tongue, and dashed off.

A taxi honked, and they hopped in. Different cab. This car had dirt caked on the floor mats. This driver didn't say a word as he sped down Milwaukee Avenue, weaving around double-parked automobiles. Vivian wanted to call Mel as soon as they got to the downtown station. Maybe he would leave work early to pick her up and drive home together to Wilmette. Maxwell Street wasn't far. She couldn't bear the train trip alone with her thoughts. Her hands shook as she asked Ethel, "Did that place scare you as much as it spooked me?"

Ethel rolled her eyes. "Oh, kid." She reached for Vivian's hand. "Did ya think it would be a Sunday School? Those folks are probably in cahoots with the mob."

Vivian's teeth chattered. "I wonder if Aunt Ruthie took Ma to a place like this after your trip to the druggist. I can't imagine how scared she must have been. She hardly spoke English."

Ethel covered her eyes with her palms. "I don't know about that, but I do know Ma was brave. Specially with how sickly she was."

"Do you think she had all of us because she loved Pa?"

Ethel snorted. "Loved Pa? Oh, grow up, baby girl. Is that what you call love?" Ethel's eyes flashed. "Ma loved all of us children, I'm sure about that. And Pa loved her, in his own way. But if you're asking my two cents, I don't think Ma ever loved Pa. When I was older, Ma told me how she had been afraid to have more children, but, oh no, Pa wouldn't leave her alone."

1937

THE NIGHT began no differently than most in their crowded flat. Ethel made up the daybed where she slept alongside teenaged Vivian. Vivian, finished with her homework, changed into her nightgown, propped up the cushions behind her, and began to read her library book. Ethel returned to the easy chair and thumbed through an issue of *Collier's* magazine, noting the summer fashions. Max leaned on his elbows as he lay on the floor next to the radio listening to the White Sox game before stretching out on the divan that was his bed. Vivian reached the end of a chapter, put in a bookmark, and soon drifted off, lulled by the smooth tones of radio announcer Bob Elson's voice. Suddenly, she was awakened by a commotion in the kitchen with no clue about what time it was.

Ma's voice was uncharacteristically shrill. "Look at you! You're a disgrace, Abraham Kolson! No wonder our son wants to move away to Los Angeles with his girl."

"Shut up, wife. What do you know about it? He wants to be his own man. Nothing to do with me. Now, come here and let me give you a kiss. Aren't you happy to see me?"

"You stink like drink."

"Don't be sore. Where's the Alice I married?"

"I never was your Alice or anyone else's. When will you see me for who I am?"

Vivian sat up and called out. "Ma? Are you OK?"

Ethel put a finger to her lips.

"Now you've woken the kinder!" cried Hannah. "Leave me alone. I'm already a mother too many times over."

"Too many times? What are you saying?" Abe got loud.

"You know what I'm saying! When I almost died, did you care? No. You come to me in my bed without a worry what the dangers might be. You do what you want when you want."

"A man is a man. You must know that by now."

"How well I do. Don't you remember? Vivian, our treasure, was also my greatest fright. I was afraid I could die."

"Stop being a Sarah Bernhardt. Having babies is what women do. Anyway, Alice, you're too old for babies now."

"Let me alone. I'm older, but not too old. Last year I thought my monthly bleeds were gone for good. Now they've returned. Get away from me. Go sleep on a chair."

Vivian lifted her head from the pillow and saw Pa grab Ma's wrist and start to drag her toward their bedroom in the back of the flat. His face was red as a bowl of borscht.

"Quiet, woman. I won't sleep on a chair like a hobo. Come to bed."

"Bed. Bed. Bed. When you come home, that's all you ever want. Do you want me to get with child again and have Ruth take me somewheres to end it? Not again."

"That bohemian hussy took you *where* to do *what*?"

Hannah made gulping, choking sounds.

Abe's voice rose higher. "I said, where did you go, Alice?"

"You don't know anything about what goes on with me, do you, Mr. Big Talker?" Hannah was sobbing now.

Vivian rose from the daybed, but Ethel pushed her back down. "Go back to sleep. Pretend you never heard none a' this." Vivian wrestled Ethel's arm away, but her sister was too strong. "Leave them be."

Abe was screaming. "How could you do such a thing without a word to me? I heard rumors from someone at Jacobson Brothers, but I said, 'Not my Alice. Not my pious wife.'"

"Stop calling me your Alice. Get away from me! Get out!"

Abe got louder. "How dare you put me out? This is my home. Where will I go?"

Vivian put the covers over her head, stuck her fingers in her ears, and hummed to herself to block out their words. At the sound of a slap, Vivian cried out.

Ethel made a fist and scrambled off the daybed to head toward the kitchen. "That sonnava bitch."

Hannah wailed louder. "I don't care where. Go!"

Their oldest brother came in to the flat wobbling. With his

asthma, he slept all day in air-conditioned picture shows and stayed out half the night in pool halls. He grabbed his father's raised hand before he could strike Hannah. "Get out, old man!"

Ethel cheered. Abe staggered back. "Not you, too? Do you all want me gone? Okey dokey, but don't go looking for me. There's nothing more for me here." He stumbled toward the hallway door.

Vivian jumped off the daybed. "Pa! No! Don't go!"

"My shaina maidele, my pretty girl. Listen to me, don't be like your ma and do the unthinkable." He bent to kiss Vivian, who coughed at the stench of tobacco and beer on his hot breath. Then, he tottered away and slammed the door behind him.

"What did Ma do?" Vivian asked Ethel.

"Don't you worry. Pa never treated Ma right. Good riddance if you ask me."

Vivian cried at the sound of his heavy boots clomping down the stairs. She touched her cheek with the memory of the tickle of Pa's beard when she was a girl. How she glowed when he hugged her after running up the stairs after a long day at the factory. She remembered her delight when he brought her a special treat—an apple, a pencil, or a ribbon for her hair.

"Quit your blubbering," said Ethel. "Go back to sleep. We're all better off without that no-goodnik."

Max roused from the divan and stretched his arms over his head. "Are Pa and Ma at it again?" Vivian was still sniffling. Max got up and went to console her. "Don't cry, sis. He'll be back. Pa always comes back."

1956

WHEN THE two women arrived at the downtown train station, Ethel paid the cabbie, unusual for her to offer to pick up a tab. Vivian thanked her and leaned over to brush her cheek with a kiss, but Ethel waved her off, mumbling, "Glad to."

Vivian headed toward a row of pay phones and told her sister she'd call Mel to ask if he'd pick her up to drive back to Wilmette.

"Suit yourself," said Ethel. "Do ya mind waiting alone? I'm gonna catch the bus to the shop. With my luck, that nervous mother of the groom will show up outta the blue for a fitting. Will you be OK until Mel comes?"

Vivian nodded, wiping away a tear. "I'll be fine. You've done a lot already."

Ethel surprised her by putting her arm around her. "Take care of yourself, baby girl."

Vivian took out her clean handkerchief and blew her nose. "Don't worry about me. Thanks for everything."

"Hey, I didn't do nothing. And remember, you didn't do nothing either. You're stronger than you think," said Ethel, wiping her eye with the back of her hand.

Vivian knew Jacobson Brothers' Central 6 number by heart. Mel answered on the first ring. He must have been waiting near the phone. "That you, Viv? Is everything all right?"

"I'm downtown at the train station. Can you pick me up here? Now?" She tried not to cry, but her gulping voice disintegrated into sobs. "I didn't go through with it. I couldn't." She choked. "That man . . . the whole place . . . it was awful."

"Honey," Mel said hoarsely. "The man must know his business because Dr. Goldblum recommended him. Listen, from what I know, the best of that bunch are stuck paying off even shadier guys."

"The man told me I have only one week left if I decide to go back."

"I told you before," Mel sounded cross. "You don't have to go back. We'd love another one same as the others."

"But I can't face starting over."

"How many times can I say this?" Mel was so loud Vivian held the receiver away from her ear. "There's no halfway. Either you will or you won't. But please, don't worry yourself sick. You don't have to decide right now. How's about I bring home corned beef tonight, so you don't have to cook?"

Her voice was scratchy. "The girls will love that."

"Stay put," he said. "I've gotta finish one more thing. I promise I'll leave in fifteen minutes. Sit tight. See you in thirty."

IN THE cavernous waiting room of the Chicago and North Western Randolph Street station, Vivian gazed up at the series of arched, multipaned windows on three walls below the vaulted ceiling. Seated alone on a hard bench in the enormous space, she felt insignificant. The station wasn't crowded at this hour, but the waiting room led to eight island platforms with two tracks on each side, with the capacity of sixteen trains coming and going at the same time. Soon, swarms of men with briefcases would come rushing by, hustling to board trains on the three commuter lines fanning out from the city to the bedroom suburbs where dinners with their families waited.

Vivian felt paralyzed by indecision. She was angry to feel wishy-washy, a woman who couldn't act. She'd long been proud to know her mind, to have goals even when buffeted by family and world events beyond her control forced her to change course. The Great Depression. The war. The night Pa left. She'd made her choices among those that life offered: school, job, marriage, children. She pinched her thigh. Many women had done what she just ran from. Hadn't they made peace with themselves? Why *had* she run? She would have survived. As Mel had reminded her, this was Dr. Goldblum's man. What did he mean when he said his *father* told him about Dr. Goldblum? But she felt sick to recall the sneering Dr. Boone with his crack about asking Mel to buy her a diamond necklace. The nerve! And that horrid assistant? She was no nurse. Nurses were kind, caring. Vivian hunched her shoulders and rubbed her naked wrist. Her beautiful anniversary watch was gone. She was certain that scheming woman had snatched it. Vivian let out a sob. She would never get it back.

If she had let him go ahead, how would she feel now? She groaned with an abdominal cramp. What would the cramping be like if she'd actually had the abortion? Would Mel change his mind and leave them? She couldn't take care of the kids on her own in their expensive Maple Street house. Where would they go? They were too many to live with Ma and Aunt Ruthie in Rogers Park. She wanted to stay in Wilmette with Mel and the children. Her throat tensed. Her tush was sore. Sitting on this hard bench distressed her bony bottom.

An announcement blared over the loudspeaker: A train with a stop at Wilmette would leave in ten minutes. She was glad she wouldn't have to endure the bouncing ride back home with its abrupt stops and starts. Waiting for Mel felt longer than a thirty-minute TV sitcom with too many commercials. Wasn't it time yet? She glanced at her naked wrist again and felt faint. She stood up to get a better look at the large clock at the far end of the waiting room. Time to scurry outside to watch for Mel's two-toned, dark green and white Oldsmobile. Outside, the wind ruffled her hair. She yearned to confide in a woman besides Ethel.

There he was. Her reliable husband had arrived precisely as promised. He reached across the front seat to push open the passenger door, and she hopped in. He leaned over to kiss her, his five o'clock shadow barely visible. The car reeked with the pungent aroma of spicy corned beef. Nonetheless, she felt as if she had entered a grand limousine driven by a movie star like heartthrob Gary Cooper.

Mel put the car in gear and drove off. Vivian clutched at her purse. She said with a wail, "Oh, Mel. That awful place already cost us three hundred dollars."

"Please, darling," said Mel. "Calm down. No use crying over money that's gone."

"I'm not even sure if that man was a doctor. He said you should buy me a diamond necklace when it's all over."

A smile came over Mel's face. "You want a diamond necklace? I know where to get one."

She laughed a little, not meaning to. "You can buy anything on Maxwell Street, can't you?"

"Isn't that why you married me?" Mel took one hand off the wheel and squeezed her thigh.

"I don't want a diamond necklace. I want you. I want Irene, Sandy, Linda, and Billy. I want everything to go back to the way it always was." Then, she burst into tears. "I left that place in such a hurry, Mel, I don't know how to tell you. The silver watch you gave me on our second anniversary is gone."

"The watch I bought for you, special? Did those goniffs steal it?"

Vivian cried harder.

"Don't cry. I'll find you another watch."

"But I want *that* one. Your beautiful gift to me before we had children."

"Forget about it. We got more to worry about than one lousy watch."

Vivian snuffled. Mel tuned to WBBM news radio.

WHEN THEY pulled into the garage, the girls were in the den glued to their afternoon favorite, *The Mickey Mouse Club*. Even Daddy coming home early, together with Mommy, couldn't shake them from singing along and spelling the words in the snappy finale until Mel yelled, "Corned beef sandwiches for dinner tonight!" Irene and Sandy shrieked with delight. Daddy's juicy sandwiches were their favorite dinner.

Mel paid the babysitter. Vivian called Jackie to say Mel surprised her by picking her up at the station. Jackie replied with a suspicious-sounding, "Really? How sweet." Vivian concurred and went upstairs to take a shower. She let the warm water run all over her body, caressed by the gentle stream. She examined her belly. Not much rounder than it was after her extreme diet to fit into the black sheath for their neighbors' long-ago party. After her shower, she stayed in their bedroom, where the relentless noise of the children's voices rose upward in a crescendo of demands. Each one needed something different. She had a crushing headache and couldn't imagine adding to this commotion for how many more years? Should she screw up her courage and go back to that Dr. Boone?

Irene's cry was unmistakable. "Mommy, come down here. Sandy hit me!"

"Irene started it!"

"I did not!"

Mel sat in his easy chair, reading the newspaper, calm amid any maelstrom. He must be accustomed to tuning out noise during his twelve-hour days at his family's wild establishment.

Vivian stood at her bedroom door and called out over the din. "Girls! Behave!" She strained to yell louder. "Mel! Please! See what's going on down there. I can't be the referee. Not tonight."

Mel came to bed after everyone was settled for the night. Vivian twisted from side to side. "Mel, maybe I should go back to that man. What do you think?"

"Put it out of your mind for now. Wait and see. You have one week. Sometimes it helps to take a fresh look on a new day."

Vivian was calmed by Mel's practical outlook.

"Do you remember how troubled I was when we first met?" he asked. Vivian kissed his cheek. "My world was upside down. I thought I would never be happy again. Then I met you and everything changed. Look at us now. Did you ever imagine we'd have four adorable children and live in a beautiful house on the North Shore?"

"Never in a million years," said Vivian, suddenly chilled. Was she cold or terrified? She'd come close to doing what she'd previously considered unthinkable. At the center of her world was Mel. Solid, steady Mel. She knew the measure of the man she'd married. Caring. A terrific father and husband. They both felt their union was *b'shert*, meant to be. On some days, Vivian was astounded by the serendipity that had brought them together after the tumultuous war years.

"It's just as well you didn't go ahead," said Mel. "Something like this, you must do with your whole heart. That goes for almost everything. If you're not sure, it's no-go. I learned that during battle overseas. No hesitations." He smoothed the blanket over her. "You're shivering. I'll go downstairs and turn up the thermostat."

Vivian pulled the blanket tightly around herself and soon slept.

WHEN MEL returned to their bed, he was wide awake. He wanted to shake Vivian. This was her fault. If she'd kept track of her cycle, they wouldn't be in this predicament. Wasn't that a woman's job? Now they were stuck. But what if she became unstable? She was already on edge all the time. What did they call it? A nervous breakdown? Mel stared at the ceiling. He wanted to give Vivian everything, but he was beyond his limit too.

In a flash, Mel recalled, to his horror, something that had happened during the Battle of the Bulge. It had been years since he'd let himself remember. He felt sick to his stomach, crept out of bed, went downstairs, and began to pace around the living room.

CHAPTER NINE
MEL'S WAR

1956

MEL STOPPED pacing, sank into his easy chair, and took a deep breath. Yes, Vivian miscalculated. But should he be angry at her for losing track? Everyone makes mistakes. She's a wonderful wife and mother, but she is only a woman. Women are not the same as men. Women carry different burdens. His ma had a hard life. Viv's ma did too. Many things were easier for women now, but the basic facts of life did not change. One way or another, together he and Viv would get through this crisis. He could almost hear his ma's faint whisper, "If we have to, we must." Being drafted shattered his world, as it had for so many others. But ultimately, it brought him to Vivian. What would his life be like if he hadn't met and married Vivian Kolson? He needed her more than she knew.

1944

THE MEN in Mel's field artillery unit, stationed at Fort Benning, Georgia, anxiously awaited deployment to Europe in the elusive countdown to the D-Day invasion. A few months earlier, during a rapid-fire drill, Mel's quick and precise calculations stood out and earned him a promotion from lowly private to the role of "computer" with the rank of staff sergeant. After years behind the cash register on

Maxwell Street, mental math was as natural to Mel as breathing. The role of an army computer was to be one of a trio of men responsible for one of the field artillery guns. One man took a sighting and called out his reading; the computer subtracted this sighting from 360, and the third man cranked the wheel of the gun to aim and fire.

In October 1944, four months after D-Day, Mel's unit landed unscathed on Omaha Beach. In December 1944, the Germans launched a massive attack on Allied forces in the Ardennes forest in Eastern Belgium. The chaotic Battle of the Bulge raged for weeks. Bursting auras and thunderous shelling replaced what would have been otherwise a calm, starry night sky among towering evergreens. The pounding noise and flashing lights were punishing. *Boom!* Mel's ears couldn't stop ringing. *Boom! Boom!* Impossible to distinguish whether explosions originated from the Allies or the enemy.

Boom! Boom! Boom! Again and again and again.

The lead man took his sighting and called out, "Eighty!"

Mel shouted back, "Two hundred eighty!"

Fire!

Boom!

Again, the lead man called, "Forty-seven!"

Mel shouted, "Three hundred twenty-three!"

Boom!

As soon as the numbers left his throat, Mel doubled over, clutching his gut. *No*!

The lead man grabbed Mel's arm. "Jacobson? Are you hit?"

Mel shook him off. He retched. His error nauseated him. Not 323. Shoulda been 313. Stupid. How dumb could he be? What if he'd caused friendly fire? He moaned. Too late now. Mel would never forgive himself if he was responsible for even one Allied casualty. He retched again.

The lead man waved over the lieutenant, who ordered Mel to take a rest. After the replacement computer stepped up, Mel staggered toward the latrine. Made it in time before his bowels exploded. Heartsick, he sat on a nearby bench, gulped short drinks of water from his canteen, and panted in between. He couldn't get his error out of his head. He took a long, slower drink, still chastising himself. How could he have made such a mistake? He tried to console himself. Of course, he wasn't perfect. No man was. He wasn't God. Only human. But still, he felt sick.

FDR's slogan, "Nothing to fear but fear itself," had become Mel's mantra to steel himself during battle. Mel never felt he was meant to be a soldier and longed to return safely to Chicago. If only Pa were nearby to bolster him. For the first time during the war, Mel prayed. He uttered a fervent "O God, may no one have been hurt by my mistake," surprising himself to be calling upon God. Long ago, he saw himself as a nonbeliever. As a boy who'd learned all the traditional prayers, he'd prayed fervently alongside his zayde to restore his bubbe, his grandmother, to good health. After she succumbed to cancer, he thought, *What's the use? God didn't answer our prayers.* His beloved zayde moved into their flat and mourned his wife until the end of his days. Mel remained respectful to his parents, honored their customs, but shed their beliefs.

Now, in the middle of a snowy European forest, Mel was distraught. He didn't deserve the rank of computer. During drills at Fort Benning, he'd silently ridiculed his fellow GIs when they couldn't do calculations in their heads. Laughing at their need for pencils and paper to do simple arithmetic. He kicked himself. He was no better.

"Jacobson! Time's up! Get back in there!"

Mel jumped. No time to let his mind wander. After another long drink, he refilled his canteen. Mel's head ached when he returned to his post. He'd have to concentrate and be more focused, if even a tad slower. He was a United States Army Computer with a job to do.

This was war.

By OCTOBER 1945, the Allies had celebrated both V-E and V-J Days. The war had been over for months, but Staff Sergeant Melvin Jacobson remained stationed in Germany among the United States' occupying forces. A peaceful equilibrium washed through him, a tranquility that forced Mel to acknowledge how on edge he'd been since landing on Omaha Beach twelve months earlier. He and his buddy John Chasen enjoyed a heady night polishing off a bottle of schnapps they'd bartered for in a nearby village for their army-issued cigarettes, to celebrate their survival and imminent homecoming. As they toasted the day they'd return home, Mel invited John to travel from Racine, Wisconsin, to share a few beers with him at Jacobson Brothers.

But Mel had celebrated too soon. The next day, Mel lost his war. The commanding officer presented him with a cable. Pa was dead. At first the words did not make sense. Can't be. Two days later, a second cable arrived from his brothers, asking for Mel's immediate discharge. Mel's heart squeezed at their futile request. They did not understand the US Army. *Discharge denied. Mrs. Jacobson has other sons at home.* For the first time during the war, Mel became angry. Angry at his country, angry at the army who had uprooted him to fight halfway around the world, angry for keeping him away from his family during his father's funeral and shiva.

Every morning and every evening during the seven days of shiva followed by the customary thirty days of mourning, Mel turned to his army-issued pocket prayer book, *For Jews in the Armed Forces of the United States*. He'd never opened the book before. Day after day, he chanted Kaddish for his pa, reciting the memorial prayer on the last page. Mel wasn't seeking solace from God; rather, he sent his prayers across the ocean to feel a connection with his family who were mourning Pa in Chicago, on the other side of the planet.

One night, Mel awoke, shivering, and pulled the coarse olive drab wool blanket up to his neck. Had John gone out to take a leak and left the tent flap open? No, the flap was tied down securely, and Chasen was snoring lightly in the cot next to him. A swirling mist filled the room and a hoarse voice addressed him by his familiar Yiddish name. Pa? Mel's heart leaped to recognize his father's voice. He rubbed his eyes, yearning to see Pa's face, but the specter remained hidden in the fog.

Melech, my son. How I ached to see you again in Chicago, to daven together in our shul, to rejoice and thank God for bringing you home to us. But we men can never know God's plan. My weak heart claimed me to join our ancestors while you were away in Germany. Remember, I will always be alongside you, my firstborn. Don't despair. You are strong. Take care of Ma.

During Mel's remaining months of German occupation, he often felt his pa's encouraging presence, reminding him that the family loved him and he would soon return to Chicago and someday have his own family. Mel was comforted and began to look forward to the hauntings. This surprised him because he had not been raised to believe in ghosts, rather to trust in the all-seeing, invisible God of his boyhood teachings.

Mel ached to return home. He had pledged his allegiance and risked his life for his country. Yes, he was proud to have helped the Allies win, but, oh, how he hated this war.

FEBRUARY 1946

HOME AT last, but Chicago didn't feel like home. The familiar landscape of the only city he'd known until he'd been drafted was unrecognizable. Everything was off-kilter, Mel couldn't find his footing. Where was he? The army first deployed him to Wisconsin, then Georgia, and then all across Europe. Although the months of waiting were finally over, Mel's stubborn sense of order was forever changed.

He floundered without Pa. After years away, Mel was adrift in post-war Chicago.

Jacobson Brothers looked the same as it had the day he left for induction at Fort Sheridan, but Mel couldn't face resuming his work routine. His uncle and brothers offered to continue to pay his salary until he was ready to return. Mel felt undeserving because the business supported several families. But they insisted. Hadn't Mel fought for their country while they were safe in Chicago?

Liza Jacobson, still grieving for her husband, found new purpose by tending to her son, the returning soldier. He must rest, not worry about staying away from the business. He'd done more than his share. Before the war, when one by one his brothers married and welcomed children, Mel worked every night, never missing a shift. Now, back in his ma's home, it wasn't unusual for Mel to stay in bed all day long until Liza called him to supper. She spoiled him by cooking his favorite dishes: chicken soup with fluffy matzoh balls, thick-sliced brisket even juicier than he remembered, glazed baked chicken, fresh-baked challah, mashed potatoes, steamed carrots, kishke, potato knishes, and crusty, sweet mandel bread loaded with almonds. After years of bland army food, the home cooking numbed him, but Mel couldn't shake an ever-present emptiness. No matter how high he piled his plate with food, he never felt full.

Nightmares plagued his sleep. He roamed through the apartment long after midnight.

The Jacobson family's collective mourning for their patriarch had ended months earlier. Here in Chicago, as in Germany, Mel mourned alone.

On the days he did go out, Mel explored the unfamiliar north side Lakeview neighborhood where his parents had moved while he was overseas. The streets were set at odd angles compared to the west side grid of his childhood neighborhood, tilting him off-balance. He hurried around a corner, expecting to find the Douglas Park Fieldhouse looming, where he might encounter a cousin, an old neighbor, or strike up a game of handball. Instead, he found the Amalgamated Meat Cutters Union's brotherhood sculpture at the corner of Diversey and Sheridan. Mel walked through the lakeshore parks where grim, bare branches reached out at him menacingly from towering trees. Only once did he consider seeking bullets for his souvenir German Luger, but he dared not bring more tragedy upon Ma or the family. He must go on.

Only in the expansiveness of Lake Michigan did Mel find peace as he contemplated the mercurial changes that stretched beyond the horizon: Some days, the water was a serene azure blue; the next day, unpredictable wild, dark green waters with white-capped waves slammed the rocks that jutted out from the shoreline. When the wind became raw, Mel took shelter in the Lincoln Park Conservatory greenhouse where the humidity and exotic foliage transported him to an alien landscape. After leaving the cozy, glass-enclosed shelter, he took a lazy jaunt through the zoo, startled by an ear-splitting *Pop! Pop! Pop!* and dived to crouch behind a bush, placing his hand on his hip, ready to reach for a phantom weapon. Coming up empty, he stood, stumbled, and collapsed onto a nearby bench. This wasn't Europe. He was in Chicago. A child bawled. No gunshots, only a burst balloon.

On his way home, relieved to live in a peaceful city, Mel decided to stop at the Greek coffee shop on North Broadway to satisfy his cravings for the greasy *traif* he'd developed a taste for in the army.

When he opened the door, Liza gave him a hug. "Mine handsome son, you look pale. Sit down and have a big bowl of soup with fresh kreplach."

MEL'S WEEKS of malingering strung together, until one day, at noontime, Liza knocked to wake him and announced, "Uncle Fred and Aunt Frieda want to throw a homecoming party for you."

When Mel imagined a crowd of relatives staring at him, he began to scratch at his arms.

"Please, Ma. No party for me."

"What's wrong with celebrating a happy occasion? Everyone in the family wants to see you. The war brought too much misery, too much tsuris. Now we are alone without Pa." Her voice cracked.

"I don't want to go."

"You can't stay at home. You're the guest of honor."

The guest of honor. Mel got out of bed and stood tall, lifting himself up to his full six-foot height. He felt a tingle, a spark to be surrounded in safety by the aunts, uncles, and cousins who'd known him all his life. Loved him for who he was. He'd even be happy to see the ones who annoyed him.

"Listen, son, I hear there's a nice-looking Jewish girl working at the Walker–Jacobson Company. Your Uncle Fred said she's got a good head, a smart kopf, for numbers. Frieda asked me if we should invite her. I said yes, but I hear she's from that Kolson family. Remember them from our old shul? I told her a Kolson won't be good enough for a Jacobson."

Mel chuckled. Ma thought no woman would be good enough for him, but he didn't feel the same; he didn't feel good enough for any girl. Look at him. The war still haunted him. He couldn't even go to work. Every night he heard bursts of shelling, his nose felt stuffed with the powder of explosions. No working girl would want any part of that. He tried to picture this Kolson girl from his uncle's office. His younger cousin's age, if he remembered correctly. But he never knew what to say to strange women and wished he were more like his charming brothers with their gift of gab. It wasn't that he didn't want a girl, but it had been years since he dated his friend Mario's cousin Gina—a sexy waitress from Mario's family's restaurant on Taylor Street. Mel and Gina had kept it on the q.t. because his parents would never have approved of an Italian daughter-in-law, and Gina's parents certainly wouldn't accept a Jew.

But that was all before the war. Overseas, he hadn't lusted after local girls like many of his fellow GIs. He and his buddy John didn't think that was right. Now he was more than ready to leave his ma's apartment and settle down with the right woman, if only she would have him. Why not go to this party?

"What would I wear? I can't go in uniform. I'm discharged."

"Don't worry, my son. I will take you shopping."

1956

WHAT IF he hadn't gone to the party? One look at Vivian, and he had never wanted anyone else. She was a knockout. On the fateful night they met, he reclaimed his desire to live. Now, ten years later, she'd given him four wonderful children. Three smart, spunky girls, and a baby boy to carry on the Jacobson name. Vivian was upset, so upset she didn't know what she wanted. He couldn't lose her. He couldn't force her to take on another child that would push her over her limits. They had to see this through together. He went back upstairs to their bed, where she lay sleeping. When Mel gently brushed the bangs away from her forehead and kissed her lightly, a small smile danced around her lips. Wasn't this predicament his fault too? How could he blame her for her mistake?

CHAPTER TEN
VIVIAN'S CONFIDANTE

THE COUNTDOWN BEGINS
DAY 1: TUESDAY

THE DAY after she escaped from Dr. Boone's office, Vivian felt like a different person. How could she have come so close to doing something she'd only heard whispers about?

When she recalled that sickly smell, her gut constricted. She felt like she would vomit and ran to the master bathroom.

All at once, she remembered what happened when she and her best friend Jean were fifteen. Jean's mom was more modern than Hannah, Vivian's immigrant ma. Jean's mom asked them about school, upcoming tests, popular songs, or which boys they thought were cute. Jean's father was long gone, and when a new man came to live with them, Jean swore Vivian to secrecy with the news that her mother was expecting and would soon marry. Before long, Jean came crying to Vivian that there wouldn't be a baby. The man had moved out. For weeks, Jean's mother was weepy, no longer interested in their lives. Overnight, she had transformed into a sad, old lady. Only Aunt Ruthie would say it aloud. She told Vivian that Jean's mother must have had an abortion. It was the first time Vivian had heard the word.

Vivian's nausea dissipated to feel this kinship with her long-ago, second mother. Vivian never dreamed that striving to be a good Jewish wife and mother could become so twisted.

With Mel at work, Irene in school, Sandy playing outside, Billy napping, and Linda babbling in the playpen, Vivian had a rare quiet moment. She felt desperate to share her situation with another woman who would understand. Not her old friend Jean. She still hadn't settled down. How about Jackie? Might she be the compassionate sister that Vivian had always yearned for? Surely, Jackie could empathize with the strain of trying to be the perfect suburban wife and mother. After yesterday, Vivian had no doubt about her own failings. Further proof was the glimmer of temptation to return to that shady doctor. Ethel would say, "Forget that smug SOB," but Vivian felt torn. She wanted to scream aloud. Only one week to decide! She called Jackie to come over for coffee.

Jackie rang the bell, coffee cake in hand. Vivian thanked her and admired her perky lime-green shell paired with polka-dotted navy-and-white capri pants. Vivian had always been impressed with Jackie's chic sense of style, dressing not in the most expensive clothes, but in flattering outfits with distinctive colors and patterns. Jackie's frosted flip, with newly cut bangs, gave her an extra sparkle. Tipped hair was in. Maybe Vivian would try it. She could squirrel away a little extra from the household fund and ask her beauty operator, but only if he promised not to charge her an arm and a leg. Vivian gulped to remember she might have to save to buy a new layette.

"What's going on with you?" Jackie asked. "You're jumpy."

No pretending with Jackie. After pouring the coffee, Vivian lit a cigarette, not sure how to begin. She drew in her breath, but before she shared any details, Jackie spooned two sugars into her cup and said, "I have a hunch about all your trips into the city."

Vivian's throat gripped. Jackie couldn't know. She must imagine something far less sinister. After Vivian blew out a long, slow stream of smoke, she said, "Really? I don't think you can guess."

"Try me."

Vivian drummed her fingers on the table. "I'm ashamed to say."

"Take it easy." Jackie looked over her coffee cup and stared at Vivian. "Are you pregnant again?"

Vivian nodded, a tear trailing down her cheek.

Jackie grasped her hand. "And you don't want it?"

"It's too much." Vivian let out a sob.

"Listen," said Jackie. "You think you're the only one? I know what you're going through. I was only twenty when Hank got me pregnant. Two months after Pearl Harbor. His draft notice would arrive any day. He promised to marry me, but we were too broke. Anyway, his mother hated me because I wasn't Jewish. You know, the evil shikse who trapped her son, the handsome Jewish prince."

Vivian let out a giggle in spite of herself. "Sorry. Shouldn't laugh."

Jackie put up her palm. "Doesn't bother me. Not one bit. I'll tell you my story. I was scared. Didn't know what to do. My mother's friend saved my life. She knew where I could go. God knows, Hank and I have enough problems now. I can only imagine how much worse it would have been had we started our family back then."

Vivian stubbed out her cigarette. "Do you still think about the child you never had?"

Jackie hesitated, but only for a moment. "Not often. I used to stop and think, how old would he be now? But after we had our two kids that faded away, like a child who was never meant to be, like a miscarriage." Jackie looked out the window, away from Vivian. "My mother had two 'misses'—that's what she called them. They made her sad because she really wanted a fourth child. But in the end, it was just as well, because when my father died of cancer, well, I'll tell you, times were tough enough." Jackie slurped the rest of her coffee. "Any more in the pot? Please don't go to any extra trouble."

"Sit," said Vivian and scrambled to her feet. "I'll bring the percolator to the table."

Jackie sighed. "Oh, Viv, you must be frantic. Remember, no one can tell you what to do. Follow your instincts. Hank was away in basic training when I found out for sure. What if he didn't come home from the war? I didn't feel strong enough to raise a child on my own. Sure, plenty of women did, including my older sister, but she was tougher than me. She was married when her husband was lost on D-Day. Their son was four years old."

Vivian gasped.

Jackie continued. "I was afraid to take that chance."

"How did your sister manage?" Vivian lit a cigarette.

"They were already living with all of us. And wouldn't you know it? A few years after the war, she married one of our neighbors. I think he'd been sweet on her since they were kids. She tries to hide it, but I know she still misses Junior's dad. You might think I'm cold, but I'll tell you the truth, I don't regret what I did."

"But it's different for me because I already have four children. Yesterday I went to a man referred by my own doctor, but I ran out. He said I only have a week if I decide to return." Vivian tapped another cigarette from her pack. "I usually don't talk about this, but when Mel and I first married, I had trouble getting pregnant."

Jackie lit up one of her own. "Well, I sure didn't have *your* problem," said Jackie with a laugh. "I know it isn't a joke, but I sure wasn't trying to get pregnant. It was only the second time we did it. When I found out, I had no doubt that I wanted an abortion."

Vivian crushed out her cigarette. "I was too scared about getting pregnant and waited until after we married to have sex. I thought that's what good Jewish girls did. Mel didn't push me. I was grateful he didn't. After our wedding, he insisted I leave my job in his uncle's office because he didn't want his family to think he couldn't support a wife. I didn't mind. I'd had enough of that one-gal office where I'd worked since high school. I thought we'd have children right away. But it didn't happen. I was bored to tears home alone all day in our cramped one-room apartment. How many times could I run the carpet sweeper? We made love almost every night, but I didn't get pregnant. I was sure something was wrong with me." She lit another one.

"Coulda been him," said Jackie. "No one ever expects something could be wrong with the man."

"That's exactly what my Aunt Ruthie said. But I was afraid to talk about it and didn't know who to ask. Aunt Ruthie isn't my real aunt, you know. She's my mother's closest friend."

"Kind of like your fairy godmother?" Vivian nodded. "So you went through hell and back and then you had Irene?" Jackie spooned another sugar into her coffee.

Vivian lit a cigarette, remembering the uncertainty of those years. "Something like that. I wish it had been that simple."

Upstairs the baby wailed.

"And look at you now." Jackie laughed.

"Yeah." Vivian exhaled a long column of smoke and stubbed out her cigarette before heading upstairs. "Look at me now."

1949

ON THEIR second wedding anniversary, Mel surprised Vivian with a dinner reservation at Chez Paree, the first time they'd dined there since they were dating.

He ordered champagne and presented her with a silver watch. Then he reached across the table to clasp Vivian's hand. "Darling, we both want children, don't we?"

Her eyes moistened, brushing them away with the back of her other hand. "Yes, of course, we do. But something must be wrong with me."

He stroked the top of her hand. "You're a wonderful wife, but honey, I've been thinking. There's a doctor who stops over to our place for a sandwich and a smoke after his shift at the maternity center around the corner. He's got a gentleness about him, a true prince of a guy."

"Are you kidding? The maternity clinic?" Tears choked her words. "Where my ma and all the immigrants in the neighborhood went?"

"Calm down. Dr. Goldblum also has a private practice downtown. Why don't I call for an appointment?"

Vivian took a deep breath and reached for her glass. She trusted her husband. Because she didn't know what else to do, she decided to go see this doctor.

Mel took off work one morning, and they went to Dr. Goldblum's South Michigan Avenue office together. The elevator operator who sat on a stool swung the gate closed and took them up to the sixth floor. When the nurse called them in, the doctor greeted Mel warmly and introduced himself to Vivian. She guessed that he was in his fifties, Jewish, about ten years younger than her ma, with a receding hairline and kind brown eyes. He didn't seem like a standoffish, snobby doctor, more like a caring uncle. Vivian liked him at once. After a few questions, nothing too embarrassing, the doctor sent Mel to the waiting room.

The doctor said to her, "I've been going to Mel's family's establishment for years. Your husband is a prince of a guy. But I'm not telling you anything you don't already know."

Prince of a guy. Mel had used those same words to describe Dr. Goldblum. Yes, she liked this doctor.

As he began the examination, she tensed at his touch. In a soothing voice he coaxed her to relax. "Pressure coming," he said. Vivian stared at the ceiling tiles. His hands moved around her private cavity, palpating her abdomen for a long time. He said nothing more. She tensed up again. Something must be wrong.

When Mel came into the room, the doctor spoke directly to him. "My initial diagnosis is that your wife has cysts around her ovaries. I'd like to do more tests to confirm this."

"What kinds of tests?" Vivian blurted out. He was talking about her as if she weren't sitting there.

The doctor paused, and then explained, "We would force gas through the fallopian tubes to see if we can get a clear passage. If you both agree to this procedure, you can set up the appointment with my receptionist on your way out, and we'll go from there. We can do this in the office."

"I'll take the bus here on my own, Mel. You won't have to miss work."

"You sure?" he said, squeezing her hand.

She could do this. How bad could it be? Dr. Goldblum was gentle. Vivian had a fierce desire to be a mother. If not, she couldn't be the proper wife her husband deserved.

After the test confirmed the doctor's suspicions, he called them both in for a consultation.

"Vivian will need surgery to remove the ovarian cysts. They are crushing her eggs as they descend before fertilization can occur. I'll remove the cysts and do my best to leave her ovaries intact. I can't guarantee that she'll get pregnant after the surgery, but this will be your best chance. Without this intervention, she will never conceive."

Vivian agreed at once. Mel looked wan and grasped her hand. They trusted Dr. Goldblum. She had the surgery, and true to the skilled surgeon's prediction, within months, the rabbit died. Vivian was thrilled to be pregnant. Mel remained cautious, but hopeful, until late in the pregnancy when Vivian began to bleed. Mel had long been haunted by his ma's tale of a failed pregnancy before Mel was born. In her ninth month, his ma fell after climbing the stairs to their tenement flat, and the male fetus was stillborn. For the first time since they'd married, Mel hurried to their synagogue to pray for Vivian's health and the health of their child. When the bleeding didn't stop, he rushed her to Wesley Hospital, where she miscarried. Dr. Goldblum pulled Mel aside and asked if he wanted to view the expelled fetus. Mel sobbed, because, like his father before him, he'd lost a firstborn son.

"No visible abnormalities," said Dr. Goldblum. "Unfortunate positioning. Placenta previa made this pregnancy susceptible to a spill. You can try again in two months."

Mel took a check from his wallet. "What do I owe you, Doctor?"

With a wave of his hand, Dr. Goldblum said, "Not a cent until I put a baby in your arms."

True to the doctor's prediction, one year later, Vivian gave birth to a healthy baby girl. They named her Irene for Aunt Ruthie's childhood friend. Mel's family showered them with gifts: a wooden crib, layette, and diaper service for a year. Mel's brothers brought a case of champagne to their apartment, where the families toasted every night. Mel presented Dr. Goldblum with a bottle of Glenlivet and a carton of Old Gold's. When Mel began to write out the check, Dr. Goldblum took the pen out of Mel's fingers. "I won't say no to a special bottle of Scotch and my regular cigarettes. But I won't take your money. You and Vivian have your baby at last. The first one's on me!"

1956

"QUITE AN ordeal," said Jackie. "Worse than most."

"Now you know why I feel like such a fool," said Vivian. "Let's move into the living room." She lifted Linda out of the playpen and sat her on her knee. "I should have known better. After my surgery, Dr. Goldblum told me not to use any birth control to increase my chances of getting pregnant. Even now, I've been careless."

Jackie shook her head in disbelief. "Even my Irish Catholic mother knew she couldn't rely on the rhythm method. No wonder you're in a jam."

"I had the babies so quick. I was surprised at how easy it was. I didn't think I could get pregnant because I'm still nursing."

Jackie gave a small, sardonic laugh. "You're not the first to fall for that old wives' tale. But it's understandable that four kids are all you can handle. Don't feel guilty if you decide to go back to that man you ran from. You don't have to like the guy. Sounds like you have a respectable doctor. He wouldn't send you into danger."

"I'm sure that's true."

Vivian stood, put Linda back into the playpen, and fluffed the throw pillows on the couch. "You know, I've been wondering about what Jewish law says about all of this. I'd like to talk to the young rabbi at the new synagogue out here. Tomorrow is Mel's day off. Maybe I can convince him to come with me to ask the rabbi."

Jackie lit a cigarette. "I don't know anything about that. I converted because Hank's mother insisted. Hank doesn't care much about being Jewish. Sure, go and ask this rabbi if you think it will help you make peace with your decision. But one thing I know for sure: Don't second-guess yourself. All those woulda, coulda, shouldas will make you crazy. You're stronger than you think. You are a capable woman who will be able to live with whatever you decide."

"Mel said the same thing and added that major life decisions aren't clear-cut."

"Good advice. Although I'll say this. Your Mel strikes me as an old-fashioned guy who pushes you to do things his way. He's older than you, right?"

Vivian nodded. "Nine years."

Jackie let out a low whistle. "And he leaves you stranded out here without a car? Listen to me. You need more freedom. How did you two meet, anyway?"

When Vivian remembered the war years before she met Mel, she cringed at how her twenty-one-year-old self had ached, afraid that she'd never meet Mr. Right, given the dearth of eligible men. She'd created a Plan B. As soon as the war was over, she would quit her dead-end job where she'd worked since she was fifteen to help her family pay the bills, and aim for a position as an executive secretary in a glitzy office in a Loop skyscraper. Even now, the independent life that she'd never had held an appeal. She laughed out loud to recall how, on a lark, she'd decided to send a letter to the "Bintel Brief," the advice column in the *Jewish Daily Forward.*

November 29, 1944
Dear Editor,
I never thought I'd write to you because I am a modern woman. When I fell for a swell Jewish guy I met on a weekend in South Haven, Michigan, I hoped marriage was in our future. After he pressured me to stay overnight with him at the resort, I said no, and he dropped me like a hot potato. Now I hear he's going out with a girl from the classy Austin neighborhood, leaving me all alone in plain old Lawndale. I'm almost twenty-one. Am I destined to be an old maid? —VK

Dear VK,
Twenty-one years old is not too late for love. If you stay true to your heart, I assure you, there will be others. Sounds to me like this "swell guy" has a swelled head. I predict after the Allies win the war, with God's help, you will find the Jewish man of your dreams.

"What's so funny?" asked Jackie.

Vivian laughed again. "How did we meet? How much time do you have? Do you want the whole story or the *Reader's Digest* version?"

"I've got time. The kids are going to after-school programs. They won't be home for hours. Give me the whole story."

"OK, I'll let the laundry sit."

Vivian lit a cigarette and began.

CHAPTER ELEVEN
COURTSHIP

1956

VIVIAN BLEW a column of smoke toward the ceiling as if she could fly back across the years. "It all started when I was invited to Mel's family's homecoming party after he returned from overseas."

MARCH, 1946

ONE FRIDAY afternoon, Frieda Jacobson went to meet her husband at his office at the edge of Chicago's Loop. Vivian Kolson had worked at the Walker–Jacobson Company since she was a teenager. There was no "Walker." Mel's uncle Fred Jacobson added a Gentile-sounding partner's name to attract Midwestern store owners who might not be inclined to buy wholesale clothing from a Jewish company.

Mrs. Jacobson stopped at Vivian's desk. "I'd like to invite you to the homecoming party we're throwing for my nephew on Sunday night," she said. "I think you two might hit it off."

Vivian had long heard about Fred and Frieda Jacobson's rollicking shindigs at the Seneca Hotel where they lived. Every so often she tried to imagine herself smartly dressed, eating hors d'oeuvres at one of their parties. But today, she scrunched up her face. She was the Help, one of the poor Kolsons from the old neighborhood, not a member of the prominent Jacobson family. Vivian didn't belong.

In the years she'd worked for their company, she'd learned all about their extended family. "Isn't your nephew too old for me?"

What she wanted to say was, "It's obvious that I'm the single Jewish girl in the office that's only invited to be fixed up with the returning soldier."

Mrs. Jacobson laughed softly. "He's not too old for you. You carry yourself in a mature manner. Mel lost prime years with his wartime service. I'll say this about him, he's a little shy, but he's a mensch."

Sounded to Vivian like this nephew couldn't find his own dates. "I don't know, Mrs. Jacobson. I really don't like to be fixed up."

"Pishposh. No one says you have to marry him, my dear."

The boss's wife was right. No need to get overly excited. "Thanks for the invitation. I'll go. I can get a ride out to the Gold Coast from the west side, but I'll need a ride back afterward."

"Of course, we'll see to it that you get home." Frieda Jacobson winked.

Vivian took a deep breath. She felt like Cinderella with nothing to wear to the ball. Like it or not, Ethel would have to be her fairy godmother.

On the way home, Vivian stopped at Woolworth's to buy a fresh tube of her latest favorite lipstick to beef up her smile: Revlon's Fatal Apple Red, a killer shade to cloak her angst. Twenty-two years old and stuck in a dull storefront office with no prospects. She went over to Ethel's flat, hoping she'd be at home. Vivian trusted her sister's eye for what was fashionable given her job as the apprentice seamstress at a chic Oak Street shop. She dressed Vivian like her own little Kewpie doll. When Vivian was younger she rebelled against her homemade dresses, but now, if Ethel told her she looked good, she was confident she did. Relieved when she buzzed her in, Vivian dashed to the second floor.

Ethel opened the door in her dressing gown, cigarette in hand. "This had better be important," she said, blowing out a stream of smoke. "It's my card night."

Vivian waved away the smoke. "It *is* important. My boss invited me to their family party at the Seneca Hotel. I've got nothing to wear."

Ethel whistled. "Hoo boy. That's a swell joint. I hear it's owned by one of the biggest mob families in town."

"Are you saying the Jacobsons are mobsters?"

"Not your precious Jacobsons. I'm only telling you what I've heard about the Seneca Hotel."

"Stop it, Eth. I need your help."

Ethel knotted the ties of her robe tighter around her waist. "I've got a little time before my game. What's the occasion?"

"A special family club party. They are going all out for their nephew Mel's homecoming."

"I remember him from their saloon."

"He was recently discharged from Germany," said Vivian.

"Isn't it a little late? The war's been over for almost a year."

"But he hasn't been home for long. The family didn't want a sad homecoming because his father passed away while he was overseas."

"I heard about that at their joint on Maxwell Street. So, you're the nice Jewish girl they want to set up with Soldier Boy? No wonder you're nervous."

"Oh, shut up! Just because you don't want to get married—"

"I couldn't count on any man to take care of me."

"I've heard your big talk before. Will you make a dress for me or not?"

"Let's go over to your place and look through your closet. I might come up with something."

"Eth, there's nothing there. What about a sample from your shop?"

"Out of the question. I already owe too much on account. I'll go see what you've got."

Ethel dressed quickly and they hurried to the rooming house on the next block where Vivian lived with their ma. Ethel flipped through the hangers in the wardrobe and stopped at a blue dress, but Vivian shook her head. "Mrs. Jacobson bought that for me after a buying trip to New York. I'm sure she'd recognize it."

"I can alter it. I've got an idea from a new line we just got in."

"Is there time? The party's on Sunday night."

"I'll start when I get home from my card game. I hate wasting my time sleeping."

THE DAY before the party, Vivian called her best friend Jean to ask to borrow her beige cardigan with mother-of-pearl buttons, a classier wrap than any Vivian owned. Jean agreed and added that her new beau had a snazzy car and would drive her to the party. At noon on Sunday, Ethel stopped by with an elegant dress. She'd added wide bell sleeves and a border of raised gold braid surrounding a lowered neckline that showed off Vivian's décolleté, but modest enough not to raise eyebrows. She'd nipped it in at the waist to fashion a belted sheath around Vivian's athletic shape, tight but not too tight. She'd appliqued gold fleur-de-lis through the fabric, giving the dress a lighthearted look.

"It's perfect! You're a genius!"

"Pa did teach me a few things before he left."

"You passed him up long ago," said Vivian. "This is beautiful."

When Jean arrived and handed her the sweater, Vivian twirled to show off her dress. "Gorgeous. That sister of yours is a marvel," said Jean. "Love the sleeves."

Jean's beau tooted the horn on his eggplant-colored Hudson sedan. "Let's get this show on the road."

Vivian applied a thick coat of lipstick to cloak her nerves and tried to squelch the fluttering in her stomach. As they drove east toward the lake, she reminded herself that she was only invited for a fix-up. No big deal. Would Mel Jacobson even notice her? At least she looked fabulous.

The Seneca Hotel was close to Lake Michigan where the winds blew stronger. Vivian pulled the borrowed sweater tight to her chest. When the doorman directed the elevator operator to take Vivian up to the penthouse, she stepped in and jutted out her chin as if she belonged. Once inside the vast party room, Vivian gasped at the expansive views of Lake Michigan. This must be what it feels like to fly in an airplane. Maybe someday she would.

Frieda Jacobson approached her right away. "You look lovely, my dear. Here comes Mel, the guest of honor."

Vivian looked over her shoulder and spotted Mel Jacobson walking toward her through the crowd. Vivian feigned sophistication, but in truth, her limited experiences made her nervous around men, particularly after being dumped by the so-called dreamboat on her summer fling to South Haven with Jean. Vivian couldn't deny that her heart beat faster to see how Mel Jacobson stared at her. No one had had that stunned look in his eye quite the way he did. It was as if all the motion in the room stopped: no bustling activity, no buzzing conversation, and no waiters passing baby hot dogs, salmon canapés, and champagne flutes. Vivian returned Mel's gaze and noted he was more attractive than she'd expected.

She felt on display, nervous, as if the whole Jacobson family were watching Mel watch her. She resisted the urge to giggle and run away. She was both excited and uneasy, wondering what might happen next. Could Mel Jacobson—a tall, strong veteran from a good Jewish family—be her match? Every time he started to walk toward her, she felt awkward and stole away to the other side of the room. She cleaved to Mel's cousin who Vivian knew from Marshall High School before she transferred to Jones Commercial. Family members toasted the returning soldier again and again until well after midnight.

Vivian had begun to worry about how she would get home when Mel came striding toward her. She froze.

"I hear you need a ride," he said. He looked shaky. Nervous or tipsy?

Her voice wavered. "I think I missed the last streetcar back to the west side."

"I wouldn't let you go alone on the streetcar at this hour in any case. I'll drive you. My brother will loan me his car."

Mel's brother tossed him the keys. His wife stood on tippy-toes and gave Mel a smooch. "My favorite brother-in-law," she said to Vivian. "The strong, silent type. Watch out. He's smitten!"

Vivian blushed.

"Naomi, you've had one too many," said Mel. "Vivian Kolson, let's get you home. Mind you, it could take an hour, even without any other cars on the road."

"Sure, let's go," Vivian answered, suddenly ready for anything. "Lucky for you to have a brother with a car."

On the elevator, Mel said, "You remind me of someone. Can't quite place her."

Vivian looked at her feet. "Some people say I look like Joan Crawford."

Mel looked confused.

"My wide brown eyes. Or is it my red lipstick?"

He stared at her face. "You're more beautiful than any movie star. Movie stars aren't real. You're the perfect girl from our old neighborhood."

Did he think she was old-fashioned? Mel opened the car door on her side. *Nice touch. He's a gentleman.* Vivian got in and sat close to the door, then dared to inch toward him on the front seat. Before he started the car, he put his arm around her and gave her shoulder a squeeze. "You're something else. And my uncle Fred says you're the best bookkeeper he's ever had."

Bookkeeper? Was that what he was looking for in a wife?

Mel took his arm off her shoulder; he needed two hands to put the car into gear. "Where exactly is home?"

She hesitated, wishing she didn't have to direct him to the rooming house. "Hamlin and Polk."

"Hope your ma isn't waiting up. I don't want to start off on the wrong foot by bringing you home so late."

"I'm old enough to keep my own hours," Vivian said and slid even closer. He had an appealing, dusky scent.

At first, their silence felt uncomfortable. Then as Mel drove, he began to tell her about his life in the army. Once he began talking, he didn't stop, like the pressure released from a singing tea kettle. He spoke of everything he'd been through—in basic training where he'd almost died of pneumonia and then had an allergic reaction to sulfa drugs until he recovered with the help of the miracle drug penicillin. How he was sent to Fort Benning, and later, overseas. Mel grabbed her hand when she asked him about the battles he fought in Europe. He told her about his job as a computer and how important it was during the Battle of the Bulge.

Her eyes widened. "In the newsreels, they said that battle was the war's turning point. You must be really smart! What does a computer do?"

He squeezed her hand harder and didn't let it go except to shift gears. "Not so smart. I was part of a team to aim our big guns to fire at the enemy. My calculations were nothing a sixth grader couldn't do."

"Weren't you scared? No one knew if we would win the war."

"That's the army. You never know where you're going on or what will happen. When we landed on Omaha Beach, we weren't in the same danger as the brave men who landed on D-Day four months earlier, but I was scared. But I thought my feet would never be warm again when we marched through France all the way to Germany.

Lucky for me, our field artillery unit was stationed behind the front lines."

Vivian gasped and gripped Mel's forearm. "You're a war hero."

"I'm no hero. Just a regular soldier fighting for his country. After the war was won, we occupied Germany near the Elbe River. It was a relief to live peacefully, trading the starving Germans our cigarettes and chocolate for liquor and goods to ship home to sell. At first, I felt sorry for the villagers, but when I saw pictures from the concentration camps, my sympathies disappeared. Everything we'd heard was true and worse than true. My unit wasn't among the liberators, but I got angry about the horrors just because they were Jews like you and me. The townspeople knew what was happening and let it happen. They turned in their neighbors. Hitler aimed to exterminate my people, our people. He was beyond evil."

Vivian agreed. "They gave hints in the newsreels at the show. When the papers began to share details, at first, we thought they were exaggerations."

"The Yiddish papers warned earlier," said Mel. "My pa told us all about what he read in the *Daily Courier*." His voice croaked when he said "pa."

Mel stopped the car on Lake Avenue near Kedzie and got out to wipe off the fogged windshield with his handkerchief. When he got back inside, he leaned over and kissed Vivian. She kissed him back. She was falling for him. The handsome veteran, just like the "Bintel Brief" columnist predicted.

Mel said in a husky tone, "My Uncle Fred and Aunt Frieda don't need an excuse for a family party. I was embarrassed to go, but they insisted. I'm glad they did. Otherwise, I would never have met you."

Vivian felt shivery. "I don't like to get fixed up, but I couldn't say no to my boss. And the chance to meet a war hero."

"Hey, I told you, I'm no hero. You must have plenty of guys to date."

"Don't be so sure, soldier."

"I'm not a soldier anymore. Just a guy who works on Maxwell Street. But without his pa." Mel brushed at his face. Was he crying? The windows fogged. Mel got out of the car and wiped the windshield again. On the rest of the drive, he couldn't stop talking about how much he missed his pa. He told Vivian all about getting the news in Germany, how alone he felt without his family.

She listened as he went on and on. "The strong silent type," his sister-in-law had called him. Strong, yes, but tonight he was anything but silent.

When they got to her rooming house, Mel shut off the engine, turned toward her, and they kissed for a long time. Vivian felt as if she'd let him, he couldn't—wouldn't—stop. She didn't want to stop either but straightened up with a start. What if the landlady locked her out? It was long past midnight.

"I'd better go inside. I've got to be at work in the morning."

Mel was weaving when he walked her up the steps, his hand steered her by her lower back. He may have had a few highballs and glasses of champagne, but Vivian hadn't felt safer with any man in years. The landlady stared out of the window. Nosy old woman, still awake in the middle of the night with nothing better to do. Vivian couldn't sneak in past her.

"Can I take you to dinner tomorrow night?" asked Mel.

"Sure thing." Vivian's heart was throbbing. She had to dash inside.

The landlady opened the door. "Vivian Kolson, is that you, coming in so late?"

She turned her face to Mel's for another kiss.

"What time do you get off from work?" he asked.

"Five."

"I'll pick you up at your office. Five o'clock sharp."

Vivian opened the door, waved, pulled off her high heels, but before she could run up the stairs to the third floor, the landlady put out her palm to stop her.

"Who's that man? He's got a nice-looking automobile."

Vivian didn't answer. She took the stairs to her room two at a time. Her heart raced as she stripped off her blue dress to get ready for bed. Mel Jacobson was a dream come true. She lay in bed, reliving his kisses. Handsome. Smart. A veteran who'd served bravely overseas. She wondered where he might take her on their date. She'd wear her best suit.

A FEW HOURS later on the streetcar, Vivian was daydreaming about Mel and almost missed her stop. She made it into the office only a few minutes after nine o'clock, still sleepy from the late night, and couldn't stop yawning all day. At four o'clock, half dozing at her desk, she was startled into alertness by the doorbell. She buzzed in the caller, wondering who could be at the door so late in the day. No deliveries arrived after two o'clock. In strode Mel Jacobson, a newspaper under his arm. He took off his brown felt fedora and placed it on the hat rack. "I know I'm early. Think you can get away before five?"

Vivian could hardly speak. "I'll say you're early. Didn't you say tomorrow night?" She was thrilled to see him again and felt a flutter in a place deep inside her that she hadn't known existed.

Mel looked flustered, but only for a moment, and then sat on the lone chair alongside her desk. "It *is* tomorrow night."

Vivian was flabbergasted. "Nooo, it was after midnight when you brought me home. When you said tomorrow night, I thought you meant . . . well, Tuesday. It's only Monday. Oh, I must look awful. Let me go freshen up."

Mel smiled. "You look just fine. But take your time. Don't mind me. I'll wait." He sat back and opened his *Daily News*.

She grabbed her compact to inspect her face. Her eyes looked droopy. She quickly added a layer of powder to hide the dark circles, grabbed her handbag, and sped to the washroom, nearly bumping into Fred Jacobson, who was rounding the corner into the main office.

"Whoa there, Vivian! What's the hurry?" He looked over her head and chuckled. "Oh, I see. Our veteran has arrived. Good to see you're wasting no time, my boy," he said loudly as Vivian closed the washroom door. "You don't want to let this one get away." Fred aimed his thumb at Vivian's empty chair. "She's a keeper."

"I'll say," said Mel.

When the doorbell buzzed again, Fred answered. "Hello, darling," he said and bent to kiss his diminutive wife. "I've got a few things to finish up in back. Won't be long."

Mel stood. "Aunt Frieda? What are you—?"

"Melvin, our brave soldier, thank God you're home safe. Your uncle and I are going to the movies tonight." She wore high heels but craned her neck to give him a sloppy kiss. She grinned. "You're not looking for a job at the Walker–Jacobson Company, are you?"

"No, um . . . I'm here to pick up Vivian Kolson for a dinner date."

She laughed. "Of course, you're not looking for a job here. Besides, we've got all the help we need with our Vivian. What a treasure. Our only worry is someone will snatch her away." She wagged a finger at Mel.

Mel didn't reply. He stood over Vivian's desk, admiring the neat columns of numbers in the open ledger book.

In the washroom, Vivian was frantic, pinning and re-pinning her hair, freshening and blotting her lipstick, frowning at her reflection. She was dressed in her plainest brown suit. She'd planned to wear her dark blue one with brass buttons and navy-and-white spectator pumps for their date tomorrow night. But instead of tomorrow night, their date was tonight. If she had known Mel had meant tonight, she might have played hard to get and said no, because she'd be dead tired. What if she had said no? His feelings might have been hurt, and he might have never asked her out again. This outfit would have to do. When she emerged from the washroom and gave an extra pat to the back of her head to check if the hairpins had secured her pompadour in place, she nearly crashed into Frieda.

"There you are, my dear," said Frieda. "Looking lovely as ever."

"I thought I heard your voice, Mrs. Jacobson."

Vivian went back to her desk, her face reddening. Were all his relatives going to track Mel's every move? The clannish Jacobsons were different from the Kolsons, whose motto was "live and let live." Growing up, her family had ignored her brothers' gambling because they needed their earnings to keep their household afloat. When her oldest brother left for California, she missed him, but everyone accepted how he'd moved away to seek his fortune in a new frontier. Some neighbors gossiped about her ma's relationship with Aunt Ruthie, but Vivian didn't care. Her ma had never been happier. Vivian wondered if she would ever fit into Mel's family. She shouldn't get ahead of herself. This was only their first date.

Mel said, "Thanks for making the beautiful party last night, Aunt Frieda."

She gave him another kiss and said, "Oh, honey. You know, your uncle and I love nothing better than a good party. What a wonderful occasion to celebrate. Our handsome nephew, safely home from overseas! If only your gentle father had lived to see this day." Mel slumped and sat down. "I'm sure he's watching over you. In fact, he may have found our Vivian for you." Mel tried to bury his face in the newspaper. "Don't you doubt it, Melvin. I have a feeling that's just what that dear man did."

Fred appeared. "Let's grab a bite before tonight's picture," Frieda said. "I hear *Mildred Pierce* is a shoo-in for the Academy Award this year."

"I loved that movie," said Vivian. "Joan Crawford's best yet."

Fred and Frieda Jacobson left arm in arm.

"Let's go," said Mel. "I've got a reservation at Don Roth's Blackhawk."

The Blackhawk! Wait until she tells Jean!

DATING VIVIAN Kolson became Mel's reason for living before he returned to work with his brothers on Maxwell Street. He wanted to impress her and swept her into a whirlwind of Chicago's nightlife, made possible by his ample savings from before and during the army. Vivian was thrilled to go to the swanky restaurants and nightclubs she'd only heard about: the glamorous Chez Paree, Eli's Place for Steak, Henrici's, the Pump Room, and the classic German restaurant the Berghoff. Vivian relived these wondrous places by recounting every detail to Jean: The deft tableside preparation of the surprisingly tasty—anchovies and all—spinning salad bowl at Don Roth's. The tingly bubbles in her nose from a glass of champagne at the Chez Paree that left her lightheaded. And best of all, one night, they sat two tables away from Cary Grant at the Ambassador East's Pump Room. Cary Grant looked more dashing in person than in the movies, but Vivian had the impression that no matter where he was, he was always acting.

Vivian was happy to have a regular date to the movie palaces she adored, although she suspected Mel wasn't as enamored of the movie stars as she was. Since childhood, every weekend, Vivian escaped into the cavernous, air-conditioned shrines during humid Chicago summers and cold winters to take refuge from their crowded flat. Vivian liked to quote lines from her favorite movies, scene by scene. At the end of their dates, they stayed in the car for more kissing, caressing, and exploring as much as they could without going all the way. Heavy petting. Between his room in his ma's apartment and Vivian's strict landlady, they had nowhere to be alone. Vivian was glad he wouldn't disrespect her by inviting her to a hotel or on a weekend in Michigan, although sometimes she half-wished he would press her for more. She wanted him, but also wanted to be the chaste Jewish wife that she was raised to assume men wanted. Why wouldn't Mel Jacobson be any different? Wouldn't he also want her to live up to this ideal?

After several months, Vivian began to worry he might never ask her to marry. He could be one of those men who never wanted a wife. She was nearly twenty-three years old. Mel was nine years her senior. They had no time to waste if they wanted children. If she didn't become a wife and mother, what would her future be like? She'd long ago given up her dream of becoming a schoolteacher. She'd gladly give up the dream of working in a Loop skyscraper to become Mrs. Melvin Jacobson.

What Vivian didn't know was that Liza Jacobson had begun to nag her son to pop the question. "That Kolson girl is the best one from that family. You'd better give her a ring. I'm not getting any younger, and neither are you!"

In the dark theaters, Mel and Vivian held hands. He caressed her fingers, one by one, sliding her Jones Commercial High School class ring on and off.

"What are you doing?" Vivian whispered. "Don't drop my ring in the dark. It took me a long time to save up for my first piece of jewelry."

He shook his head and whispered, "Don't worry. I won't lose it. Keep watching your movie."

Vivian often met Jean after work to dish about their boyfriends. It wasn't unusual for Jean to be dating two guys at once, hoping neither would find out about the other. Vivian was afraid to tell Jean too much about Mel. She didn't want Jean to wonder, if he was so great, why weren't they engaged?

One afternoon at the soda fountain after work, Jean told Vivian she had the best news. "I've found a doctor to bob my nose. Not too pricey. Let's do it together. Two for one. Maybe he will give us a deal."

Vivian was tempted. Jean must have known how this would appeal to her lifelong friend. Vivian was vain to a fault and particularly sensitive about her bulbous nose with a bump at the bridge, just like her father's. When she shopped for hats in department stores, Vivian tried on each one, gazing at her face in the mirror, from every angle, hoping the style could distract attention from the center of her face, disappointed when even the latest style couldn't disguise her prominent facial flaw.

"If you do it, I will too," said Vivian. "Call for the appointments."

"Already did," Jean said with a laugh. "Back-to-back. In three weeks."

The next night over dinner at Eli's Place for Steak, between bites of Lake Superior whitefish, Vivian asked Mel. "I need to know what you think about something. It's important."

"Anything wrong?"

"My nose." Vivian hated to draw his attention to her eyesore. She gave him her sweetest smile. "I'm thinking about getting it fixed."

He stared at her with a look of genuine concern. How she loved his face, those caring, velvety brown eyes, thin eyebrows, warm rosy lips, and his perfectly shaped, straight little nose.

He grabbed her hand. "Why? Are you having trouble breathing?"

She nearly toppled her water glass. "Trouble breathing? Don't you see how ugly my nose is?"

"There's nothing ugly about you, Vivian Kolson. Nothing at all."

That settled it. Mel was the man for her. Proof that he loved her as she was.

The next day, Vivian called Jean, told her to cancel her appointment, and related her conversation with Mel. "He asked if I was having trouble breathing! Can you believe him? I won't go for a nose job."

Jean laughed. "You lucky dog. If I wish on a star, maybe someday I'll find a man as blind to my faults as Mel Jacobson is to yours. Until then, I'm not taking any chances. I'm going through with the operation, no matter how much it might hurt. I've got the money saved up. You know what, Viv? If you ask me, Mel showed up just in time for you. Remember our trips to South Haven during the war? When that guy broke your heart?"

Vivian certainly did remember. That chump wasn't half the man Mel was.

A few weeks later, Mel made a reservation for them at the ritzy Chez Paree nightclub. Vivian wore her best black dress with the brooch that Frieda Jacobson bought for her in New York. She turned her dark hair into a French twist and wore high heels.

After his usual cocktail, Mel cleared his throat. His hand shook and his voice cracked as he took a ring box from the inner pocket of his dinner jacket. Vivian's heart leaped into the back of her throat. She nearly jumped up from the table. She'd been waiting for this moment, ready to say yes, but when she saw the box, she couldn't speak. She looked deep into his pleading brown eyes. She swallowed hard when he snapped open the box and took out the ring. The exquisite, square-cut diamond in a platinum setting took her breath away.

After a moment, in a small voice, she asked, "For me?"

"Of course, it's for you." Mel sounded gruff. "Who else? You're my girl."

He slipped the ring onto her finger. It fit perfectly.

Could this really be happening to her? She felt like the girl from the other side of the tracks, the secretary from the west side who would marry the handsome prince. She tried to remain calm as she adjusted the ring on her finger and stretched her hand out to admire the sparkling stone from a distance. She couldn't wait to show Jean.

1956

"I LOVE how Mel was blind about your nose," said Jackie. "I've got a new appreciation for your husband. But how did he guess your ring size?"

"He told me later," said Vivian. "During our movie dates when we held hands, he took off my class ring and placed it as far as it would go on his own pointer finger. Later, a string around that knuckle revealed my ring size. He's always been a numbers guy and planned for a perfect fit to improve the chances that I'd say yes. He would have been devastated if I'd handed it back. But he shouldn't have worried. Never in a million years.'"

"What a story!" said Jackie. "Time for me to get home. Good luck with your rabbi. Let me know how it goes. I'm curious."

Vivian couldn't stop thinking about what Jackie had shared. She wasn't the only one who had terminated an unwanted pregnancy and wished she'd asked Jackie for more details. What did the abortion feel like? How long did it take her to recover? She chastised herself as she vacuumed. Why did it matter? Most likely, she wouldn't be going ahead with it. She could tell that Mel was against it.

THERE WERE several interruptions during their private dinner-time. Vivian didn't have a chance to ask Mel about going to the rabbi the next day. She was keen to have Rabbi Bornstein explain the Jewish perspective on abortion. The rabbi also had a young family. He might be sympathetic to what they were going through. Wilmette's modern Conservative synagogue was perfect for the Jacobson family. Not strictly Orthodox like their immigrant parents' old shul where you were criticized if you didn't follow every rule. This was another positive indication of their family's good timing to move out here. Times had changed. Vivian couldn't imagine her observant mother daring to approach her traditional rabbi about any womanly matter.

Vivian and Mel had both attended the same west side shul, but when they were dating, Vivian had been shocked when Mel confessed that he didn't believe in God. How could this be true? She knew Mel to be an honest, caring man and a learned Jew. He might say he was not a believer, but his actions spoke otherwise as well as his regular observance of Jewish customs and holidays. That was enough for Vivian. She'd learned from her ma what Hannah's own mama had taught her daughter: How you treat your fellow human beings in this life is what's most important, not how many prayers you recite. That's what it means to be a Jew.

WHEN THEY lay together in bed, Vivian asked, "Mel, are you still awake? I want us to go and talk to Rabbi Bornstein tomorrow. To ask him about what we should do."

"Are you kidding? What can a rabbi tell us? Go to sleep."

"I mean it, Mel. I want his advice."

Mel liked to please his wife. He wouldn't say no to her, but what a waste of time. He stroked her arm. Vivian soon slept, a peaceful look gracing her face.

Talk to a rabbi? Now Mel was wide awake. He had sloughed off formal religious beliefs long before his slog across Europe. Mel observed fellow soldiers who talked tough before the battles and then cowered when the shelling began. That night in Wilmette, when Mel finally fell into a deep sleep, he felt a cool mist surround him. He hadn't felt that familiar presence since his lonely nights in occupied Germany. He reached out his hand and whispered, not wanting to wake Vivian.

"Pa? Is that you?"

"I'm here, my son. I'll always be near you."

"What shall we do about another baby? Do you know what God would tell us?"

"You are a man, my son. A man cannot expect God to make man's choices. You must act with your best judgment as the true mensch, the human being, that you are. Does your wife want another baby?"

"I don't think she knows what she wants." Mel's tears streamed.

"Trust yourself. The answers will come. Az me muz, ken men. If you have to, you can."

"That's what Ma always said. If you have to, you can."

"IF WE have to, we can. If we have to . . ."

Vivian shook him awake. "Mel! You must be dreaming. You're talking in your sleep. What are you saying?"

Mel brushed his face with the back of his hand and reached for her. "We'll do what we have to do. We'll face life's challenges together, whatever they may be. That's how I felt on the night we met."

"That was ten years ago, Mel. You sound schmaltzy. Don't tell me you're getting sentimental? What happened to my no-nonsense, practical husband? Now, go back to sleep."

"We make beautiful children, don't we, Viv?"

"Please. Don't make this any more difficult than it already is."

"Five couldn't be so different from four, am I right? Business is picking up. If we have to, we can."

"Stop it, Mel. I mean it. Everything looks different at night. We'll decide what to do after we talk to the rabbi."

"Don't expect too much from him. I'll go, but mark my words, he won't have the answers. No religion does. That's a truth I learned long ago. We cannot predict the future. Can't know what life has in store for us. Whatever it is, we must find a way to keep going. Get some rest."

Now Vivian was wide awake. Why *did* she feel the need to see a rabbi? Her husband was as wise as any Talmudic scholar. He was right. They would face this challenge together.

CHAPTER TWELVE
RABBI BORNSTEIN

DAY 2: WEDNESDAY

VIVIAN SUGGESTED a white dress shirt and striped tie for Mel to wear to the rabbi's office. He quickly nixed the tie. "I don't need to dress up. It's my day off. And remember, a rabbi is just another man. Do you think he has a private hotline to God?"

Mel had seen too many scams on Maxwell Street to trust anyone who made their living in the religion business—any religion. The only thing Mel liked about this Wilmette rabbi was his modern interpretation during the Rosh Hashanah service. The rabbi didn't pretend that anyone should be as willing to sacrifice a son as Abraham was to prove his faith in God. Barbaric. Mel treasured each of their children and couldn't imagine being willing to sacrifice any one of them. Nothing would ever make him put any of his children purposefully in danger. On Rosh Hashanah, Rabbi Bornstein acknowledged that such a sacrifice would be unthinkable in today's world, but they could learn from the story of Abraham's devotion.

Mel didn't expect any great wisdom from the rabbi about their predicament. He would go along only because Vivian felt Rabbi Bornstein might have answers that could give her peace about her decision. The synagogue administrator led Vivian and Mel into the rabbi's study. Up close, the rabbi looked even younger than when he stood on the bimah during services. When the rabbi motioned them to sit in the two chairs in front of his desk, Mel took note of the sparseness of the man's neatly trimmed light-brown beard and photographs of his smiling blond wife and three laughing children on the credenza behind him. The rabbi's children were not much older than their own four little ones.

"How can I help?" he asked. "Questions about the nursery school? I recall you've got one of the bigger families in our new congregation."

Vivian positioned her pocketbook on her lap to try to hide her stomach. She gripped Mel's forearm and began. "No, Rabbi, we're here about a different family matter. We need your advice."

A worried look crossed the rabbi's face as he looked first to Vivian and then to Mel. "You certainly look to be a happy couple. Well-matched."

Vivian interrupted. "No, no. Our marriage is fine." She turned to smile at Mel.

Mel said, "We have to make a critical decision."

"Go on," said the rabbi.

Vivian said, "It's just, well, I was . . . we were . . . wondering about how Jewish law would apply to something."

"Something we might do. But not for sure," added Mel.

"We only have a few more days to decide," Vivian said.

The rabbi leaned back in his chair and cracked his knuckles. "Only a few days?"

Mel bumped Vivian's arm with his elbow. "Tell him, Viv."

"I'm pregnant again, Rabbi."

"Congratulations! What a sizable family you have!"

"But Rabbi, I don't . . . I don't want—"

The rabbi gave her a solemn look.

"It's too much for me. I'm upset every day. I don't think we can . . . I can . . . genuinely care for a fifth one. We just moved to Maple Street last year, you know. There's no more room in our house. Our oldest is only six—" She began to cry. The rabbi pushed the box of tissues on his desk in her direction. She took one and blew her nose loudly.

Mel spoke up. "Rabbi, my wife is concerned that we could be going against Jewish law if she has an abortion."

The rabbi pulled on his sparse beard and looked from one to the other. Vivian wiped her eyes and gazed at him intently. He said, "You wouldn't have come here today unless you already understood this to be a serious matter. I can't presume to tell you what to do. No one can. But know that the act of abortion is not mentioned anywhere in the scriptures: not in our Torah nor in any other Bible. What comes to my mind are the famous words our ancestor and great teacher Rabbi Akiba wrote in *Wisdom of our Fathers*: 'All is foreseen, yet free will is given.'"

Vivian took a deep breath. She said, with a catch in her voice, "Are you saying we have free will? How can this be up to us? I'm going crazy. You have children. You must understand. What should we do?"

Mel covered her hand with his. "Vivian, this is our decision. Not his." He jerked his thumb toward the rabbi. "As he said, it's not up to God either."

"Your husband is right," said Rabbi Bornstein. "Remember, according to Jewish law, a fetus carries potential for life, but it's not entitled to the same rights as a living person. Even a late-term stillborn is prohibited from burial in a marked cemetery plot. I've known situations when an Orthodox rabbi will mandate an abortion if a woman's life is threatened."

"My own mother considered an abortion when she worried her life could be in danger"—Vivian looked at Mel—"when she was carrying me. How could she? I wouldn't be here!"

The rabbi did not look shocked. "Trust me. I understand how that could be upsetting."

The rabbi swiveled to glance at his family photos on his credenza. Vivian twisted the handle of her pocketbook until he spoke again.

"I have family stories, too," he said, "from before I was born. You and your husband are facing a quandary that many have faced before. I'll share a personal story, one I rarely speak of. I am the youngest of four boys. We were not a family of means. When I was in rabbinical school, my father told me that he and my mother had considered an abortion when she was pregnant with me. Many experienced hard times during the Depression years, but when my father revealed this to me, I became upset. Here I was, about to become a rabbi. What if I had never existed? I went to my head teacher. He told me to remember that we Jews consider the spirit to be indestructible. Ashes to ashes, dust to dust. God holds our souls in His keeping forever no matter what happens: miscarriage, stillbirth, death, and yes, also an elective abortion. In Ecclesiastes, we learn the spirit returns to God."

Vivian began to weep. "I still can't believe it's up to me." She wiped her eyes. "It's too much."

The rabbi's tone was even. "Living with young ones is unpredictable and can be hectic. Many have wrestled with this dilemma. Trust yourself and your husband to make this decision together."

"I trust our doctor too," said Vivian. "He referred me to a man he believes is safe. I'll admit I went to him on Monday, intending to go through with this, but everything about this man scared me—the place, his assistant. I ran out. Before I left, he told me if I want to do this, I must return by next Monday, otherwise it will be too late. Now I don't know what to do."

Mel stood. "Viv, you can't keep going around and around on this. Enough already. Let's go."

"Sit down, Mr. Jacobson." The rabbi looked intently at Mel. "What do *you* want to do?"

"Me?" He looked at Vivian. "Rabbi, we have four beautiful children. My Viv is a wonderful mother." At these words, Vivian sniffled and reached for another tissue. After what she admitted to the rabbi, she felt more like a terrible mother than ever. Mel added, "I may work on Maxwell Street, but don't think our business isn't good enough to support another child."

"I'm not doubting you, Mr. Jacobson, but would another child upset the peace in your home? How would you feel about adding to the strain on your wife?"

Mel leaned over and placed his hand on the rabbi's desk. "Look, I don't want anything to happen to her. I'll go along with her decision as long as she's sure. No second-guessing."

Rabbi Bornstein smiled. "Contemplation of the consequences of our actions is a hallmark of a thoughtful life. But you two must agree, whatever you decide. I often rely on a quotation from Proverbs when I confront a situation without a clear direction, 'For wisdom shall come to your heart, and knowledge will be pleasant for your soul.' Mrs. Jacobson, as long as you and your husband go forward as one, rest easy that you made this choice together. I wish you peace."

Vivian squeezed Mel's hand.

The rabbi asked, "What about coming to services next Saturday morning? You might find answers in the week's Torah portion. Last week we read the last section of Leviticus about the laws surrounding the Jubilee, the biblical fiftieth year, the year of renewal before we begin again. The year when all of the lands, animals, and people must lie fallow and rest. The Jubilee year is a year of forgiveness."

Mel tapped his foot. "Rabbi, I learned about all of this before I was a bar mitzvah. My zayde was a cheder teacher. I mean no disrespect, but I can't attend on Saturdays with our business on Maxwell Street. Weekends are our busiest days."

The secretary knocked and opened the door. "Rabbi, an emergency call is waiting on Line 2."

Rabbi Bornstein stood and said brusquely, "Another congregant needs me."

Vivian and Mel hurried to their feet. "Thank you, Rabbi," said Vivian, still snuffling. "I'll try to attend on Saturday even if Mel can't. Maybe my mother will come with me." She took another tissue before following the secretary out of the office.

As they got into the car to return home, Vivian shook her head. "Can you believe our rabbi's parents considered aborting him?"

"Our lives are not so different from any others'," Mel said. "Are you surprised because he's a rabbi? Remember, we're all human. None of us is better than anyone else."

"Now *you* sound like a rabbi."

"I told you," Mel said, "we don't need a rabbi to decide what's best for us. I would never force you to have a child you couldn't care for. You don't give yourself enough credit. You can take on more than you think." He squeezed her hand.

"Are you saying five won't be so different from four? What would you know about it?" She shimmied out of his grip. "You're away all day long. I can't tell you how often I feel like the kids are driving me crazy. It's hard to be the mean one all day, every day. Easy for you because the children adore you."

"Don't say that. Of course, they love you too," Mel said. "Please don't pick a fight. Not today."

"If I go back, can I be certain this Dr. Boone will be safe? Think about the story of your Aunt Addie. I could be risking my life. What would our children do without a mother? You'd have to find another wife."

"I don't want another wife. Look at me, Vivian. I don't want another wife. I want you." He put his arms around her. "I want you to be happy."

Vivian's mouth drooped. "I can tell that you want this baby," she said. "I'll have him."

*

THAT NIGHT. Vivian slept fitfully, waking many times to check on Billy after hearing his cry. But every time she padded into his room, he was sound asleep, a small smile curled around his bow-shaped, rosy lips, as if he'd just kissed a soft puppy dog in his dreams.

Vivian's unsettled feelings remained. The rabbi asked Mel what he wanted, but he didn't ask her what *she* wanted. What did she want?

She believed Mel when he said he didn't want another wife. She thought back to when they first met, after he returned to Chicago from the war. He'd wanted her more than he'd ever wanted a woman before. She'd decided to give up any notion of an independent career to marry Mel Jacobson and have a family. She'd had no doubt that he was the man for her. She'd felt the electric connection as soon as they met. She'd pledged to be the best wife she could and a devoted mother for their children. She'd be loyal to her husband.

Vivian couldn't imagine life without Mel. She snuggled closer to him. He was truly one of a kind. He respected her. Hadn't he let her take the lead on this big decision? Many men would not do this. She ached to wonder if it would change how he thought about her if she did end this pregnancy. When they married, Mel had lifted her into a world of comfort and stability she'd dared not dream could ever be hers. But she was no longer a naive, unmarried young woman from a poor family, as Ethel liked to remind her. As a child, Vivian's teachers encouraged her to aspire to college and a teaching career, but during the war, she'd resigned herself to less lofty goals. Becoming Mrs. Melvin Jacobson had emboldened her. Didn't they say marriage was built on compromise? She shouldn't be selfish and think only of herself. But what was Mel risking? What was he giving up if they had a fifth child?

Was Mel truly intent on having another one? She would do it for him, but she wasn't certain another child was what he wanted. Could it be only that he didn't want her to think less of him as a man?

A voice inside told Vivian she was fooling herself if she thought she could go through having another child and not fall apart. But didn't both Jackie and Mel say she was stronger than she thought she was?

She would have this baby.

But nagging doubts remained.

CHAPTER THIRTEEN
THE ANNIVERSARY WATCH

DAY 3: THURSDAY

BEFORE VIVIAN opened her eyes the next morning, visions of the women who had borne unwanted children or risked their lives to avoid bearing them floated across her fluttering eyelids: Ma, Aunt Ruthie's teenaged friend Irene, Mel's Aunt Addie, Jackie, and now, Rabbi Bornstein's mother, too. Each with her own reasons. Vivian accepted her situation. She would not risk upsetting the secure family life she shared with Mel.

She rifled through the hangers in her closet looking for maternity clothes. Three months after Billy was born, she'd donated them all to the Wilmette synagogue's rummage sale, vowing never again to wear another tentlike overblouse with an outsized, clownish bow planted above her breasts. It was futile to think she'd find even one remaining elastic-waisted skirt. Another pregnancy would mean she'd have to spend money on those shapeless fashions. Maybe Ethel had a source for castoffs with an unusual flair.

She sighed and threw on her everyday housecoat to retrieve Billy from his crib and take him down to the kitchen, groaning at the sheaf of notes piled on the mail table that Irene had brought home from school the day before. No time to read them now. One errant paper fell to the floor. Vivian bent to pick it up. Large block letters caught her eye. *QUARANTINE: Chicken Pox*. Two children in Irene's class had been diagnosed. This was the season when all of the childhood diseases emerged. Vivian would have to be on the lookout for any telltale lesions among her brood. Chicken pox was nasty. Hard to soothe an afflicted child.

Mel had already made coffee, but he was fidgety as he awaited his breakfast, eager to bolt for work. He quickly ate the soft-boiled eggs and toast Vivian set in front of him. When he finished, he threw down his napkin, rose, and said, "Don't worry, we'll make do," and gave her a quick peck. Then, he grabbed an apple, headed to the downstairs bathroom, and then out to the garage, calling, "See you tonight!"

Within an hour, Billy had thrown up all over Vivian's housecoat, and Linda was wailing for her from upstairs. She could hear Irene and Sandy talking in their room. Vivian's head felt like it would swivel off her neck. As soon as she turned in one direction, she was wrenched without warning to move in another. After all the kids were fed and Irene left to walk to school with the girl from across the street, Vivian called Jackie.

"How'd you do with your rabbi?" Jackie asked her. "Did you decide?"

"Mel wants another one. I can tell. I won't go against him."

"You know, I hate to hear you say this. You should be the one to decide what you want. But I understand you'll do what you have to do. But you'll be the one who will go through another pregnancy and delivery. Not him. We all know what that's like. Then taking care of the new baby, along with the others, will also fall to you. You may think your Mel is a prince, but from what I see, he leaves all the dirty work to you."

Vivian had sworn that she would not cry about this again. "Don't most husbands do that? That's life. Growing up the way I did, I never thought I'd have a home like this. Before I met Mel, I'd begun to think I'd be an old maid stuck working in his uncle's little schmate company, living out my days in a rooming house like Ethel."

"Ha! Vivian Jacobson, I don't believe that for one moment," Jackie said with a laugh. Vivian heard the snap of her lighter. "Now you're feeling sorry for yourself. You can't fool me. You were always a glamour girl with high hopes."

Vivian choked back a laugh. "I don't feel glamorous when I'm rinsing a stinky diaper in the toilet with another slung over my shoulder reeking of spit-up. I could cry when I know that in a few months, I'll be as big as a house again." She let out a sigh. "All after I worked so hard to get back into that dress I wore to the Cohens's kid's bar mitzvah party."

Jackie laughed. "You must have been irresistible that night. That was your downfall. Mel couldn't control himself."

"Not funny. But one way or another, somehow I've got to get back to that awful place and steal back my silver watch. Any ideas how I'm going to do that?" Vivian lit a cigarette and blew out a wavy stream of smoke.

"Why not call your Aunt Ruthie? Maybe she'll save the day."

"Great idea. Listen, if Aunt Ruthie can pick me up, I'll take Sandy with us, but could you come over and watch Linda and Billy for a few hours? It would be during their naptimes. I won't be too long."

"Sure, I can do that. I'm off to the beauty shop in fifteen minutes, but I'll be back by noon."

"You're a lifesaver. I owe you."

When Vivian called Aunt Ruthie and told her she'd decided to go ahead with this pregnancy, she thought she heard a dejected sigh on the other end of the line. Aunt Ruthie didn't question her, only asked if there was anything she could do to help. Vivian explained that she wanted to retrieve the watch she'd left behind on Monday. Could she drive her back to that place? Aunt Ruthie agreed at once. When Vivian shared the address in Chicago's Jefferson Park neighborhood, she thought she heard Aunt Ruthie gasp before saying, "Yes, I know exactly where that is. Oh Vivian, dearest, I'll get to you by one o'clock."

Miss Satwick answered Vivian's call to the office and said curtly, "So you've decided to get back on Dr. Boone's schedule after all?" Before Vivian could object, she went on, "Sorry, he's out for the rest of day. How about tomorrow? Or Monday morning, latest? Those are the only times he's got left for you."

Vivian could picture Miss Satwick's sneers as she peered at the ledger book.

With the strongest voice she could muster, Vivian said, "I don't want an appointment, but I do want to stop over this afternoon to pick up my silver watch."

"I'll say again, like I told you on Monday, dearie, I don't have it. If you insist on coming here, feel free to take another look, but I'll be leaving early today."

AFTER AUNT Ruthie pulled into the driveway, Vivian called Jackie to come over, assuring her they would be back soon, and took off with Sandy in the back seat. Aunt Ruthie gunned her Chevy back toward the city. She only drove on the surface streets, never on the highway, but knew her way to the Jefferson Park neighborhood. The greystone loomed as prominently as ever, with a distinctive, almost regal, elegance compared to the frame buildings on the block. Aunt Ruthie turned off the engine, stepped out, and looked up at the building.

"Hard to believe it's been over thirty years," she said. "A little shabbier, but in many ways, this block looks exactly as I remember it. A step back into a time I never wanted to reenter."

"Is this the same place you took Ma?"

Aunt Ruthie nodded. "Good thing she didn't come with us."

Vivian tried to imagine what this street must have looked like in Ma's day. The trees in the parkway would not have been as tall, but the same two-flats must have been standing. She guessed they were all built after the Chicago fire and soon after the turn of the century, about the same time her parents arrived in Chicago from Russia, and Mel's too. These residences were grander than both the dilapidated wooden structures near Maxwell Street where her parents first lived and the more substantial, but still crowded, buildings of the Great West Side where Vivian had grown up. Would Ma have been less frightened if Aunt Ruthie had brought her to a man in a familiar neighborhood?

"Where are we?" asked Sandy. "Aunt Ruthie, this looks like the street where you and Bubbe live."

"Sandy, no questions," said Vivian. "I told you. Little girls must be quiet here."

The buzzer released them into the entryway, and the three climbed to the second floor. Aunt Ruthie rapped at the door with the brass knocker.

"I wasn't sure you'd show up," said Miss Satwick. "I told you. Dr. Boone isn't here today."

"I'm only here for my watch," said Vivian.

"This doesn't look like the doctor's," said Sandy. "Where's the machine where I see Irene's bones?"

"No fluoroscopes here, kiddo," said Miss Satwick with a chuckle.

Vivian put her finger to her lips. "Sandy. Enough."

"My name is Sandra too," said Miss Satwick, breaking into an uncharacteristic smile.

Sandy perked up. "That's my real name. But I like Sandy better. Is back there where the dining room is?" Sandy pointed to the closed pocket doors.

Her daughter was right to notice the familiar layout. Thank goodness, today there was no stinky smell of gas. The bright early afternoon sun had the surprising effect of softening the room, smoothing its sharp edges with a clarity leading to an unexpected coziness, a stark contrast to the harsh aura when she and Ethel had been here on Monday. The flocked wallpaper looked tired and worn. Nothing to be afraid of.

The etchings? Aunt Ruthie laughed as she pointed to them. "How long have those tired drawings been on the walls?"

Miss Satwick eyed Aunt Ruthie. "No wisecracks. Who are you anyway? Something about you looks familiar."

"Long before your time," said Aunt Ruthie. "But your high forehead, stiff black bun, round blue eyes. You look familiar to *me*."

"You knew my Aunt Agnes?" Miss Satwick looked startled and then composed herself and patted her lacquered hair. She narrowed her eyes. "Don't get smart with me. I know your type."

Aunt Ruthie jerked her thumb at Vivian, who was frantically searching the cushions of the club chairs and was about to open the door to the bathroom. "C'mon, Sandra, or whoever you are. Give her back her silver watch. We didn't come all the way here just to go home empty-handed."

"Hold your horses." Miss Satwick walked over to the desk and pulled open a drawer on the opposite side where the gun had been stashed and stared at Vivian's midsection. Vivian reflexively put her hand on her still-flat stomach as if shielding herself from nuclear radiation. "You sure you don't want me to put you into Dr. Boone's schedule?" She opened the ledger book. "He's still got time on Monday. Didn't he say that day was your last chance? Mind you, you won't get your money back whatever you decide. Might as well go on ahead with it."

On Monday, Vivian had been ready and brave enough to do this, until she panicked and fled. Last night, after the meeting with Rabbi Bornstein, she was ready to acquiesce to what she thought Mel wanted. She remembered Jackie's insistence that she should do what *she* wanted. Today this place didn't frighten her as it did before. Her arms prickled. Could she be bold enough to return on Monday?

Sandy pulled at Vivian's skirt. "Not now, Sandy," Vivian said. "This lady stole my watch. I've got to find it."

"I did no such thing," said Miss Satwick. "How dare you accuse me."

"Your beautiful watch, Mommy?" said Sandy in a shy voice. "Irene and I like to play dress-up with your pretty watch."

"Quiet down now, Sandy."

Aunt Ruthie stooped to ask Sandy. "What did you say about your mommy's watch?"

Sandy started to cry. "Irene put your watch in her sock drawer. She didn't want you to find out."

At first, Vivian wasn't paying attention and then Sandy's words exploded in her ears. She shook her child's shoulders. "You did *what*?!"

"Irene told me not to tell. She said you'd be mad."

"I *am* mad. At you *and* Irene." She waved Aunt Ruthie toward the door. "Now let's go."

"I told you I didn't have it, missus," said Miss Satwick. "Why would I keep your watch? Dr. Boone runs a clean business. We're no thieves."

"Goodbye, Sandra," said Sandy.

"The lady's name is Miss Satwick," said Vivian.

Miss Satwick smiled and waved. "Goodbye, Sandy."

In the car, Vivian said, "Don't tell Daddy you came here with me today. You and Irene will both be punished for taking my watch without asking. No TV tonight."

Sandy wailed, "Not even *Mickey Mouse Club*? *Wagon Train* is on tonight!"

"I don't care if the Miss America pageant is on. I said no TV!"

When they pulled into the driveway in Wilmette, Irene was on the sidewalk. "Aunt Ruthie! What are you doing here?"

"Your mommy needed a ride," said Aunt Ruthie and then turned to Vivian. "Think about what that woman said. I can't tell you what to do, but you do have a few days left to go back and take care of this. I want you to think seriously about it."

Jackie greeted them as they walked in. "Did you get the watch?"

"Long story. It's here. Irene and Sandy hid it."

Jackie raised her eyebrows. "So it was never there in the first place. Tell me, how did it feel to go back?"

"You know, not half as bad as I thought. It didn't stink of that chloroform or whatever he uses. It's just an ordinary, two-flat apartment on the northwest side. Nothing sinister. Of course, that sarcastic doctor wasn't there."

Vivian remembered how Aunt Ruthie recognized the greystone as the same place she'd taken Ma years ago. She'd keep that to herself and not tell Jackie. She also decided not to tell Mel that it was the same place.

Irene tugged at her sleeve. "I have papers from school. The teacher said every mommy should read them right away."

"Put them on the counter with the mail. I'll look at them later. First let me say goodbye to Aunt Ruthie and Mrs. Reisman. Thanks a million. Really, you two are the best. I don't know what I'd do without you."

"Think nothing of it," said Jackie.

Aunt Ruthie added, "You know you can always count on me," and gave her a hug.

Jackie dashed out the door. "I've got to run and get my pineapple upside-down cake into the oven."

Irene raced Sandy to the TV. Vivian hung their jackets in the closet.

"Hold on, girls. Remember, your punishment. No TV today. Bring me my watch. Right now!"

Irene gave Sandy a little punch on the arm. "You told?"

"She made me."

Irene dragged her feet up the stairs and returned with the silver watch. Vivian affixed it to her wrist, pausing to admire the glittering face and clasp she'd never expected to see again. Those rascals! She must have been such a wreck on Monday on her way into the city to meet Ethel that she didn't realize she hadn't worn the watch that day. She'd forget her head if it weren't attached to her neck.

What could she make for the kids' dinner? Nothing fancy. Salami sandwiches for the kids. Open a can of Campbell's chicken noodle soup. A pan of red Jell-O with fruit cocktail was in the fridge, ready to go. Upstairs, the baby was crying. Time to get him up. She had veal cutlets for her dinner with Mel later.

Upon his return home, Mel ran through his usual routine. When he perused the mail, he called out to Vivian in the kitchen. "Viv, you didn't tell me about this. Did you see what Irene brought home from school?"

"In a minute. I'm fixing our dinner."

"Honey, this is important. Children in her class have the German measles."

German measles?

Vivian felt the blood drain from her hands. Mel went upstairs to wash up. Vivian set the table for the two of them and, shaking, she walked over to read the school paper: *Quarantine: Three children in your child's class have German measles. Dangerous to pregnant women if exposed.*

What had been her pa's favorite Yiddish saying? "Man plans, and God laughs." She and Mel always contributed to the March of Dimes. This year Vivian had been Maple Street's block captain, collecting door-to-door for the worthy cause to end polio. Now with Dr.

Salk's vaccine—how her girls had hated those lifesaving but painful shots—there was a possibility it would no longer be a crippling threat. Impossible to imagine they might see this in their lifetimes. Vivian had received a notice that the March of Dimes would soon shift its support away from finding a cure for polio to fund research on causes of birth defects. Why babies were born with deformations remained a mystery, but it was common knowledge that if a pregnant woman contracted German measles early in her pregnancy, the baby could be born blind, deaf, or worse. Vivian wasn't sure if she'd ever had the German measles. If she had, she might be immune. But in her family, no one had kept track of who had what or when.

Vivian sat down, her head spinning. She knew she would love any child that she and Mel would have, handicapped or not, but the extra difficulty to care for such a child alongside the other four felt overwhelming. She remembered the child who lived downstairs from them in the city, one year older than her Irene, who was born with brain damage. Everything had been fine until during the delivery, oxygen was cut off to the infant's brain. The baby survived, but she would never live independently. A tragedy.

Mel came downstairs. "Vivian, I know what you're worried about, but don't panic. Keep Irene home from school tomorrow. I see you picked up your watch."

"You won't believe this. Irene and Sandy had it all along. They were playing dress-up with my watch and hid it from me!"

He laughed. "The little tricksters!"

"Not funny. I'm punishing them. No TV."

"No wonder the house is quiet."

"I could use some peace," said Vivian. "Let's eat before our dinner gets cold."

He nodded, and she went to the stove. The room spun around as if she were riding the Tilt-A-Whirl at Kiddieland amusement park.

"Are you OK? Viv, sit down. Take it easy."

"Easy? Now I've got to call Dr. Goldblum to ask what to do about this German measles scare. Should I call his answering service right now?"

"Wait until morning," said Mel. "What can he do? Better watch out if he prescribes any medicine. We've both read about those drugs that cause babies to be born without arms."

"Don't even say it, Melvin Jacobson. Don't you think if we know about those drugs, Dr. Goldblum does too? I'm scared enough as it is. If Ma heard you talk like that, she'd call out 'keinehora' faster than you can say Jiminy Cricket."

"Foolish superstitions," he said. "I believe in science."

"But you're no doctor," said Vivian. "That's why I rely on Dr. Goldblum. I don't feel hungry anymore. I'm going upstairs to lie down. You clear the dishes tonight."

CHAPTER FOURTEEN

DR. GOLDBLUM'S GUIDANCE

DAY 4. FRIDAY.

"IRENE SEES a spot on my tummy!" Sandy cried from the bedroom as if she'd identified a rare bird in the wild.

Vivian took in a sharp breath. What to do? Mel would still be in traffic en route to work. Can't reach him for another hour. "Be right there." She rushed up the stairs.

"See!" Irene proudly pointed out her discovery alongside her sister's belly button. "Our teacher told us to be on the lookout."

There was one blazing scarlet raised spot. But was it a sign of German measles? Unlike the usual measles that Irene and Sandy had both contracted last spring, one after the other, Vivian had heard that symptoms for the German measles were mild—few spots or none at all. She tried to keep a poker face, not wanting to alarm the girls. Sandy was already shaking and whimpering. No matter if close contact would put her at risk, Vivian had to care for her child.

"Quick! Sandy, let's get you into the tub."

Vivian ran the water as Sandy stripped off her pajamas. Linda was wailing to get out of her crib. Baby Billy was crying too. They would have to stay put for now. She had only one pair of hands.

Irene followed her into the bathroom. "Why is Sandy having a bath in the morning?"

"Irene, please. Leave Sandy alone. Go downstairs and make toast for everyone."

"OK, I'll be the mommy today."

Ha! Her daughter should know how ready Vivian was to hand over this job.

In the tub, Vivian patted Sandy gently all over with a washcloth and Dial soap. Tears ran down both of their faces.

"Do I have the Germans?" asked Sandy.

"I don't know, honey. It's probably nothing."

Vivian hoped saying the words aloud would make it true. She bundled her trembling child into a towel and settled her into the overstuffed easy chair in the bedroom with its connected bathroom that she shared with Mel. Vivian's sanctuary, where she rarely had the chance to retreat.

Irene came back upstairs and perched on the ottoman in Vivian's bedroom. "Am I staying home from school today?"

Vivian nodded. She didn't need another one at home today, but she had to keep her from further exposure to the children in her class.

"Goody," Irene said. "Sandy, let's play."

"Irene, listen to me. Stay separated from Sandy. Just in case."

Irene kicked at the floor. "Just in case, what?"

"In case Sandy has German measles."

"If she does, will I get it too?"

"I don't know. I don't know." She shook Irene's shoulders. "Did you make toast like I asked you to?"

"Hasn't popped yet."

Vivian took a deep breath. She went to Linda, who had finally stopped wailing and shaking the rails of her crib. She lifted her out, brought her down to the kitchen, and set her into the high chair. Irene trailed after her and went to the toaster. Vivian hurried back upstairs to retrieve Billy and brought him into the kitchen. With a loud sigh, she settled into a chair and unbuttoned to feed him.

Irene looked away from her and said, "I'll cook breakfast for Linda." She painstakingly spread margarine over a piece of toast and placed it onto Linda's highchair tray while Vivian nursed the baby.

"When will he eat real food?" asked Irene.

Vivian had been wondering the same thing. "Soon. Very soon."

Linda threw the buttered toast onto the floor.

"Irene, pick that up. Please."

Irene asked, "When can Sandy play?"

"Please. Don't bother her. Turn on the TV. Isn't *Ding Dong School* on now?"

"That's not real school. I'll put on one of Daddy's army shirts from the closet and play war. Sandy will be an enemy German. I'll hide from her."

Vivian held up her hand. "Don't. She might be sick." Her voice rose. "I won't tell you again. Leave your sister alone."

"Did Daddy almost die in the war?" asked Irene.

"No, he fought in Germany, but he wasn't wounded," said Vivian. "Thank goodness he came home safe. But he did get sick in Wisconsin. He caught pneumonia. And he was allergic to the sulfa medicine."

"Are me and Sandy allergic too?"

"I hope not. Now go turn on the TV."

Vivian finally called Mel and told him about Sandy's spot. He spoke harshly. He didn't have time to talk. She held back from demanding he'd better not speak to her like that.

"Wait a minute, Mel. What if Sandy does have German measles? What if I catch it?"

"Vivian, please. You don't know anything for sure. Anyway, what can I do about it? Look, I'm busy here. The insurers of a damaged railroad car sold us the whole lot of whiskey at ten cents on the dollar. Only a few bottles are broken. It's all-hands-on-deck to unload and stack the cases in the basement. Call me later."

"Careful you don't get a hernia."

Mel had already hung up and didn't hear her last wisecrack.

Didn't he understand how serious this could be? When Mel was away on Maxwell Street, it was his whole world, as if nothing in Wilmette mattered. She'd have to take care of this herself, like everything else around here. She decided to call Dr. Goldblum to ask his advice despite what she knew Mel would say: "Doctors aren't gods. Make up your own mind."

Vivian carried Billy up to his crib and went back down to the kitchen to call the doctor. She was poised to dial the number until Linda tossed her toast again, this time along with the plate, onto the floor. Thank goodness it didn't break. Vivian hung the receiver back on the wall and brought Linda a handful of Cheerios to scatter over the messy breadcrumbs on the highchair tray. The toddler picked them up daintily, one by one, as if she were a grand lady at high tea. Vivian sank into a chair, panting, as winded as if she were the first mother training to break the four-minute mile.

Vivian settled herself, picked up the phone again, and hesitated before dialing the last digit. She took a deep breath, and completed the call. When the receptionist asked if this was an emergency, Vivian said not exactly, but she must speak with the doctor today.

"Expect a callback during his lunch hour."

Hours to wait. Vivian called Jackie. When she answered, Vivian couldn't hold it in any longer and began to sob.

"I can't understand what you're saying. What's this about Sandy? Hold on. I'm coming over."

"No, no, you can't. She might have the German measles."

"Don't worry. We've all had everything over here. Oh wait, now I get it. Talk to me."

"I put a call into Dr. Goldblum's office. He is supposed to call back around noon. To tell you the truth, I'm embarrassed to keep calling him. He must think I'm a basket case."

"I'm sure he's heard every woman's tale of woe from here to

Timbuktu. Don't be ashamed. He knows you. And Mel. Call me after you talk to him."

Linda was pounding on the tray. Vivian made a soft-boiled egg and spoon-fed it to her. When she checked on Irene, she was lost in a book.

"What are you reading?" Vivian called.

"*Ginger Pye*. The librarian gave it to me to borrow when Daddy and I went there on Wednesday after school. She said it's a book for good readers."

Her bright girl. Maybe Vivian was doing something right, after all. If all went well, Irene would outshine her mother and graduate from college. Vivian was proud of Irene, but she was wistful to recall how she'd had to transfer from the college track at Marshall High to Jones Commercial secretarial school. She wanted their children to have the best opportunities, but tried not to be resentful of all she'd missed.

Vivian went up to her room to check on Sandy. Asleep. Good. Let her rest. She went back to put Linda in the playpen, then back up to gather a load of laundry to take down to the basement. All was still. For now. In the rare quiet, she began to fold the clothes she'd brought up earlier from the dryer.

The phone rang at noontime, startling Vivian, who was making peanut butter and jelly sandwiches for the girls' lunch. She poked her head around to see Linda kicking the bars of the playpen, took a deep breath, and lifted the receiver.

"Vivian? Dr. Goldblum here. How can I help?"

Everything tumbled out in a rush: how she went to Dr. Boone and left, but had until Monday to return, how she thought Mel wanted to have another and she'd agreed, but wasn't completely sure, but now—she could hardly croak out the words—this morning when it was possible Sandy had German measles, she didn't know what to do.

She asked, "Could the baby be at risk?"

“Calm down,” he said. “First, no one can say with certainty if she has German measles or not. It’s hard to detect because the symptoms are mild. Keep an eye out to see if she develops a fever. And Vivian, even if I could determine whether she contracts it and you catch the virus, I couldn’t know whether or not the fetus would be affected.”

Vivian’s tone was high-pitched. “Whatever I decide is wrong.” Her words came out in uneven splashes like water from a clogged kitchen faucet.

“Vivian, take two deep breaths. Sit down.”

She obeyed. Vivian stretched the phone cord to the kitchen table and sat. In the playpen, Linda began to whine.

“Listen closely, I don’t have long to talk,” said the doctor. “Down deep, what do you feel you want to do about this pregnancy? Can you and Mel wholeheartedly welcome another child into your family?”

Vivian was silent at first. “I’m not sure about Mel. But when you asked me this same question in your office last week, I was absolutely certain I couldn’t take care of another.”

“That’s why I referred you to Dr. Boone.”

Vivian sighed. “He scared me. No one except you had ever examined me before.”

“Vivian, be reasonable. I’m not the only obstetrician in Chicago. You may not care for him, but trust me, I would not send you to anyone who would put you in danger.”

“I know that, but I was scared. After running out, I feel ashamed to go back. But now I’m confused. I think Mel’s pride won’t let him admit that supporting another would be a strain. We’re already stretched to the limit. But in my heart, I don’t want another. What do you think I should do?” Her words came in spurts, her breath jagged.

“Calm yourself,” he instructed. “No one can decide except you. Not even Mel. You’re an intelligent woman, Vivian. I’ll share my strategy when I’m faced with a difficult decision. Do you ever make a list of pros and cons?”

"Not for something this important."

"I understand it's complex. Yes, there are significant consequences with whatever you decide, but you might be surprised how this process can provide clarity. I have confidence in you to decide what's best for you and your family."

Dr. Goldblum's belief in her meant the world to Vivian. She was proud how he trusted her to make this choice.

"Do you have pencil and paper handy?" he asked.

She always kept a notepad and ballpoint pen on the countertop next to the phone.

"Take another deep breath and write this question across the top of the page: 'Shall I continue this pregnancy?'" He directed her to write two columns: *Reasons to Continue* and *Reasons to Abort.*

As Vivian wrote the words, her breathing became even. Her ideas tumbled out, and she listed them under each column. She was still writing when Dr. Goldblum said, "I must get back to my appointments now. Keep going. Take a break and later come back to review your lists. Add and cross off those items that don't feel right. Consider the overall effect. If you do decide that you want to go back to Dr. Boone, call this afternoon to make an appointment for Monday. You can change your mind up until the last minute, even on Monday morning. Trust yourself. No human being can predict the future. Be proud you made a difficult decision based on how you felt and what you knew at the time. As you know, my answering service is available twenty-four hours. They can reach me anytime, but I trust you won't need to call me this weekend."

"Thank you, Doctor."

"Vivian, you must know how fond I am of you and Mel and your family. I wish you all the best. Goodbye for now."

He was wise and so kind. She hated to hang up. As soon as she did, she jotted two more notes on each side. Then, she checked on Linda and took her upstairs to change her. Thank goodness, Billy was napping. She peeked in on Sandy, who was still asleep and curled around the big-eared, stuffed monkey she adored. Vivian bent down to feel her forehead and then pressed her lips against it to be certain it was cool. No sign of the fever that Dr. Goldblum had warned about. Perhaps she wasn't sick.

Before Vivian returned to the kitchen, she took a few steps down to the den and saw Irene doggedly working on a jigsaw puzzle with a picture of the Eiffel Tower. Maybe someday she and Mel could find a way to travel to Paris. He'd been there during the war. Vivian had always dreamed of taking a European vacation.

She sat gnawing on her ballpoint pen and reading over what she'd written. She lit a cigarette, exhaled slowly, and added a fourth idea under *Reasons to Continue*:

I couldn't have any children ten years ago. It's selfish to say I don't want this one.

Her stomach rumbled. She went to the Frigidaire and took out what was left of Jackie's coffee cake and brought the plate to the table. She cut a thick slice, took a few nibbles, chewed slowly, and swallowed. Another reason for the "cons" popped into her head. Dare she be so bold to add it? Why not? She scribbled down her deepest yearning, gasped to see it in her own handwriting.

Vivian stubbed out the cigarette burning in the ashtray and read it again:

Otherwise, I might never go to college for a teaching degree.

She remembered how Miss O'Grady had encouraged her to study hard in high school so that she could go to college. Vivian had given up her childhood dream long ago to take the one-gal office job at Walker–Jacobson Company, years before she met Mel. A few weeks ago, she had been ready to take the beginning course at the Teachers College in September. A fifth child would mean she would have to put the plan on hold again—maybe forever.

The phone rang. Jackie. "How was the call with your doctor?"

"Better than I expected."

"What are you going to do?"

"I'll tell you later. After I'm sure I'm sure."

The phone rang again. Aunt Ruthie, this time, reminding her about Shabbos dinner.

Vivian's voice cracked, but refused to reveal dismay. "We can't go. Sandy might have the German measles."

"Stay put. Your mother and I will bring dinner to you. You won't have to do anything. It'll be just us. Ethel's going out to play cards tonight."

"Are you sure you're not afraid to catch what she has?"

"Vivian, we're too old for that to be any danger to us. Stop worrying about every little thing. Your mother and I can take care of ourselves."

When Mel called, she told him Ma and Aunt Ruthie were bringing over dinner. "That's a break," he said. "Did you talk to Goldblum?"

"Yes. I'll tell you all about it when you get home."

Vivian looked at her list again.

"Give me a hint. What did he say about the German measles?" Mel sounded hoarse.

"Nothing definite, but he made me stop and think about what it is I feel about continuing this pregnancy."

Mel's voice was muffled as if he were covering the receiver to talk to someone else. "Tell him I'll be right there." He came back to her and said, "What about how *I* feel? Don't we need more time to be sure?"

"Mel, we're out of time."

He sounded tired. "Let's talk more tonight. I'll leave as soon as I can, but remember, rush-hour traffic on Fridays is slow."

After she hung up, Vivian lit another cigarette and read over what she had written one more time. Dr. Goldblum was right: This was not easy. The final decision would be irreversible. From her first misgivings, Mel promised she'd have the last word to decide what was best for her and for their family. It was time she stopped deferring to him. She'd been inclined to do that automatically because that was what women were supposed to do or because she was a Kolson who wasn't good enough for the Jacobsons. She was stronger than that. She wanted to accomplish more than she had, not just for herself, but she wanted her children to be proud of her. Not to see her as cook, housecleaner, and laundress, nagging at them all the time.

VIVIAN READ over her list again:

Shall I continue this pregnancy?

Pros: Reasons to Continue

1. *I love each one of my babies. Each child is different.*
2. *Another unique sibling for the other children—maybe a brother for Billy?*
3. *Mel is a good provider for all of us. He's proud to do this.*
4. *Mel fears for my safety if I have an abortion.*
5. *I couldn't have any children ten years ago. It's selfish to say I don't want this one.*

Cons: Reasons to Abort

1. *My nerves are shot. I can't handle another. Some days I feel like I'm losing my mind.*
2. *No more room in our house.*
3. *Extra expenses—maternity clothes, diaper service, college savings accounts.*
4. *Less time to pay attention to the four children we have. I already neglect them more than I like to admit.*
5. *Otherwise, I might never go to college for a teaching degree.*

Vivian pondered number five on the list of *Reasons to Abort*. Yes, it was time to consider what she wanted. To do what was best for her and her children's futures.

She dialed Dr. Boone's office.

"Monday. Ten o'clock sharp," said Miss Satwick. "You're in the book. Are you sure this time, dearie? No running away?" Her gravelly voice sounded like a character on one of the girls' cartoons. She cackled. "And remember, don't wear that fancy watch of yours." She paused. "Only kidding."

Vivian responded with a sad little laugh. One by one, she tore off both sheets on the notepad that detailed her list, smoothed down the pages, and folded them neatly in half. A strange flicker rose up from deep in her low abdomen, a fluttering that flowed through her body, down to her toes and up through her torso, arms, fingers, and spiraled around her chest. The warmth radiated through her neck to the top of her head. She'd rekindled a flame of hope for herself: who she was, who she might yet become, and what she might yet accomplish as her own woman—separate from being Irene's, Sandy's, Linda's, and Billy's mother; and Mel's wife.

FRIDAY NIGHT

MEL HAD walked in the door only a few minutes before Aunt Ruthie and Hannah rang the bell. "Let me help you, Mother Kolson," he said, taking a tinfoil-covered platter from her hands.

Aunt Ruthie, carrying a tureen, nodded her head toward her car. "After you put that away, there's another vegetable dish on the back seat and a lemon poppyseed cake on the floor."

"Bubbe!" screamed Irene. "And Aunt Ruthie! Why aren't we going to your house? Is it because of Sandy's spot?"

"Your bubbe and I are happy to take a ride," said Aunt Ruthie.

Hannah added, "Can't be too careful."

Irene hugged Aunt Ruthie around her knees. "Can you sleep over?"

Vivian spoke harshly, hands on her hips. "Irene, you know better. There are no extra beds in our house."

"Bubbe could sleep in my bed, and Aunt Ruthie could sleep in Sandy's. We'll put our pillows and blankets next to them and sleep on the floor like we are cowgirls on a ranch."

Aunt Ruthie laughed and then joined Hannah, who was scurrying around, setting places at the dining room table.

Mel strode in. "What's all this? Nobody sleeps on the floor in my house!"

They gathered around the table. Hannah asked Vivian to bless the candles because the meal was in her home. Vivian covered her eyes with her hands, mimicking what she'd learned from her ma and what Hannah had learned from her mama in Russia. Vivian murmured the traditional blessing and lingered, keeping her eyes covered, adding prayers for continued good health for Mel, the children, Ma, Aunt Ruthie, and the whole extended family. Whenever Vivian had a chance for a silent prayer, this was always what she prayed for. Today she also added a prayer for compassion to accept her decision.

After dinner, Irene asked, "Is Sandy all better? Can she help me with the jigsaw puzzle?"

Vivian gave her the OK. She hadn't seen another spot, and Sandy had no signs of the fever Dr. Goldblum had warned about. Before dinner Vivian checked for the spot Irene spied in the morning. Disappeared. Perhaps it had been only a mosquito bite. The girls raced each other to the den. Vivian took Linda and Billy upstairs and settled them in their cribs. The other adults relaxed around the table, drinking tea and coffee.

Mel helped himself to another slice of cake. "Delicious. Reminds me of the lemon poppyseed cake my ma baked."

"Couldn't possibly be as tasty as that," teased Aunt Ruthie.

Vivian returned to the table. "I want to tell you my news."

Mel tapped his thumb on the tablecloth.

Aunt Ruthie stared at Vivian and put down her fork.

"News?" asked Hannah.

Vivian took a deep breath. "Mel has agreed. We are happy with the four children we have. I made the appointment for Monday morning."

"Thank goodness," sputtered Ruth.

Mel squirmed. When Vivian had shared her decision with Mel, he'd voiced his concern that she might regret this later, but promised he wouldn't block her.

Hannah said, "Melvin, let's hear from you."

Mel spoke slowly, "If Vivian is sure, I am, too."

Vivian met his eyes with a million thank-yous.

Aunt Ruthie's eyes were somber, but her mouth widened into a crooked smile. "What do you need from us?"

Vivian looked from her ma to Aunt Ruthie and back to her ma. "Would you go to services here in Wilmette with me tomorrow morning?"

"I like that idea," said Hannah. "Shul is always the best place to think. And the best place for God to find His way to you. Every woman has her own reasons to make such a decision."

Vivian reached for Mel and squeezed his hand.

Aunt Ruthie said, "Vivian, dearest, you are your mother's daughter. Tomorrow I'll drive you two to the synagogue and pick you up afterward, but I won't go inside with you. I no longer feel the need for formal religion."

Hannah said, "We'll talk over lunch afterward."

Ruth gazed out the window into the nighttime backyard. The glowing eyes of a raccoon stared at her through the window. "Like your mother said, many women throughout generations have made this decision for their own reasons. No matter how urgent, it doesn't lessen the agony each one feels. I remember my friend Irene's anguish and wish she could have found a way to end that pregnancy without taking her own life. I think of her often and miss her deeply."

Hannah wrung her napkin. "I, too, had such a secret."

"Aunt Ruthie told me what you wanted to do," said Vivian. "But, Ma, here I am."

Ruth and Hannah exchanged serious looks. The Shabbos candles were close to burning out, flickering as erratically as the last gasps of a drowning man. Hannah twisted her fingers around her napkin.

"Ma?" Vivian reached for her hand as the girls raced up from the den. "Was there another secret?"

"What secret, Bubbe?" asked Irene, who had come back from downstairs.

"This is grown-up talk," said Mel. "Not for children."

Vivian stood up and said, "Upstairs." She pointed. "Now. It's past your bedtimes. Brush your teeth and get into your pj's."

"Do we have to?" whined Sandy.

Mel insisted, "Mommy said *now*. I'll come up to read you a story."

After they left, Vivian asked, "Ma, what happened?"

Hannah examined her long fingers where the reflected light from the candles danced across her fingernails.

Aunt Ruthie said, "Not here. We'll tell you tomorrow."

Mel returned with the girls, dressed in matching navy-and-white striped pajamas.

Vivian said, "Now say your good nights, get into bed, and recite the Shema prayer together."

Mel added, "Then go to sleep. Mommy and I will check on you later."

"Listen to Daddy," said Vivian. "It's a special night for me to visit here with Bubbe and Aunt Ruthie. Good night, sleep tight."

"Don't let the bedbugs bite," Irene and Sandy sang in chorus.

"What do these girls know of bedbugs?" asked Hannah.

"Mommy taught us the rhyme," said Irene.

"Oy," said Hannah. "What nonsense are you teaching these girls?"

Vivian looked sheepish. Of course, her girls didn't know about bedbugs. They were growing up in Wilmette. Locusts, maybe, but no bedbugs. Vivian was the youngest, but she remembered. All the Kolson children did.

With the girls safely upstairs, Vivian spoke softly, because the noise carried to every part of their open-plan house. "For my appointment on Monday, Ma, will you and Aunt Ruthie take me to Dr. Boone?

"Dr. Boone?" Hannah gasped and grabbed Vivian's hand. "How can this be? I swore I would never go back to that man. And now, my miracle child, my Vivian goes to him?"

"Can't be the same man," said Ruth. "But who knows? Perhaps, the man is his son."

Mel returned. As he collected the dirty dishes, he said, "You don't know. Boone may not be his real name. Abortion has always operated under the table, like any illegal operation. Where there's money to be made, unsavory people will swarm in. They'll be payoffs for protection from the police and anyone else who wants to challenge them. But I'm sure this guy is as good as you can expect from any of them, because Dr. Goldblum gave you his name. Goldblum has been around for a long time and knows what's what. On Monday, I insist on going with you, Viv. Afterward, I can take you to your ma's and Aunt Ruthie's place to rest. I'll go on to work and pick you up at the end of the day to bring you home."

Vivian put her arms around Mel's neck. Her dear husband. None better.

Aunt Ruthie said, "Mel, sit. I'll take the plates," and began stacking them.

"No," said Mel. "Let me wash up. If you're driving to the city and back out here again in the morning for services, you'd better leave now. Vivian will return your serving pieces tomorrow, all clean."

"Good plan," said Aunt Ruthie. "After I drop you two off at the synagogue tomorrow, there's a bookstore I've been meaning to explore not far away, in downtown Winnetka. I'll go there while you two seek your peace."

Hannah jabbed her with her elbow. "Don't be a kidder. Have respect."

"I'm not kidding, my dear friend. I used to find peace there, but no more."

AS RUTH drove them back into the city, Hannah tapped her hand on the dashboard. "Are you sure what our Vivian will do is right? She might regret this forever. She's strong and healthy. Doesn't she have the perfect life in Wilmette? What's one more baby?"

"You know far better than I do," said Ruth, "because I never wanted children. But I'll tell you, from what I see, our Vivian is overwhelmed out there so far from the city. I worry she could have a nervous breakdown if she's pulled in too many directions. And what about her dream to go to college to become a teacher? She mentioned that again only a few months ago. Another baby would make that impossible."

Hannah stared out the window into the darkness. "Yes, she'd wanted to be a teacher ever since she was a girl. But now she's a married woman and a mother too. She can't go to college."

"Why not?" said Ruth. "What would be the harm in making a life for herself away from Maple Street?"

Hannah spoke quietly, as if speaking more to herself than to Ruth. "She did like to stay after school to help that favorite teacher of hers. Came home full of chalk dust all over her good sweater. Do you remember that teacher's name?"

"Of course I do," said Ruth. "Miss O'Grady."

Hannah said, "Yes, I remember now. She encouraged Vivian to go to the World's Fair." She put her hand on Ruth's shoulder. "I remember your boyfriend who worked in the mayor's office got us the tickets. What a treat you gave us that day." Hannah had a faraway look in her eyes. "Maybe it *is* possible. My Vivian, in college? My mama would have been proud. None of my other children made it. Ethel has a harder life than she deserves, but insists it's the life she chooses. This country has much to give, but also there are many places to stumble. I didn't do enough for my children."

Ruth reached for her hand. "You did everything you could."

Hannah sighed. "Vivian wanted to stay in school, but when my eldest moved to Los Angeles after Abe left, Vivian had to go to work. So young, but we needed her. I kept her from college."

At a stoplight, Ruth turned to face Hannah. "Stop blaming yourself. Those were rough times. I shouldn't have to remind you how this life holds many surprises, no matter when or what country we live in. We all lived through the Depression and the Second World War. Don't blame yourself, and don't criticize your daughter's decision. She will need us when she returns after the procedure with this Dr. Boone."

"Do you think it's time I told her about why her pa left us? Because of what I did?"

"Yes, it is time. I've got a hunch that she was old enough on the night he left to already have an idea about what happened. We'll tell her together tomorrow after services at our lunch. I'll be right next to you."

CHAPTER FIFTEEN
FORGIVENESS

DAY 5: SATURDAY

VIVIAN'S HEART soared every time she entered the gleaming building that housed Wilmette's Congregation Beth Shemesh. At her first visit, when she and Mel attended the prospective members' coffee hour, the stark lines of modern architecture left her in awe. The gleaming building was nothing like the old west side neighborhood shul with its dirt-caked limestone facade. Inside, Wilmette's new synagogue was unfinished. The unpainted women's bathroom patiently awaited its first wallpaper treatment like bare tree limbs poised for springtime's leafy coverings.

As a married woman respectful of her ma's custom, Vivian wore her best beige boiled wool hat with a broad brim and grosgrain ribbon. Today, alongside her daughter, Hannah wore a brown felt fedora. Unthinkable for Hannah to enter a house of worship with a bare head, no matter that many women in this congregation did not wear hats.

Rabbi Bornstein, dressed in a gray business suit, hurried past them toward his study. "Mrs. Jacobson! Good morning! I'm glad you're here."

"Let me introduce my mother."

"Welcome," he said. "Your daughter has a beautiful family. Go inside. Make yourselves comfortable. Services will begin shortly."

Hannah smiled. "The rabbi looks so young," she whispered as Vivian steered her into the sanctuary. "Not much of a beard." Vivian put a finger to her lips.

No permanent seats—only folding chairs lined up squarely in rows with an occasional one pushed aside. Vivian chose an empty row away from a group of noisy teenage girls and boys in an attempt to put her mother at ease. She recognized a friendly middle-aged couple whom they'd met at the new members' dinner and waved.

Hannah looked puzzled. "Can women sit anywhere?" She scanned the space. "Even near the men?"

"Ma, please. These are modern ways."

"This shul feels like a church to me," said Hannah, and pointed to a geometric array of colored glass windows.

Vivian was annoyed by her mother's disapproval. She found the windows stunning. On bright days, as the sun moved across the sky, the windows changed from burnt orange to yellow, from deep purple to a shimmering pale lavender. The changing colors mesmerized her during the prayers.

"I shouldn't criticize," said Hannah. "I'm used to the old ways. Maybe it's time to change." Hannah spoke in a softer, more contemplative tone. "Shemesh means sun. The House of Sun. I see how these beautiful windows bring in the sunlight to renew us all."

Vivian squeezed her mother's hand. She was grateful to live in a changing world striving to equalize the divisions between men and women. At their old shul, Jewish education wasn't offered to young girls. Her oldest brothers weren't interested. Vivian yearned for the studies offered to Max. How unfair. How could women's roles be less consequential than men's? Weren't women responsible to keep the household traditions? Responsible to teach the children? Vivian didn't want her daughters' dreams to be shortchanged and settle for less in life.

Hannah mused, "Now that I'm old, I can laugh at myself. I used to think there was only one way for everything in this life. Ruth jokes with me, saying, 'There's a right way, a wrong way, and Hannah's way.'"

Vivian laughed. "Leave it to Aunt Ruthie to understand. I used to be angry with your old-fashioned traditions. I didn't want anything or anyone holding me back. Now I know it was how you were raised. You did the best you could."

"I tried. I wasn't as smart as you are."

"You were plenty smart, Ma. And strong." How hard it must have been to care for the household in their small flat. She'd had to rely on Ethel, and later, Aunt Ruthie, especially after Pa left.

Hannah pointed to the front. "I do like the wooden Ark doors." Mounted on the rich oak were the first ten letters of the Hebrew alphabet in two vertical lines, representing the Ten Commandments. The brass letters gleamed.

Vivian said, "My favorite is the unusual Ner Tamid." The eternal light next to the Ark glowed with an understated radiance. An illusion as if it were behind a block in the wall, not emanating from a standard light fixture.

Hannah remembered as a girl, she had asked her mama why a candle always burned at the front of their village's wooden shul. Her mama said it was to honor God's divine presence shining whenever they gathered to pray. When young Hannah asked if it only burned during a minyan, the requisite gathering of a quorum of ten men needed to conduct a service, her mama had become cross. "Don't forget how important we women are in our homes and community. Never ever think that anyone, man or woman, is better than you!"

Now she whispered to Vivian, "I, too, like this Ner Tamid. Like none other I've seen. It will shine forever."

The rabbi invited the congregation to read the first prayer together in English. Hannah couldn't keep up despite Vivian's guiding finger under the lines, but she loudly sang the Shema and

Ve-Ahavta ancient prayers, squeezing Vivian's fingers at the Hebrew line: "You must teach your children."

After the tall, lanky rabbi took the Torah from the Ark, he carried it through the sanctuary, stopping to greet congregants with a wide smile. He slowed down at the aisle where Vivian and Hannah stood, close enough for them to see his sparse blond beard and long-lashed gray-blue eyes. Vivian touched her prayer book to the velvet Torah covering and then brought the book to her lips and brushed it with a light kiss.

Hannah's hand trembled. "I've never been this close to the Torah. Only men touch it with their tallis fringes. Women have always been kept far away."

Vivian understood her ma's awe, remembering the first time she had seen the Torah up close, almost like trespassing where she didn't belong. She gripped her mother's forearm. "Women aren't sent to the rafters at Beth Shemesh. We're on equal footing here."

Up on the bimah, in preparation to read from the Torah scroll, Rabbi Bornstein announced, "Today we read from the beginning of the Book of Numbers. The portion, BaMidbar, translates to 'In the Desert.' Next week we'll celebrate the festival of Shavuot commemorating a great event for our people: when God gave us the Ten Commandments. You may recall Moses broke the first set of tablets when he returned to find the people he left behind had created a golden calf to worship. I interpret this story not as punishment, but as the challenge to practice forgiveness, to give people a second chance. What one person deems to be an unholy act may come from a desperate need. We are human beings, not God. We must not judge another's actions but rather develop compassion to understand and forgive our neighbors and ourselves."

"I like this young man's message," said Hannah. "He is brilliant." She squeezed Vivian's hand. "I'm sorry for what I said earlier. Thank you for bringing me here today."

"This is a new Jewish world, Ma, not blindly following rules made long ago based on reasoning I can't understand. Whatever our actions, we must live with the consequences of our choices. Sometimes we don't know how we will feel about what we do until afterward." Vivian looked rueful.

"You're a wise woman, my beautiful daughter."

Vivian grimaced. She wondered how wise she would feel next week.

AFTER SERVICES, Aunt Ruthie waited in her car outside the synagogue and drove them to Mister Ricky's, a restaurant in nearby Skokie. Hannah wouldn't go out to eat unless she could choose dairy, fish, or vegetarian dishes. She'd never risk eating meat that might not be kosher. Hannah was delighted to see cheese blintzes on the menu, exactly what she had a taste for. She never made them at home.

After they ordered, the three women discussed the rabbi's sermon. Vivian said it had been many years before she could forgive her brother for moving to California and Pa for walking out on the family.

"Life is funny," she said. "I was upset when they left, but if they hadn't, I might not have gone to work at the Walker–Jacobson Company and met Mel."

"I don't think that's funny," said Hannah. "It was God's plan."

"Believe whatever you like. You may say it's God's plan," said Aunt Ruthie. "Some things in life are happenstance, serendipity, not God's doing. Hannah, I think it's time you told Vivian why her father left."

Hannah's face contorted.

"What happened?" asked Vivian. "Does Ethel know?"

Aunt Ruthie said, "Ethel probably has a good idea. Let me make it easier for you, Hannah. I'll begin." Aunt Ruthie took a sip of water.

"A few years after you were born, your mother came to me, crying. Your father had forced her when she tried to refuse him. He became rough. She was scared she might be pregnant again. I feared for her safety."

Vivian's face became red. "How could Pa treat you like that?!"

Hannah's voice was soft. "Don't be harsh. Remember your rabbi's words today. Forgive him. Your pa wasn't so different from many husbands in those days."

"No woman should ever have to endure such things!" said Vivian.

Aunt Ruthie continued. "I knew your mother had been warned that she might not survive another childbirth. She'd taken a great risk to have you. It was near the end of the summer; the High Holidays would occur later than usual that fall. I told her if there was still no sign of her monthly by Yom Kippur, I would take her back to Dr. Boone."

"I would never go back to him!" said Hannah.

"Listen. When it became clear your mother was pregnant, not only was her health at risk, but upkeep of the household was in peril."

Hannah said, "I didn't know where to turn, so I called the only person I knew who could help: the midwife."

"She took pity on your mother," said Aunt Ruthie, "and gave her a special herb tea that caused a miscarriage a few hours later. There was a lot of blood. Your mother began to run a high fever. She panicked and sent a neighbor to find me at work. Your father was off somewhere. I was terrified she would die. I insisted on taking her to Mount Sinai Hospital. After two weeks, she came home and remained in bed for at least another month. All the neighbors helped out."

"I had to keep it secret from your pa."

"Ma, you almost died! And you couldn't tell Pa?" She put her head in her hands. A cry escaped from her lips. Vivian couldn't imagine keeping such a dire medical consequence from Mel. Even when they differed on important matters, Vivian was glad she could be open with her husband, not like Ma hiding her fears of pregnancy and termination attempts.

Hannah twisted her napkin. “Can you forgive me, Vivian?”

Before she could answer, Aunt Ruthie said, “Don’t blame your mother. *I* suggested she keep Abe in the dark. I didn’t know what he might do to her if he became angry. Some nights I agonized that I should have insisted she return to Dr. Boone, because he may have been safer. Finally, she regained her health, and I rested easier.”

Hannah said, “Your pa was between jobs, as he often was in those times. Many years later, one night he came home stinking of drink and wanted to . . . to do what I didn’t want to do . . . I got angry and told him how I didn’t want to have Ruth take me somewheres again. He was angry. We said many harsh words. That was the night he left us for good. Do you remember that night?”

How could Vivian forget their fight? The shouting, the accusations. She had been frightened by the intensity, as if they had let loose years of hatred in one barrage of bullets from a Tommy gun. Ethel told her to grow up, their pa was a no-goodnik who had never treated Ma right. A tear came to her eye to remember how Max tried to comfort her, saying Pa always comes back. But he didn’t. Not after that night. Soon after Vivian’s oldest brother left with his bride-to-be, Vivian transferred to the new high school with guaranteed job placement upon graduation. The promise of that downtown job was derailed by the war.

Vivian remembered how desolate she’d felt after Pa left, thought he didn’t love her anymore. Pa always told her she was his baby, his American princess. She was a daughter with smarts—a good head, a good *kepi,* as he called it—that would lead her to success. She missed Pa after he left, despite his faults. He praised her and gave her the courage and desire to seek a better life. He had escaped anti-Semitic violent pogroms in his village near Odessa to follow the dream of creating a prosperous life for himself and future family amid the freedoms of the United States of America.

"Of course, I remember that night," said Vivian. "Tell me, Ma, did you miss not having another baby?"

"Don't ask this question," said Aunt Ruthie. "Your mother's health was at risk. And your family didn't have the means to care for the ones they had."

Hannah put up her palm to silence Ruth. "In truth, I didn't want another one, even if my health had been perfect. I loved all of you, of that I had no doubt. But I had enough. Dayenu. As I think about your rabbi's words today, eventually I did forgive Abe, no matter all the trouble he caused me. Look at you. Look at my beautiful grandchildren. But when I think about those days, if I am honest, every once in a while, I wonder about the one who is not here."

Missing a child who never was. Would Vivian feel the same?

"You forgave Pa. Did you forgive yourself?" asked Vivian, thinking about the rabbi's message. She had a searing notion that would be the deepest wound to heal.

Hannah was silent for a moment and then said, "I did what I had to do. Yes, I forgive myself, but every Yom Kippur, I beg God to forgive me again."

Her ma found comfort in the annual High Holiday Day of Atonement, the most solemn day on the Jewish calendar. If Vivian believed Aunt Ruthie's bravado, Aunt Ruthie wouldn't ask any god to forgive her. Vivian was different from both women. She embraced her Jewish identity as a proud Beth Shemesh congregant but would not leave her fate in God's hands. Her marriage to Mel was based on trust. Vivian had learned King Solomon's lesson. On a matter like this, there was no compromise, no middle ground.

THAT EVENING in bed, Vivian told Mel about the rabbi's sermon with its theme of forgiveness.

Mel said softly, "Yes, an important message. You must forgive yourself," and winced to recall his wartime computation error. "I should give that rabbi more credit."

Vivian shared what Aunt Ruthie revealed about her ma's induced miscarriage and snuggled closer to him to feel his warm strength. "All this time, I thought Pa didn't love us. It was really all between him and Ma."

Mel sighed. "Life isn't like a story in the movies. Will we be able to forgive ourselves if you go ahead with this on Monday?"

They fell silent. Vivian acknowledged that yes, that was the big question, but yes, she felt strong enough to do this and live with her action. "Ma said she didn't want that next baby, but she says sometimes she wonders about the one she didn't have. I don't understand what she means. Not really."

She grabbed Mel's shoulder. Would she understand better next week?

Mel cleared his throat and pushed the hair off Vivian's face. "We must accept the unknown. We will never know the future or what might have been. We are simple people, no better, no different from anyone else. This is the human condition."

"Now who's the rabbi?" she asked.

They laughed together. A somber, sweet laughter.

Despite his lack of formal education, her Mel was a learned man. She was a lucky woman to be his wife. Perhaps it was not luck, as her ma would say, but *b'shert*, meant to be. Was there a God watching over her? Vivian could not bring herself to beg God not to punish her like her observant ma does on Yom Kippur, but she could thank God for protecting her, Mel, and their children. A dull ache nagged at her from her depths. She loved each of her children, but this one, this one was not meant to be. Vivian found herself asking for forgiveness. From whom? From God? From Mel? No, from herself, as Rabbi Bornstein urged.

"Mel," said Vivian, "let's go back to meet with Rabbi Bornstein when this is all over."

"Oh, Viv. You know I don't go too much for that. No rabbi, not even this guy Bornstein, would be a help to me. I've been through too much. Trust me, we can live with this. We won't be the first."

No, not the first. Not by a long shot.

"Please, no more worrying," he said. "Now that you've decided, be confident as you go forward. Get some sleep."

Mel soon slept, snoring lightly. He was right. Many women had taken the same action, across generations, rich and poor, in cities, small towns, and farms, women of all ages, backgrounds, and religions. Women risked their lives and their health because it wasn't the right father, the right circumstance, or it wasn't the right time in her life to bring a child into this world: too young, too old, too many children, or too busy with a career or studies. Or sadly, after a rape. No matter that abortion was against the law, women risked their lives to get the services they needed. Many did not survive. Weren't pregnancy and childbirth dangerous too? Choosing to risk an abortion must be a personal, individual woman's decision.

Vivian understood the courage she'd mustered to make this decision. Did women forgive themselves after an abortion? *Truly* forgive themselves? When she heard her ma and Jackie talk about their experiences, it wasn't the same as adding up a column of figures to balance in a ledger book. Each woman had her own reasons, reasons that at the same time were both rational and irrational. And for those who couldn't find a safe way to end an unwanted pregnancy? She remembered Mel's Aunt Addie and Aunt Ruthie's teenaged friend Irene. Tragic. Desperate. Vivian was grateful that she had the opportunity to make a safe choice. Too many women did not.

Vivian slowed her breathing to try to calm herself and invite in peace. The peace she needed to forgive herself and accept her human limitations. For the first time in recent weeks, she fell into a sound, dreamless sleep.

CHAPTER SIXTEEN

DELIBERATE, BUT NOT DELIBERATE

DAY 6: SUNDAY

VIVIAN AWOKE with a start. The sun streamed through her bedroom windows, stark evidence that she'd slept later than usual. Time to get up. What day was it? She reached toward the other side of the bed, but Mel was gone. Sunday. He must have chosen not to wake her when he left for the busiest day on Maxwell Street. She stretched her arms languidly and yawned until she remembered. Tomorrow. Monday. Her ten o'clock appointment with Dr. Boone.

From her crib, Linda bleated, "Mom-mee. I want Mommy." Before going to her, Vivian ran down to the basement to start a fresh load of laundry, stepping over scattered toys, and hustled back upstairs to Linda and Billy. She brought them to the kitchen as she prepared breakfast for the older girls, who were laughing over the Sunday comics. Irene read them aloud to Sandy. Vivian tried to relax with a cigarette and coffee as she scanned the *Sun Times*'s "Woman's Page."

Her head ached to ponder how slowly the twenty-four hours would tick by before tomorrow's appointment, as unrelenting as the *drip, drip, drip* of a leaky faucet. Her pulse throbbed as if counting beat by beat. This week had already felt longer than a month. So much had happened. Billy cut two new teeth; she'd soon have to stop nursing him. Irene was exposed, but hopefully did not catch the German measles. Rabbi Bornstein shared his reaction to his parents' dilemma before he was born, uncannily similar to her own response when she learned of her ma's crisis when pregnant with her. But yesterday was the biggest shock of all: the action Ma took a few years after Vivian was born, but revealed to Pa ten years later. Now Vivian finally understood why Pa left.

Vivian trembled when she considered the finality of what she'd decided to do. What unknown consequences might surface in the future? Her head felt as heavy as if she were balancing a stack of books in practice for a job as a Conover model. After tomorrow, there would be no going back.

She called Jackie.

"Viv! Thank goodness! I've been dying to talk to you."

Vivian said, "I wasn't sure if I should bother you on a Sunday."

"Sunday? No bother. I'm here all by myself. Hank left to play golf at the crack of dawn, Peggy won't be home from last night's sleepover party for hours, and Chuckie rode his bike to the park to play baseball. He might be home to take a break for lunch, but maybe not."

"Could you come over here?" Vivian's voice sounded scratchy.

"On my way. You sound weepy. Listen, I have something you've got to read. I hope it will make you feel better. Less alone."

When Jackie arrived, Vivian ushered her into the kitchen and poured her a cup of coffee. The girls were still engrossed in the Sunday comics. Linda was in her playpen pretending to read to her bunny. Billy was dozing upstairs in his crib.

"So what's the word?" asked Jackie. "Yea or nay? Isn't tomorrow the day?"

Vivian launched into the whole story of all that had happened since they'd talked, including Dr. Goldblum's guidance to make a list of pros and cons.

"You're more scientific than I thought," said Jackie. "Ever think of becoming an engineer? And I don't mean the one who drives the train."

"Don't make fun of me. Not an engineer, but maybe someday, I'll be a teacher." She paused. "I made the appointment. For tomorrow." Vivian could hardly croak out the words. She replaced her cup on the saucer, her hands shaking, causing a few splashes to slosh over the rim. Whatever Jackie, the rabbi, or Dr. Goldblum suggested, it was her decision. Mel had given her the green light to choose, and she had made her choice.

"Is the chance to become a teacher what pushed you over?" Jackie's voice rose. "Are you sure you want to teach?"

Vivian looked out the window to the nest in the tree next to the patio where a mother robin flew in to feed her baby birds. "I've wanted to be a teacher since I was ten years old. But I could never afford college. No one in my family went. Not like yours. Ethel never even finished high school." She felt ignorant compared to her neighbor. "Should I bring out some Oreos to go with our coffee?"

When Vivian returned with the cookies, Jackie said, "My sister is a Chicago teacher. You know that, but you might not know that it's a tougher job than you think. During the school year she works all hours, preparing lessons, grading papers, and getting involved with students and their families. Last year, when a student ran away from home after her mother died, my sister counseled her for weeks. I don't want to put a damper on your dreams, but be careful what you wish for. Are you ready to trade your children for your students?"

Vivian took a sharp intake of breath. Would teaching really be like that? Mel and their children must always come first. No doubt she would care about her students to try to live up to the standard of being the excellent teacher she would want for her own children. It might be easier when her children were older to give herself over to her students like Jackie's sister or the dedicated Miss O'Grady had done for her. Miss O'Grady had seen a spark in Vivian and had inspired her to strive toward a better future. What would Miss O'Grady think of her now? Vivian clutched at her abdomen and felt nauseated.

"Have a sip of water," Jackie said. "Slowly, don't gulp. Listen, don't get me wrong. I admire my sister's dedication. She continued teaching after she married again and had another child. She would never give it up because she loves her students too much."

Vivian took another sip of water. Her stomach settled. She said, "Someday I want to be a teacher like your sister."

Jackie held up a book. "Speaking of my sister, I want you to read this. She gave it to me for Mother's Day. A book of poetry."

"Poetry?" Vivian wasn't interested, but wanted to be polite. "What's the title?"

"*A Street in Bronzeville* by Gwendolyn Brooks. My sister taught one of these poems in her eighth-grade class, but not the one I want you to read. Brooks is the first Negro woman to win the Pulitzer Prize for poetry. She lives on Chicago's South Side."

"You're the college grad, Jackie. I haven't read a single poem since I memorized Edgar Allan Poe's 'The Raven,' in seventh grade."

"Don't tell me," said Jackie. "'Nevermore.'"

They laughed, but Vivian remained skeptical. She liked reading novels and had recently finished *Marjorie Morningstar* for a second time. *A Tree Grows in Brooklyn* was her all-time favorite. But poetry?

"You'll appreciate this poem, called 'The Mother.' It's as if Gwendolyn Brooks was sitting with us right here in your kitchen. She made me think her poem could be about any of us mothers. That is, any of us mothers who have had an abortion."

Vivian covered her mouth with her fist. "No? Are you kidding? A prizewinning poet wrote about having an abortion?"

"Not exactly about having the abortion, more like her feelings afterward."

Vivian stared down at the book in Jackie's hand. "How did she feel?"

"Mixed. Her mood is thoughtful, she may have some regrets, but she's not punishing herself. She admits how she thinks about the children who were never born, the ones who never had a chance to grow up."

"My ma said she also thinks about the one she never had. I've got to read this poem."

Jackie handed her the book.

Vivian opened it to the page marked with a bookmark. When she read the first two lines, she gasped. It was as if the poet Gwendolyn Brooks had crept inside her.

Abortions will not let you forget.
You remember the children you got that you did not get.

Vivian put the book down and took out a cigarette. Her fingers shook, and Jackie held the lighter for her. Tomorrow's abortion suddenly felt real. "I never asked you, Jackie. Is having an abortion like childbirth?"

Jackie was quiet for a moment. "No, not really. It's different. For one thing, it's over much quicker." Vivian gave a nervous laugh, but Jackie did not join in. "But you know what, Viv? I've been thinking about that late-term miscarriage you told me about. Before you had Irene. Did your doctor do any 'cleaning out' afterward?"

"I was so upset when I lost that baby. I don't remember much about that night. They put me under. When I woke, I knew my baby was gone. Dr. Goldblum told me he did a D&C. I had on a pad and was bleeding like I was having a heavy period. I had tried so hard to become a mom. I wanted to collapse in tears, but I couldn't let myself because I knew how sad Mel was too."

"I'd guess tomorrow's procedure will be similar to what you went through back then. Probably not as much bleeding. You're still in the first trimester."

Vivian remembered how after she miscarried, Mel had tried to cheer her up with a trip to Los Angeles to see her family, but she'd stayed in their hotel room for most of the visit, not wanting to go out. Her brother pulled her aside to ask if she and Mel were having marital problems, but she assured him they weren't. She couldn't tell her brother what she'd been through or her fears that she might never have children and be a proper wife. Before she and Mel flew home from California, they drove across the border to Tijuana, Mexico, where Mel bought her jangly charm bracelets and a bright red-and-orange shawl. He was trying to console her, but she was not consoled. In the weeks and months that followed, the physical aftermath from the D&C was forgotten, but her fear of never being a mother wasn't gone until one year later, when she gave birth to Irene. That seemed so long ago.

"How long does it take to recover?" Vivian asked.

"In a couple of days, you'll be back at full strength."

Full strength. She'd have to be. Being a mother at 336 Maple Street meant running up and down the stairs all day long, feeding, hauling folded laundry up to the bedroom level from the basement, and preparing meals in the kitchen located on the level in between. This time there would be no need to banish the dread that she might never have children.

She heard Irene and Sandy giggling. Vivian loved hearing their joyful sounds and brushed away a tear thinking how this one would never have a chance to laugh over the Sunday papers.

In a quiet voice, she whispered to Jackie, "I never asked. Where'd you go to have your abortion?"

Jackie, usually flippant, turned pale and lit a cigarette. "I went to the old Italian neighborhood on Taylor Street, you know, not far from where Mel works. My sister took me. She was angry that I was doing this, but she agreed. Our mother was a devout Catholic. We didn't want her to find out. When we arrived at the storefront office, a woman took our cash and blindfolded us. Two men led us out the back and through the alley. I was never sure where we ended up. After it was over, they drove us to a street corner over a mile from the original office and dropped us off."

Jackie had been brave and confident of what she wanted to do. Vivian felt timid by comparison, but at least her eyes would be open. She would be gassed, but not blindfolded, in Dr. Boone's office with its faded red wallpaper and scuffed oak pocket doors. At least his space was clean. Dr. Goldblum knew Boone, and he knew of Goldblum. Mel would be in the waiting room. Vivian pictured Miss Satwick—Sandra Satwick—with her starched white coat over her blazer, placing the cone over Vivian's nose and mouth. She squeezed her eyes shut at the vision of Dr. Boone's dark, wooly eyebrows and gagged at the memory of the ghastly smell that filled the entire space, a swirling fog wafting around her eyes and filling up nose and ears. She pressed her forehead into her palms to try to stop a pouncing headache pain.

"Are you OK, Viv? Need more water?" Vivian shook her head no and rested her hands on her abdomen. The two women sat in silence for a few minutes. Linda began to cry, "I want Mommy." When Vivian went to pick her up from the playpen, she heard the front door slam after Irene and Sandy ran to play outside. The locusts that had scared Irene so badly a few weeks ago had disappeared, save a few stragglers. Vivian came back to the table with Linda in her lap. She thought of her list of pros and cons. Did it add up? Maybe it did and maybe it didn't, but she was haunted by the fears that if they added another baby, the children they already had would run wild without the care and oversight they needed.

"Don't second-guess yourself," said Jackie. "You've decided. Of course, you know this, but after tomorrow, there will be no going back. But remember, you aren't the only one who's made this choice."

Vivian reached for a Kleenex to blow her nose. "Did you forgive yourself afterward?"

"To tell you the truth, I don't think about it like that. You know, you could be worse off." Jackie winked. "Mel adores you. Sure, Hank and I started off in love, but now, who knows? Some days I think I'd be better off without him when I suspect he's fooling around with his secretary. All I say is he'd better not be. I'd divorce him faster than you could blink."

"I don't believe you'd do that," said Vivian. "You'd have to go to work and move away from Maple Street."

"I could if it came to that, but you may have called my bluff. Maybe I'm just blowing off steam like the old married couple we are. I don't envy you your decision. If you want my two cents, take care of this tomorrow and don't look back. You've got a loving husband and beautiful children and a nice house. Don't get bogged down by taking on too much. None of us are in the running to win a gold medal for Mother of the Year."

Billy began to cry. Vivian stood to go to him and carry Linda upstairs too.

"I take that back," said Jackie. "Maybe you *are* trying for that gold medal. But remember, none of us go through life untouched. I'll head home now, but don't forget to read the rest of that poem. Keep the book as long as you like. Try to relax. Call me later."

AFTER BILLY was changed and settled, Vivian called the girls inside for lunch: peanut butter and jelly sandwiches, cut in two triangles just how Sandy liked it, with Jays potato chips and two butter cookies each. They wolfed down the food and ran back outside with Vivian calling out a warning to stay on the block. The weather was fine, and she didn't expect them to be back until dinnertime. She put a brisket in the oven to simmer all afternoon for their evening meal. She wanted to make it special for Mel, to show her appreciation for his patience during these weeks.

Linda played quietly in her playpen. Vivian sat nearby in Mel's easy chair, opened the book Jackie had loaned her. Vivian shivered when she reread the first two lines and then read them twice more. As if Gwendolyn Brooks wrote this poem just for her. Jackie was right. The poet wrote about the ambiguous, murky feelings that she and Jackie had talked about over coffee. Her ma mentioned her own version of this ambivalence. There were no words to describe what a woman goes through when she seriously considers this choice, no matter what she decides.

Vivian read the poem all the way to the end. Plain words. Understandable. Powerful feelings. Vivian kicked herself for believing the poem would be beyond her comprehension. She shouldn't doubt her abilities. Didn't she have a woman's sensibility?

Believe me, I knew you, though faintly, and I loved, I loved you
All.

Vivian offered up thanks to the poet for giving her a glimpse of how she might feel afterward. There was no indication that Gwendolyn Brooks had deep regrets or wanted to reverse her action. Vivian wished she could be as eloquent to express how much she ached about her decision. She reminded herself that's why Brooks was a prizewinning poet. They don't hand out the Pulitzer Prize for no reason.

How insightful Brooks had been to see the abortion as both deliberate yet not deliberate. Yes, Vivian felt the contradiction deeply. Her pros-and-cons list masqueraded as a calculated method. In her heart, Vivian understood that her reasons in each column did have meaning, but could never add up to a quantifiable action. She would have to trust her feelings, however mixed.

Vivian reread the poet's words. Linda began to chortle, playacting as if her stuffed animals were having a conversation. Her darling girl. Vivian's tears flowed as she read "The Mother" again from start to finish. The noise from the children playing on Maple Street merged into an indistinguishable roar. She imagined this was how a group of ponies, donkeys, or cows might sound braying alongside one another. A cacophony of living creatures. She gazed out the window to the backyard and caught a glimpse of a pair of blue jays yakity-yakking back and forth in a stream of raucous syllables. Were they arguing about who would build and clean the nest and bring food for the baby birds? All creatures had their families. Vivian couldn't resist reading "The Mother" another time. She lingered on that line again:

You remember the children you got that you did not get.

Jackie had her version of this line. After tomorrow, Vivian would also wrestle with these feelings. Didn't Ma say as much at yesterday's lunch with Aunt Ruthie? She remembered her ma liked to repeat the saying: "Rich are those who appreciate what they have." Vivian appreciated what she had, but she did want more. She wanted a life beyond the pseudo-dignified moniker of "homemaker" instead of "housewife."

Vivian dozed on her prized couch, absorbing the rare, fleeting peacefulness inside their Maple Street home. All was well. How easy it would be to upset this balance. One wail, one lost toy, one unexpected fall, or a string of muddy footprints could unleash chaos, upsetting a tentative calm and send Vivian into a screaming frenzy. Was that what it meant to lose your mind? To go crazy when a random occurrence upsets your orderly world and shattered your routine? Was that a nervous breakdown? Paralyzed and careening out of control at the same time? A new baby six months from now could upset their family's equilibrium. Could she handle an unwanted little turkey at Thanksgiving?

Mel's sister always invited their family to her home to celebrate this American holiday. Vivian could imagine everyone cooing over their latest little one with his or her freshly powdered, shampooed, brand-new baby smell. Irene would try to be the conscientious big sister, as ever—bringing diapers to help her mother. But how did Irene really feel inside? Sandy would tease the infant to tears and then rush to kiss the baby to stop him from crying. And where would five children sleep? She couldn't solve that puzzle now. There were too many pieces. Soon Linda would grow out of the tiny baby's room she shared with Billy. Either she'd have her own room or squeeze into a corner of the girls' room depending on the sex of the newborn. When Billy grew, he'd need his own room away from the girls. Vivian would not be a proper mother if she could not give each of her children the space she or he deserved along with the support of a loving home.

It was rare for Vivian to nap during the day. She was startled awake by the rumble of the garage door. Mel? So soon? What time was it? Irene and Sandy followed him in from outside, calling, "Daddy's home! Daddy's home!" They sang out, "Happy birthday, Daddy!"

Mel was all smiles, carrying a boxed cake, yellow with chocolate frosting, from their favorite bakery around the corner from Jacobson Brothers. The girls surrounded him, hugging his knees.

Vivian straightened her blouse, greeted Mel with a kiss, and said, "You're home early."

"Tomorrow's a big day," he said softly, putting his free arm around her waist.

Vivian combed her hair with her fingers and wiped away a sweaty lock of hair from her forehead. She must look a fright, having stirred from a nap without time to freshen up. She whispered in his ear, "I've decided to keep the appointment with Dr. Boone tomorrow."

"As long as you're sure." He nuzzled her ear.

"I am."

She had to accept the indeliberate nature of her deliberations. Gwendolyn Brooks, the prizewinning poet, made it clear. No matter how much one deliberated, the gut-wrenching decision was full of emotion. No formula would make it add up. Vivian must trust herself.

Before Mel went upstairs to shave, he ambled down to the basement for his end-of-workday shot of Scotch. Tonight, he downed two in rapid succession.

Vivian assembled the brisket dinner as quickly as she could, adding little roasted red potatoes to absorb the juices into the pan of simmering meat. She made a salad with iceberg lettuce, green peppers, and tomatoes. The vegetables from her backyard garden wouldn't be ready to harvest until later in the season, if they ripened at all. Vivian whipped up chunky mashed potatoes as a bonus—Mel's favorite side dish—adding a full stick of margarine and plenty of salt, then heated up a can of Green Giant peas.

Mel took his usual seat at the head at the table, beaming and smelling of Aqua Velva aftershave. He said, "My beautiful family. Look how you're growing."

"Billy is still little," said Sandy.

Mel said, "I predict Baby Billy will grow bigger than all of us."

Vivian smiled at his words and at the same time felt sad to imagine Billy all grown up. Shaving? Hairy legs? He would be her last baby.

After they ate, Vivian brought the cake to the table, and they sang "Happy Birthday." She thought about the child who would never have a birthday song.

"Make a wish!" said Irene. Mel hesitated and then blew out the candles.

"What did you wish for, Daddy?" asked Sandy.

"He can't say, or it won't come true, you dummy," said Irene.

"Don't call your sister names," Vivian scolded as she cut the cake. "If I told you once, I told you a thousand times, Irene. I don't like that kind of talk."

"Give Daddy the first piece," said Irene. "He's the birthday boy."

Sandy clapped her hands. "Bring out his presents!"

Vivian gave him *Blue Rose*, Rosemary Clooney's album recorded with Duke Ellington. Mel glowed. His favorite singer. Irene and Sandy handed Mel a crayoned card made from folded yellow construction paper.

"Daddy, I wrote all the words on our card," said Irene. "Sandy drew the pictures."

He laughed. "Read it to me, Irene."

"Happy birthday, Daddy. Today you are forty-two years old. Roses are red, violets are blue. We love you!"

Irene hugged Mel around his neck. "My teacher told me how to spell violets."

Below the greeting, there were pictures of each one of them lined up alongside one another, their heights descending like stairsteps: Mel, Vivian, Irene, Sandy, Linda, and Billy.

"I wrote the ages under each of Sandy's pictures," said Irene. "Forty-two, thirty-two, six, three, two, and one. I put 'one' for Baby Billy because he will be one in July. Linda just turned two in April."

"What a beautiful card, Irene," said Mel. "I must say, your numbers are perfect. Just like your mommy's."

"You practiced with me, Daddy."

Yes, Mel certainly loved their children and rejoiced in teaching them. What a terrific father.

"Thank you, girls. Viv, look at Sandy's beautiful pictures."

"It's our whole family," said Sandy.

"Yes," Irene echoed. "Our whole family."

Vivian and Mel looked at each other. Vivian said, "Yes, this is our whole family."

They cleared the table together. Vivian put the dishes into the dishwasher. They relaxed in the living room until Mel said in a tired voice, "Do you want to know what I wished for?" Vivian was somewhat fearful about what he would say. He held out his hand. "I'll tell you upstairs."

As soon as they entered their room, Mel locked the door. They undressed in silence and got into bed. Mel put his arms around her and said, "Sitting around the table tonight it was clear to me. I already have my wish. Our life with you and the children here on Maple Street in Wilmette is what's most important to me. Whatever I said earlier, forget it. I don't need more. I don't want to do anything to upset what we already have."

"Do you really mean it?" Vivian wiped away a tear.

Mel added, "My zayde liked to quote, 'Rich is the man who is happy with his lot.'"

Vivian nodded in recognition. "My ma liked that saying too."

Vivian hugged Mel's neck and pictured the Chicago Teachers College's colorful catalog sitting on the bookshelf in the den. She remembered the day it arrived in the mail. Yes, she was happy with what she had, but she did want more. More than ever, after this was all over, she was determined to find a way to take that first teacher education course.

CHAPTER SEVENTEEN
VIVIAN'S CHOICE

DAY 7: THE DAY

VIVIAN AWOKE with a start. Monday? Oh, what a Monday this would be. She looked at the clock, and her chest tightened. Mel was still puttering around in the bathroom. She spoke aloud the first line of Gwendolyn Brooks's poem as if it were written on the ceiling.

Abortions will not let you forget.

"Time to get up." Mel was at her side, rubbing her forearm. "Billy's crying for you."

She heard him. She could be in the basement with the washer and dryer on the loudest cycles and hear the baby all the way upstairs in his crib. A mother's ear. She resisted the urge to pull the sheet over her head. She had to get moving. It was Monday. *That* Monday.

"Can you make your own breakfast today?" Vivian asked Mel. "And give the girls their cereal? I'll take care of Linda and Billy."

Before going to them, she sat up and reached for the thin volume at her bedside. She read the two-page poem again. Upon each reading, different phrases made her tingle. At the last line, her breasts ached.

Believe me, I knew you, though faintly, and I loved, I loved you
All.

Linda cried, "I want Mommy."

Billy wailed.

Yes, their four children were more than enough. Vivian was happy with her lot.

She took Linda to sit on the toilet—why not try?—and then picked up Billy to nurse him while sitting in the rocker in the babies' room. She tickled the soles of his growing feet. His face was soft and warm, and his delicately delicious baby smell, like talcum powder mixed with the clean scent of Dreft laundry soap, filled her nose but was growing fainter. How long would it be until he smelled like a little boy and no longer a baby? When would Billy come home with his neck as dirty as a chimney sweep and his pants scraped with permanent grass stains like Jackie's son? Jackie complained she could never get Chuckie's pants clean. How long until Vivian would have the same lament? She sniffed back a tear as Billy hungrily guzzled until one breast was depleted. She moved him onto the other side, then lifted him to her shoulder to pat out a burp. What a sweet boy. She shouldn't doubt herself. She *was* a good mother.

Linda called from the bathroom, "Mommy! Pee-pee."

"Wonderful, Linda." Vivian hurriedly put Billy back in his crib. "You're a big girl now."

"Big girl," echoed Linda.

Irene ran up from the kitchen, clapping her hands. "Sandy, Linda made pee-pee in the toilet. She's not a baby anymore."

Linda was on her way out of diapers. Hooray! Only Billy would be left to train. Vivian had no nostalgia for a houseful of reeking cloths, always worrying about running out, not to mention the diaper service's ever-increasing charges.

Mel called from the kitchen. "Irene! Susie is here. Time to walk to school."

"Wear your raincoat. Don't forget your hat," called Vivian. "Looks like thunderstorms."

Vivian dressed hurriedly in plain comfortable slacks and a blouse. No dressing up today. She knew better. The doorbell rang. The babysitter, Mrs. McElroy.

Vivian rushed downstairs and ate only one of the two slices of buttered toast Mel made for her. Miss Satwick warned her to eat lightly. Vivian put a bowl of Gerber's cereal on the high chair for Mrs. McElroy to feed to Linda.

"Not sure what time I'll be back," Vivian told Mrs. McElroy. "Irene will go to a friend's house after school. Her friend's mother will bring her back home. Their phone number is on the pad near the telephone. Mr. Jacobson's number at work is there too. There are cream cheese and jelly sandwiches in the refrigerator for Sandy and Linda. One for you, too."

"I brought my own lunch, Mrs. Jacobson. Like I always do."

"Well, just in case. There are two spare bottles for Billy in the fridge. Heat them up in a pan of water. Test a few drops on your wrist to be sure they're not too hot."

"Mrs. Jacobson, how many times have I sat for you? Not just for you, but for all the mothers on Maple Street. You act like I'm one of those know-nothing bobby-soxers."

Vivian was glad that experienced, gray-haired Mrs. McElroy was sitting today. She was a widow and a grandmother whose son and family had moved to Ohio. Vivian didn't know the whole story, but she'd heard that years earlier, Mrs. McElroy had had another son who was struck by a car and killed while riding his bicycle. Ten years old. An unimaginable loss. Vivian blinked. May she never know it. Sandy complained that Mrs. McElroy was grouchy. She preferred Jackie's college-aged niece, but Vivian trusted Mrs. McElroy's judgment if, God forbid, there was an emergency.

"I don't mean to insult you, Mrs. McElroy. Of course, I know you know what to do. I'm just a little nervous today."

"What do you have to be nervous about?" Mrs. McElroy's voice was sharp. "With your beautiful house and big family? You young Jewish mothers around here don't know how good you have it."

Jewish? This old lady was not polished enough to hide her prejudice, although Vivian knew many Wilmette residents hid similar narrow-minded perspectives. True, most of the families in their new development were Jewish. The McElroys were an old-time clan who lived in the lone brick bungalow nearby that predated the development. Her disdain was as evident as if she put out a sign saying, "Go back to the city, you Jews." Vivian was crestfallen that Mrs. McElroy had the same attitude that Vivian and Mel had encountered when first house hunting in neighborhoods closer to the lake. But she couldn't stew about this now. Not today. Mel was waiting. He wore his tan windbreaker, tapped his foot, and held out her coat.

"Time to go," he said. His voice was tense, absent of his usual even tone.

"Bye, Mommy. Bye, Daddy," said Sandy.

Sandy, her wild one. Each of their children was different. Vivian couldn't pour them into a mold even if she tried. Irene was serious and bright. She imagined Linda would become headstrong and physical—an athlete? She was different from both Irene and Sandy. And Billy, oh, her Billy. Well, she couldn't know about her dear boy, not yet. How did the rhyme go? *Snips and snails and puppy dog tails, that's what little boys are made of.* No puppy dogs in this house. She and Mel staunchly agreed there. They had more than enough living creatures to care for. Vivian's heart melted when Billy gazed at her with his adoring eyes that turned from blue to green to hazel when they locked on hers. When she returned home, would Billy see her differently? Would he recognize her as his mother? That was silly. Of course he would.

WHEN THEY arrived at Dr. Boone's greystone, Mel turned off the ignition and held her close. "Be strong. Remember how much I love you and our family. More than I can say. Don't punish yourself. I support your decision."

They walked up the stairs together. Miss Satwick led them to the same two chairs where she and Ethel sat only one week ago. On that day, the red-flocked wallpapered walls felt like they would close in and crush her. Today, when Mel squeezed her hand, she looked around at a space that felt oddly familiar.

Mel leaned over and whispered, "What's that odor?" He scrunched up his face. "Some kind of gas?"

Vivian lifted one eyebrow. "That's how it smells in here."

When Miss Satwick came through the pocket doors and called her name, Vivian stood, finally ready.

"I'll be sitting right here waiting," said Mel, a worried look on his face as he grabbed again for her hand. "I won't move." Vivian gave him a small smile. Men couldn't understand what women endured with respect to childbearing. A great mystery.

Vivian followed Miss Satwick, but before going through the pocket doors that led into the procedure room, she turned, brought her fingers to her lips, and blew Mel a soft kiss. He brushed at his eye. Vivian didn't want to cause him any additional worries thinking she was still wavering over this decision. She stepped over the threshold. Miss Satwick slid the doors closed behind her. Vivian undressed quickly. Miss Satwick gave her a sheet and helped her onto the table. Dr. Boone appeared from the side door. Solemn, but boyish-looking despite his furry eyebrows. Why had she feared him?

"Lie back," he said as Miss Satwick covered her nose and mouth with the mask. "Count backward from ten." Vivian didn't remember reaching number seven.

"All done, dearie," chirped Miss Satwick.

When Vivian stirred into consciousness, her private parts felt as if they'd been Hoovered out. Her gut cramped worse than any menstrual pains she'd ever experienced. She tried to soothe herself by rubbing her fingers over her low abdomen with scant relief.

Dr. Boone was nowhere in sight. Vivian remembered what Jackie had said: Quicker than any childbirth, even Linda's, who'd almost been born in the cab when they were stuck on Lake Shore Drive before reaching Wesley Hospital.

Vivian staggered to standing and dressed slowly. Miss Satwick gently led her to the waiting room. There was Mel. What a beautiful face he had. He put his arm around her shoulder, steered her to the leather club chair, while he went to pay Miss Satwick. Then, he returned to Vivian, gently led her to the stairway, and tipped his cap to Miss Satwick, who held the door for them. Vivian was depleted, but strong enough to clutch Mel's arm with a grip that turned her fingertips as bloodless as moonstones. He guided her carefully as she crept down the stairs, wishing he could lift her up and away from this place forever.

On the drive to Rogers Park, Mel asked how she felt.

Her grogginess had lifted. "As OK as I can be. It's over." She groaned. "Already seems like a bad dream."

"Are you in pain?"

She winced. "Not too much." How could he understand? Not only the cramping physical pain, but the emptiness. She thought of the lines from "The Mother."

I knew you, though faintly, and I loved, I loved you
All.

MEL HELD the wheel with one hand, and with the other, stroked Vivian's forearm. She dozed for the rest of the drive to Rogers Park. Ma was waiting at the open door. Aunt Ruthie had prepared chamomile tea with honey. After Vivian gingerly settled onto the forest green velour couch, Mel kissed her goodbye and said he'd be back to pick her up in a few hours.

After Mel left, Aunt Ruthie said, "How brave you are. On a day like this, I think of my friend Irene."

Vivian choked back a tear. "I honored her memory with the name of our firstborn."

"You honor her every day with your courageous life," said Aunt Ruthie. "And all of us, too. You are a caring person and a wonderful mother."

"Today I chose not to be a mother again," Vivian said and began to sob.

"It's OK to cry," said Hannah. "Remember, every woman makes the best choices she can and goes on from there. Time will pass. You'll find your peace."

Vivian was relieved but didn't know how she would get over this. Now she understood. She would never forget.

Hannah gazed out the window. The clouds had blocked the sun again. "I made up the bed in my room with clean sheets. Go lie down. You must rest."

"Do you need to use the bathroom first?" asked Aunt Ruthie. "We bought a box of Kotex. Is there anything else you need? Do you want an aspirin?"

"I'm OK. I'll try to sleep."

When Vivian woke, she remembered how Mel's face brimmed with relief when she stepped into Dr. Boone's waiting room. As long as he loved her, she could go on. The cramping had eased. She changed the pad. Not too much bleeding. She'd be fine. Dr. Boone was indeed competent.

She went into the living room, announced that she was feeling much better, and gingerly settled herself on the couch.

Aunt Ruthie went to her and grasped both of her hands. "I've been eager to tell you something. I was going to wait, but I've decided now is the time. I want to be certain that you will have the opportunity to do what you wished for when you were a young girl. I have enough savings. As my gift to you, I will fund your college degree."

"*My* college degree?" Aunt Ruthie always knew Vivian's deepest dreams and made them come true. Her personal Glinda, the good witch of the North, like Dorothy's benefactor in *The Wizard of Oz*. "*My* college degree?" Now Vivian was stunned. Could she do this? Was she smart enough to go to college now? Could she compete with the young coeds who had just finished high school and weren't caring for four young children?

"Are you sure? What about my children's college educations?"

"They'll make their own ways. You are first in my heart. I've always felt as if you were the daughter I never had. I want you to follow your dream."

Today was a new beginning. Vivian knew it would be, but never imagined today would also be the day when earning her college degree would become possible. She'd have to begin slowly, of course. Caring for the children and the household still came first. But someday was not as far away as it had been yesterday. She was certain now. She would become a teacher.

MEL ARRIVED with a concerned look on his face, but his expression soon changed. "You look refreshed, darling. Your color has returned. Thank you, Mother Kolson and Aunt Ruthie, for taking good care of my Vivian."

"*Our* Vivian," said Aunt Ruthie.

"Mel, you won't believe this," began Vivian. "Aunt Ruthie is going to—"

Aunt Ruthie interrupted. "Tell him later, dear."

"Yes, plenty of time for all that," said Hannah. "Go home to the children. You'll need more rest."

Mel helped Vivian put on her spring coat. He put his arm around her, led her out to the car, and opened the passenger door for her to slide in carefully. After he got into the driver's seat, he reached over to kiss her. "Are you sure you're all right?"

Vivian murmured she was grateful that it was all over. She was eager to get home to the children, back to 336 Maple Street in Wilmette, Illinois. As they drove along, she felt every bump along Edens Highway, every pothole that hadn't yet been filled after the long winter.

In the days that followed, Vivian didn't weed the garden. She talked to Dr. Goldblum, who cautioned her to take it easy for the next two weeks. She let the laundry mount up. She cooked simple meals with meat they had in the freezer. Jackie sent over her cleaning lady to help Vivian keep up with the household chores. This rare idleness gave Vivian moments that caused her throat to constrict when she recalled the stench of Dr. Boone's office and those creepy framed etchings of naked women. She calmed herself by remembering Mel's brimming brown eyes when she stumbled out through the pocket doors. She had felt safe to have him nearby as the anesthesia took effect.

Soon her recollections diminished. Became hazy. What remained was the lingering feeling of guilt—no other word for it—and the nagging reminder that what she'd done was against nature and against the law. She had been as desperate as many women had been before her, but with her respectable referral from Dr. Goldblum and with Mel's ready cash, she was fortunate she could safely have an illegal abortion. Still, she wrestled with her conscience and reread "The Mother" many times before returning Jackie's book. She tried not to say out loud the words that bubbled up, such as, "Maybe I shouldn't have . . . I wish I could . . ."

When she asked Mel if he was certain that they did the right thing, he waved his hand over her head as if he were a magician with a wand who could make it go *poof!*

"It's done now," he said. "Over. Don't dwell on this. Try to forget about it and love the beautiful children we have."

Of course, Mel was right. He was always right. At least, most of the time, he was right.

While Vivian rested, she reread the descriptions of the teacher certification requirements in the college catalog. Could she really do this?

In the next room, she heard Billy cry out, "Da-da."

His first word.

Her last baby was growing up.

CHAPTER EIGHTEEN

NO GOING BACK

JANUARY 22, 1973: ROE V. WADE

DID SHE hear correctly? Finally. Hurrah! Vivian Kolson Jacobson turned up the radio on her drive home from Evanston's Lincoln Elementary School. Her gut clenched as she gripped the steering wheel as if she could hold back the rush of people and events tumbling through her consciousness. If only Mel were alive to celebrate this day with her.

Irene must know already. Vivian would call her as soon as she got home. She shivered in relief, relieved that her eldest, a member of Jane, the underground abortion collective, would not go to jail. That's what the group's lawyer told them while they awaited the imminent Supreme Court ruling. Thank goodness, because Irene had a promising future as a chemist. How Vivian yearned to celebrate this day with her late ma and Aunt Ruthie. How proud they'd be of Irene. Her daughter combined Aunt Ruthie's boldness with her grandmother's scholarly legacy.

Vivian hung her coat in the front hall closet, put Mel's bulky sweater over her thin frame, and breathed in his lingering, musky scent that still clung to the wool. She went to the kitchen, opened the refrigerator, and poured herself a glass of rosé from the open bottle of Mateus. A rare indulgence on a school night, because her third graders demanded her full attention every morning. But tonight, Vivian felt a quiet celebration of this remarkable milestone was in order. She offered up a hopeful toast. May no one ever go back to those days of fear and unnecessary deaths.

What would Mel say after he added a *l'chaim* and they clinked glasses? He'd likely give her a kiss and paraphrase his mother's favorite Yiddish maxim: "We did what we had to do." She missed her lovable, practical Mel. Her heart pounded at the memory when she was called out of her classroom to rush to Michael Reese Hospital after his collapse at Jacobson Brothers. She'd arrived too late for a last goodbye. She wiped away a tear. He knew she loved him.

Mel had always worked too hard, even after his first heart attack. Later, Jacobson Brothers only sold liquor directly to retail package stores, leaving their tenant, Jimmy Hot Dog, as they called him, to handle the restaurant business, cooking great quantities of hot dogs, Polish sausages, and pork chops every day. Vivian laughed to remember how Mel would come home smelling of the *traif* she'd never cook at home.

Before shopping malls, Maxwell Street had been a thriving marketplace and port-of-entry home for those arriving in Chicago from around the world and migrating from the South. Her parents and Mel's, too, lived there when they first arrived in Chicago from Russia at the turn of the twentieth century. You could always find bargains and haggle over prices of shoes, custom suits, socks at ten pairs for a dollar, the latest hats, every style of hubcaps, and a vibrant array of fabrics. Those days were rapidly fading. Now, stellar blues musicians played for donations from appreciative fans. Many buildings had been razed to make way for the new Chicago campus of the University of Illinois.

Vivian clicked on the radio in the dining room before settling onto the couch to hear the monumental announcement again. Women were celebrating all across the nation. She was certain that many ached with memories of their own stories or of those they knew. Vivian rarely told her story. Most of the time, the days of that anguished spring remained far from her consciousness. Her day-to-day existence was fulfilled as a teacher and keeping up with the four children that she and Mel had raised.

She took another sip of wine as she remembered that spring. How grateful she was that Mel agreed for her to make the decision. He respected her right to determine what was best for her and for their family. Not every man would have done that. She knew from the start that she'd married someone special. She pulled Mel's gray sweater tighter around her. How fortunate she'd been to have been his wife for twenty-five years. She'd never wanted another husband. Who could replace the partnership they'd shared in their hectic household? But Vivian never could have become a self-supporting teacher if she hadn't taken that action in 1956. Thanks to Aunt Ruthie, too.

She gazed around her living room. Five years earlier, she and Mel splurged to reupholster the designer couch and replace the worn carpeting in a different shade of green, but otherwise their home looked much the same as it did when they'd moved in. She loved their Wilmette home where tall maple trees now shaded the street. She never wanted to move.

She thought of the women who might have lived had abortion been legal before today. Among them, Aunt Ruthie's childhood friend and Mel's Aunt Addie. Vivian took a sharp inhale to imagine thousands of others whose names she'd never know. But tonight was not a time to look back in sadness, but rather, a time to look ahead with hope. What a moment! A true dividing line. Tonight she knew the feeling of freedom under the law, guaranteed by the Supreme Court. Her daughters and future generations of women could seek jobs previously off-limits, not only because they had been traditionally restricted to men but also because they would have the freedom to control when and if they had children. Her daughters—Irene, Sandy, Linda—and their daughters would have legal options not needing to be clandestine. Of course, not all would choose as she did. Sandy and her high school boyfriend were raising a daughter on a California commune, despite Mel's offer to finance Sandy's trip to New York, where abortion had been legalized ahead of today's ruling. But Sandy refused. She wanted her child. Her choice.

Vivian decided to stay up later than usual and wait until the long-distance rates dropped at eleven o'clock to call Ethel, who now lived in Los Angeles, and Jackie, who lived in Miami, to celebrate the news. Dear Jackie, who had widened Vivian's outlook when she'd shared Gwendolyn Brooks's poem. Her fifth child with Mel would be sixteen years old now. Sweet sixteen? Or getting his driver's license? As Miss Brooks, the poet, penned, that one was among the ones "you got that you did not get."

Vivian stood, pushed back the cuffs on Mel's sweater, finished her glass of wine, and rinsed it in the kitchen sink. As she stared out of her frosty kitchen window, she remembered more details from those long-ago weeks in May, a few months before her son Bill's first birthday. The stench of Dr. Boone's office, the stiff-necked assistant, and how her Sandy had admitted she and her sister had hidden their mother's silver watch when the misplacement nearly unhinged her. Vivian smiled with the knowledge that the watch was safe in her jewelry box upstairs. She let herself laugh. It was all over now.

She'd carried the weight of her actions far too long. On this wintry evening, Vivian stood tall, threw back her shoulders, and tilted up her chin just like Aunt Ruthie always taught her to do. A cascade of forgotten tensions melted away. No more punishing herself at the odd moment. She forgave herself for whatever misgivings remained. At long last, Vivian proclaimed her own freedom. There would be no going back.

She dialed Irene.

"Hello, Mom? Yeah, I heard. Isn't it great? I'm off to a party in Hyde Park. I'll call you tomorrow night."

JUNE 25, 2022: The US Supreme Court declares *Roe v. Wade* unconstitutional. Lawmakers across the country began to usurp women's personal decisions by passing abortion bans and other related reproductive services with no exceptions.

AUTHOR'S NOTE

AS I await the April 2026 publication of my debut historical novel, I reflect on the importance of libraries. My visits to libraries are among my earliest, most treasured memories. I've always held authors in high esteem, but until the last decade, I never dared to try to count myself among them. Now, with the release of *Vivian's Decision,* I can claim the title "author" and hope that librarians will make my book available to their patrons.

When we lived in the city, every week, on his day off from working on Maxwell Street, my dad took me to the Belmont branch of the Chicago Public Library. I remember proudly earning my own card when I proved I could write my name. Even now, I smile when I drive by that small yellow brick building to recall the thrill of finding a trove of books that went beyond Dick and Jane. When I was five years old, we moved to the suburbs. There, two women—Miss Jacobs, the kindly, gray-haired children's librarian in the public library, and Miss Martz, our bespectacled elementary school librarian, whose glasses did not hide her twinkling eyes—continued to propel my reading choices. Frances Hodgson Burnett, Beverly Clearly, Eleanor Estes, Sydney Taylor, and P. L. Travers were among my favorite authors. After the entire student body crammed into the library to watch Alan Shepard take his historic space flight on the school TV, I couldn't decide whether I wanted to become an astronaut or a librarian when I grew up.

Yet not only the stories from books drew me in. I was captivated by my parents' repeated tales about growing up during the Depression as Chicago-born children of Russian Jewish immigrants on Chicago's West side. At holidays and special occasions when our extended family gathered, I listened intently to stories that revealed family secrets and illustrated life lessons about people and events from before I was born. This lost world was my legacy.

My early drafts of *Vivian's Decision,* focused on immigrant Hannah Kolson, were stoked by my curiosity about my mother's immigrant mother. I ached to imagine the life of the grandmother for whom I'm named but never met. Each of Grandmother Della's seven children named a child in her memory. On visits to my mother's family in Los Angeles, where all six of my mother's siblings moved after WWII, I asked my aunts, uncles, and grandfather for their memories of Della Linson. I wondered, *Who was Della?* These recollections melded with my father's fond memories of his Russian Jewish immigrant mother. My father's mother bore six living children across the same time span and in the same Chicago neighborhood where sections of this novel are set. In those times, there were many potential perils to women's health. Both of my grandmothers passed away in their sixties.

I spent many valuable hours in the research centers of the Chicago History Museum, the Harold Washington Chicago Public Library, and Chicago's Newberry Library guided by knowledgeable librarians. Among other resources, local neighborhood newspapers' advertisements, columns, photos, and letters to the editor revealed rich details of daily life on Chicago's west side during the early 20th century. Composites of women from that era emerged to paint the vivid portraits of people and places found in *Vivian's Decision*. This is a world that no longer exists.

It was a time when the risks of childbearing were great. Women's reproductive concerns loom large throughout the pages of *Vivian's*

Decision. My own perspectives were shaped as a member of the Chicago Women's Liberation Union in the early 1970s, where I read Juliet Mitchell's *Women's Estate* (1971). Mitchell posited four pillars as a lens for analysis of women's history: 1) Production, 2) Reproduction of the Family, 3) Sexuality, and 4) Socialization of Children. The synthesis of these four constructs were the foundation for the more just and egalitarian society I yearned for.

After many revisions, my novel shifted its focus from Hannah Kolson to her daughter Vivian. Vivian is a woman struggling to conform to an unreachable 1950s feminine ideal. She's a loving spouse and devoted mother but still wrestles with her desires for an independent identity beyond "homemaker." *Vivian's Decision* is a fictional, multigenerational saga. I've aimed to fashion Vivian, Mel, and their children as composite characters who represent many women and many families while maintaining the sensibilities of this post-atomic, Eisenhower era in the United States. Another world that no longer exists, but I believe it's important that future generations are offered a view into women's constraints in these times.

As ever, Vivian's ultimate decision remains a deeply personal one. Throughout the ages, many women have faced their own versions of her crisis, and they continue to do so today. Currently, in the United States, despite advances in medicine, new, punishing laws restricting reproductive options are enacted almost daily. These laws exact harsh consequences upon women, families, and medical professionals. Let's claim Vivian Jacobson's story as our own and fight to protect reproductive freedoms.

I remain honored beyond measure for the opportunity to place this novel in your hands.

Thank you for reading *Vivian's Decision.*

Della Leavitt

December 2025

ACKNOWLEDGMENTS

WHERE TO begin? In many ways, because this novel sprung from stories I half-heard since childhood, the essence of *Vivian's Decision* has been with me most of my life. Yet I pinpoint my new beginning as a novelist with the notion to write the story of my parents' serendipitous meeting as a present to my (now, late) mother upon her ninetieth birthday. Although I'd been an eager reader from an early age and member of the late Jill Rohde's women's book group for thirty years, I'd never before dared to attempt creative writing. When I spied a closed wooden door, stenciled STORYSTUDIO, across the hall from the Tai Chi Center of Chicago, I asked our incomparable tai chi master, Elizabeth Wenscott, what it was. She urged me to open the door to "Jill's place." Jill Pollack was a fellow tai chi student and StoryStudio's founder. I took the risk, strode across the hall, stepped over the threshold, and fell into the hands of a patient teacher and accomplished author, Abby Geni. Abby guided me through the tangles and twists of how to write a story. Several months later, my mother was thrilled with her gift.

Assuming a novelist's vantage point unleashed my imagination to tap into a wellspring of stories I felt compelled to write, but soon it became clear to me how much I needed to learn to craft an artful story. I became a regular student in StoryStudio's evening classes where I met dear friend and fellow writer Susan Levi, who widened my vision. Susan convinced me to travel from my Lincoln Square neighborhood to Winnetka for weekly craft lectures at the long-running Off Campus Writers' Workshop (OCWW) led by President Fred Fitzsimmons. Without Susan's encouragement throughout these years, *Vivian's Decision* might never have become a book. At OCWW, I found a wondrous array of writerly resources: from editor Fred Shafer's annual September lecture series to extra critiques from noted authors. My identity as a writer became intertwined with this community. I served on OCWW's board for four years and forged meaningful personal and professional relationships, and contributed to three published anthologies with another one scheduled for 2026. Of special note is my friendship with Judy Panko Reis, sparked by our discovery of several significant people who crisscrossed our lives decades before Judy and I met through OCWW.

In support of my previous careers in technology and mathematics education, I'd earned several advanced degrees. I was determined that my writing studies would be an intensive DIY pursuit. Over the years, my writing improved as I took advantage of the wide-ranging resources in the Chicago area and throughout the Midwest, including the Iowa Summer Writing Festival with author Sandra Scofield as my teacher, private seminars around Goldie Goldbloom's dining room table that seats twelve, and Ragdale weekend retreats sponsored by StoryStudio and OCWW. After I met Gilded Age researcher Laurie Toth in a class at University of Chicago's Graham School, she suggested that we enroll together in "Writing Chicago," a Newberry Library adult education course taught by Donald Evans, founder and executive director of the Chicago Literary Hall of Fame. In Don's class, I wrote a fanciful story set in a Maxwell Street tavern on the night of Prohibition's repeal that sprung from my father's eyewitness recollections. Don suggested that I expand this into a novel. During the pandemic lockdown, Don's critiques of my pages led to completion of my first draft. His work complemented regular Zoom meetings with my valued critique partners, Lisabeth Weiner and Caryn

Green, with the added bonus of Sue Monshaw's insights during the year she lived in the Chicago area.

I'm grateful for the support that my work-in-progress received under the title *Beyond Maxwell Street* with a grant from the Individual Artists Program of the City of Chicago's Department of Cultural Affairs & Special Events (DCASE) and a short-term historical novel fellowship from the Newberry Library. I'm honored that Brooks Permissions granted licenses to quote lines from Pulitzer Prize winner Gwendolyn Brooks's poem "The Mother," an important turning point in *Vivian's Decision*. Thank you to Marcia Albert, subscriptions manager at Parnassus Books, who facilitated communications with author Ann Patchett to grant permission for me to cite Ann's mother, Jeanne Ray, in the epigraph that I heard Ann recount at her book tour for *Commonwealth* in Chicago.

Thank you to many who read my work over the years and spurred me to seek publication. Rickie Jacobs, Mary Anne Joyce, Andrea Change, Sarah Bornstein, and others too numerous to list. You know who you are. I found camaraderie and accountability alongside the Women's Fiction Writers Association's (WFWA) Write-Inmates led by Michele Montgomery, Amy Sue Nathan's Early-Birders, and Joan Fernandez's Tuesday Noontime Historical Fiction group.

My years under the tutelage of the incomparable editor Fred Shafer and critiques from the women in Fred's ongoing Thursday novel workshop deepened development of these characters and their stories. They influenced and shaped what became the final version of *Vivian's Decision* that Brooke Warner accepted for publication by She Writes Press (SWP).

I am grateful for Brooke Warner's publishing industry acumen and my SWP project manager, Megan Milton, for their patient efforts to bring this novel across the finish line. Thank you for the timely support I received from my new sisters in the Spring 2026 cohort, especially authors Leslie R. Schover, Amy S. Peele, Meryl Ain, and

Jane A. Ward. I appreciate the publicity consultations from Julia Borcherts and Lainey Cameron, with timely suggestions from experienced Chicago publicist, Sheryl Johnston.

Several themes of this novel have burned strong throughout my adulthood and remain etched in my consciousness. As a first-generation college graduate, I joined the socialist feminist Chicago Women's Liberation Union (CWLU) on the cusp of the passage of *Roe v. Wade*. The courageous women of Jane, the underground abortion collective, formed the heart of the CWLU. They are my s/heroes, then and always.

I'm grateful for the life I've shared with my spouse, Roy Bossen. We have been through many changes throughout the decades. Your steadfast love and belief in me mean more than words can say. With good health, may we continue to walk new pathways together in the years ahead. Being Morrie's parents has been our greatest collaboration. My hope for Morrie and Lilla is may they experience as much joy as we did raising Morrie with their sparkling Nora Shirley, born shortly after the 2024 election. May Nora be our light in these dark times as she grows and finds her way in our uncertain world.

ABOUT THE AUTHOR

photo credit: Ronit Bezalel Photography

DELLA LEAVITT draws inspiration from the lives of resilient women. After careers in technology and math education, she embarked on an intensive study to write fiction within Chicago's vibrant writing community. Della earned a historical novel fellowship from the Newberry Library and a grant from Chicago's Department of Cultural Affairs & Special Events (DCASE) while writing this novel. She lives in Chicago with her family.

Looking for your next great read?

We can help!

Visit www.shewritespress.com/next-read
or scan the QR code below for a list
of our recommended titles.

She Writes Press is an award-winning
independent publishing company founded to
serve women writers everywhere.